REMEMBER THIS

DINITIA SMITH

REMEMBER THIS

(.) . (.) . (.) . (.) . (.) . (.) . (.)

HENRY HOLT & COMPANY · NEW YORK

Library of Congress Cataloging-in-Publication Data
Smith, Dinitia.
Remember this / Dinitia Smith.—1st ed.
p.   cm.
ISBN 0-8050-1036-X
I. Title.
PS3569.M526R4   1989
813'.54—dc19   88-39555
CIP

Henry Holt books are available at special discounts for bulk purchases
for sales promotions, premiums, fund-raising, or educational use.
Special editions or book excerpts can also be created to specification.

For details, contact:

Special Sales Director
Henry Holt and Company, Inc.
115 West 18th Street
New York, New York 10011

First Edition

DESIGNED BY CLAIRE M. NAYLON
Printed in the United States of America
1 3 5 7 9 10 8 6 4 2

To the memory of my mother,
Helen Allen

I wish to thank the National Endowment for the Arts and the Ingram Merrill Foundation for the fellowships that have enabled me to write this novel. I also wish to thank my editor, Jack Macrae, and my agent, Virginia Barber, for their support and encouragement.

O brother so delayed by time,
I hold you against hope—

—*Euripides*

REMEMBER THIS

ONE

At six o'clock that evening, Laura stood up from her desk and walked to the window. She raised her arms above her head and stretched, staring by habit across at the darkened windows of Rosenstein's Cord and Tassel. She realized suddenly that she wasn't alone. There was someone in one of the black windows opposite watching her.

The palms of her hands prickled with a fine sweat. Her arms dropped. A strange feeling, this sense of a pair of eyes upon her.

Laura's first thought was embarrassment. It was winter, the lights had been on for most of the day, and her body had been lit up by the tensor lamp on her desk. She wondered if she'd scratched herself in some immodest place while she concentrated on her work.

Maybe she should hang a sheet over the window. She'd never put up a curtain or a blind because she didn't want to block the light. The light was one of the loft's greatest assets, and besides, no one was ever in the buildings opposite after five. Her platform bed was in the corner of the room and hidden from view. When she climbed up there, she couldn't be seen.

She'd lived in the city for six years now and she was used to negotiating its perils. Her work carried her to many strange places. Laura had a quality of fearlessness. Now, standing by the window, she experienced only a mild fear, and then annoyance, because it was inconvenient, it disrupted her peace and her work.

She decided to let it be. If she suddenly put a curtain up, or a sheet, it might *engage* him, whoever he was. She moved back into the shadows of the loft, near the kitchen area, where she couldn't be seen.

For the past few weeks, Laura had experienced a constant uneasiness and restlessness and she'd found it difficult to concentrate on her work. This morning, for instance, she'd sat down at her worktable by the window to finish her review—it was of a book on a woman archaeologist and her editor wanted her to cut the piece down to five hundred words. Editing it should have been a relatively easy task. Yet she'd been sitting there when suddenly she felt a strange anxiety. It was as if an electric field were playing across her skin. She had sometimes felt this way before, when she was about to get sick, as if her body were on a sudden alert. But she knew there was nothing wrong with her—she'd had a checkup, she was in perfect health. The doctor had even quoted *Lear* to her, "When the mind's free, the body's delicate," he had said. She was having anxiety attacks, she knew. A few days ago, she had been sitting in a restaurant and the feeling had become so unbearable that she'd suddenly had to get up and leave.

Then, at lunchtime today, she had taken a break and, striding through the neighborhood, she had felt the excitement surging through her body again, a manic glee. The light, the street sounds pressed down upon her with a brilliant, jagged vividness.

This afternoon, coming back to the loft and sitting down to work again, she couldn't focus on the page in front of her. She could hardly sit still. Her eyes danced across the manuscript. There it was again, the electricity on her skin. She was having anxiety attacks—but she couldn't afford anxiety.

Now, though, standing here in the early evening, she had the feeling somebody was watching her.

She was safe. Both the doors, upstairs to her loft, and downstairs leading to the outside, were steel with bars across them. There was no way anyone could get in. As a single woman she was used to negotiating these hazards.

She walked back to the worktable. She continued cutting the article down. But then again her attention wandered to the window, to the warehouses and factories and the sky beyond. The sky that afternoon had been strangely beautiful, the clouds like sheets of silver shot through with light. There would be snow soon maybe, she thought.

A few minutes later she sat up straight—that sense again of being watched. She glanced across at the building. Nothing there, only the shining black windows, the weathered red brick, and the sign, ROSENSTEIN'S CORD AND TASSEL.

At six-thirty, she walked over to the refrigerator, took out a bottle of already-opened red wine, and poured herself a glass. She carried the glass to the window, turning off the desk lamp, which had cut a swath of light across it, and stood looking out at the rain drizzling down on the narrow street.

Nothing could make her leave this loft. Although this area seemed to some inhospitable, the loft was her home—she owned it. She had bought it when lofts were cheap. The space was by some standards small, really a large studio, but nonetheless worth a great deal these days. It was the only real home she had ever known. How right that Iola, her grandmother, had been the one to give her the money, to assure her of this security. Laura had found some of the furniture on the street—the door she used as a desktop, two wicker chairs she'd had repaired, the butcher-block countertop; and at the Salvation Army, her dark blue velvet couch.

She was hungry. There was chicken left over in the refrigerator from last night's dinner and she took a drumstick, a piece of celery for a vegetable, a second glass of wine. She reached up and put her plate and glass on the platform bed and climbed up. Switching the TV on, she ate her dinner.

At eleven, she watched the news and fell asleep with the television going.

She must have been asleep for several hours when her consciousness was penetrated by a ringing sound. She opened her eyes. For a moment, she didn't know where she was, she couldn't identify the insistent noise. Then, she realized—it was the phone. She picked up the receiver.

"Hello."

But there was no answer. Only a vague static, the distant rumble of a car engine.

This had been going on for the past week; there had been several phone calls like this. The phone would ring. She'd pick up the receiver and there would be simply atmosphere. When she came home and checked her answering machine, she found hang-ups. Or else whoever it was would listen to her message and then stay on the line, and Laura would hear the crackling of electricity, the moaning of wind in the wires.

She had decided that it was her father, Hal, calling her up anonymously from South Carolina, where he and Barbara, her stepmother, had retired. He was probably drunk, phoning just to hear the sound of her voice, afraid that if he talked to her, she would only berate him—for drinking, for moving around so much, for retiring, for the past, for what happened to her mother, for a host of other things. Maybe he was finally going senile, his brain rotting with the alcohol. After the first few phone calls, she'd yelled into the phone, "Listen, Dad! I know it's you!" But there had been no answer, and she had just sat there listening to whoever it was listening to her. At other times, earlier in the day, Hal would call her and be perfectly rational, ask her about her assignments, talk about the weather down there, the renovation on their new house.

But it was midnight now, it couldn't be Hal. It was too late for Hal. He'd be fast asleep by now from the drinking.

She peered over the edge of the platform bed out the window. The rain had cleared, the street was empty. And yet she had the feeling that the street was alive; in the wet shadows and corners, there was a palpable presence, not a dangerous presence necessarily, but someone there nonetheless.

She sank back in the bed, covered herself. She was imagining it, it was all part of these anxiety attacks.

And if she didn't get some sleep, she'd never be able to work tomorrow.

She lay there, forcing herself to relax. She tried to imagine each limb, finger, toe, growing loose. She thought about how up here in the loft it was dark and she was hidden and soon her natural tiredness overcame her and she was asleep again.

In the morning, with the arrival of daylight, the sensation of being watched had vanished. She remembered the night, but the idea of someone there seemed impossible.

She brewed a cup of Spanish coffee, took a shower, and set out to deliver her manuscript.

As she stepped outside, she glanced mildly up and down

the street to see if there was anyone strange, but there were only the truckers unloading their wares into the factory buildings. She waved and smiled. She knew some of them by sight, felt reassured by their presence, protected by them, even if they did wake her up every weekday morning at six.

Pulling her woolen cap down over her hair and tucking her chin into her scarf, she turned down Greene Street toward Canal.

As she walked through the glittering, cold morning, an inexplicable, transcendent joy surged through her body. Maybe it was the reappearance of the daylight world. All fear must end sometime, she thought. And then there was the satisfaction of finishing a piece of work, of putting it away finally.

The buildings were green and pink, a tangle of fire escapes clinging to them by their last threads. Suddenly, to her right, she saw an ivory-colored building glowing in the sun; it had elaborate, arched windows, a colonnade. She loved the architecture of this neighborhood.

This was her home, her own small town. She was like millions here, people dispossessed of a past, trying to reinvent themselves as adults. She belonged among them, and these streets, with their exquisite variety, the pageant of language and sight and smell, were hers. The air was clear, the coldness gave the illusion it was clean.

She turned the corner and glanced up. Her eye was caught by the sight of a huge blimp hanging between two tall buildings. The great balloon seemed very near, hovering motionless. The great shape was an intrusion. For a moment, it seemed to darken her mind. Blimps always made her vaguely fearful. Perhaps, she thought, it was because they reminded her of her stepmother Barbara's barrage balloons, her stories of German bombers getting caught in their chains. Laura stared up at the silent mass a moment, then continued walking.

She made long, slender, awkward strides, and then she stumbled. Quickly, she recovered, glancing around to see if anyone had seen her—pretending her foot had been caught in a crack in the sidewalk. She could be clumsy sometimes, with her long, thin legs.

The tears streamed down her cheeks from the cold. Gratefully, she descended into the foul, comforting warmth of the Canal Street subway station.

She walked through the underpass and waited for the Number 6. The train came, and she pushed her way in. She found a seat—it was the latter portion of the rush hour. The subway started up, rocking and speeding north. She sat lulled by the warmth and motion. All around her, people stood or sat in a quiet and orderly fashion, reading their morning papers. Mingling with the stale air was a vague smell of shampoo and soap and perfume and clean linens, people washed and bathed and spruced up for work.

Laura sat in the subway car, at peace. Lazily, she surveyed the people opposite her. There were a couple of men in business suits and vests, their hair damp from their morning showers. A woman in a tailored dark green coat with a briefcase. An immaculately turned-out Hispanic-looking woman. Laura's eyes wandered along the row of people, a man reading Gurdjieff, someone else a computer manual.

The subway rocked and shuddered and screeched; she was almost falling asleep. At the other end of the car, a child in a stroller bundled up to the gills in his snowsuit—what damage must this loud noise do to a child's ears? she wondered.

Laura's eye fell upon another face. She saw a tall man,

maybe in his early twenties, a large man with broad shoulders, pale blue eyes, dark blond curly hair worn long around the face.

Suddenly the face took on a form, all the features coalescing like shards of a shattered vase reconstituting themselves. The face—the pale blue eyes, slanting. She stared hard. Could it be? No. Him? Here, without telling her? And the thing about it was he probably wouldn't even recognize her or she him. *Everybody* ends up in America in the end. Maybe some kind of business had brought him here. And now, before her, a ghost. But she didn't cry out, didn't even sit forward. There was only a refocusing of her eyes. And then she knew that it wasn't him.

This had happened a hundred times before. In a crowd, strolling past St. Patrick's Cathedral one spring day, she had seen him—a tall man with the pale eyes, walking right next to her. And then—the saner thought—that's probably what he would have looked like. In a restaurant, in the park, she thought she saw him. Of course, he never looked at her, never acknowledged her. Always looked right past her. Sometimes she thought of him as an automaton, a soul inhabiting a strange body, a being who could not, somehow, control himself, who had no feelings, a man who couldn't love or even really hate.

Once a month maybe, Laura saw the face, the curly hair—hair that as a child she had twisted around her fingers, hair appearing to be dark blond, but composed actually of many colors, bits of white, of gold, black too. And the blue eyes expressionless. But she had no way of knowing for sure what he looked like now. After all, the last time she had seen him they were children.

Never, in nearly twenty years, had it occurred to Laura to

tell anyone else about these—visitations—if that was what they were, and she hardly even articulated them to herself. They were part of the subterranean world of her private thoughts, the stream of impressions that passed daily through her mind, second nature, as much a part of her as breathing.

She focused again on the young man with the pale eyes as he stood up. The train stopped and he moved to get off. Of course, it wasn't him. And even if it were, there was no way of knowing for sure. She wasn't going to run up to a complete stranger and yell out, "Remember me. I'm Laura. Is that you?" She gazed after the man listlessly.

At Grand Central, she got off the subway and walked across to Third, where the magazine's office was. She left the manuscript with the receptionist.

She was home by eleven, and spent the day cleaning the loft, throwing out the detritus of her article. A good feeling, preparing for a new task.

When dinnertime came, she fried herself a hamburger and drank a beer. She had another piece due tomorrow, a short one on a black woman foundation executive, fifteen hundred words. She'd already interviewed the woman and gathered her clips. There was a chance she could get it written in one day.

She undressed, climbed up onto the platform bed, under the covers. With the television set going, she drifted off to sleep.

That night, she had a dream. In the dream, she was a child again, standing at the top of the stairs. There was a shape in front of her, a dark, rounded object, something like an hourglass, only solid, and beyond the object there was light, a whiteness, and vague figures moving. She was trying to see the figures, but she couldn't; the dark-shaped thing kept blocking her line of vision. There was a ringing sound, a ringing in her ears.

She was coming awake. A new layer of light and air was intruding on the dream. She heard muffled voices, applause.

She was pulling herself out of the deep water now. The ringing sound was outside the dream. It was her own phone ringing. And the voices, the applause, they were the television set. She must have left it on when she fell asleep.

She was awake now. The phone wasn't stopping. It must have rung ten times. She pulled herself over to the edge of the bed, reached for the receiver, and dragged it toward her.

This time there was a voice at the other end of the line.

TWO

Laura remembered standing at the top of the stairs. She was dressed in her flannel nightgown and supposed to be in bed—she was seven years old at the time, and yet she recalled the moment exactly. Her father was a Foreign Service officer stationed in London after the war, and they were living in the house at number 10, Cambridge Road. That evening, she stood on the second floor, looking down through the spools of the banister at the entry hall below. The doorbell had rung and she saw Ruth, her mother, and Hal, her father, walk quickly, nervously, across the polished floor to answer it. Her mother was wearing a gray serge dress that night, with box shoulders in the fashion of the times, her fine, fair hair rolled up away from her face the way she always wore it.

Laura saw her mother open the door and three people, two men and a woman, enter. The woman had short, almost black hair, cut like a boy's, and dark lipstick. She had pale, slanting eyes and she was wearing a dark brown beaver coat. It was winter, and a gust of cold wind blew in behind her and brought the scent of her perfume all the way up to the second floor, a deep, rich, sweet scent.

Next to the woman stood a man with shining black hair, and large, dark, sad eyes. The man was stooped and smiling, and he seemed shy. Laura didn't know either the man or the woman.

The third person with them was Dr. Severance, the family doctor. He was short and round and red-faced, with green eyes and a little mustache, and now his booming laugh resounded across the entrance hall. Dr. Severance was her father's friend and he was always at their house. Laura felt a small fear pass through her. Severance was treating her for eczema. Sometimes the edges of her mouth, the crooks of her arms, and the backs of her knees were raw and red and cracked with it. Seeing Severance now, Laura remembered the sudden cold of his metal instruments on her warm skin, the pain of his needles stabbing her arm.

Down below, her mother was smiling at the visitors.

"Ruth, this is Barbara Reed," said her father. Laura saw her mother reach over awkwardly and extend her hand, and the other woman smile and take it.

"And my husband, Owen," said the dark-haired woman, Barbara Reed.

Behind them, Laura's father stood back, tall and slender, wearing his black dinner jacket, his soft brown hair brushed away from his high, domed forehead, watching them.

There they were, all together, the five figures framed in the curve of the staircase. Something in Laura's mind clicked, and took a photograph of them for all time, the five players standing together there in the entrance hall below.

That night, Laura, as usual, couldn't sleep. She must have gone downstairs a half-dozen times—she remembered the five adults sitting in the living room around the coffee table with their drinks. The beautiful dark-haired woman was wearing a navy blue suit with a narrow waist, and very high heels. The neckline of her suit plunged deep and there was a choker of big pearls at her throat.

When Laura appeared at the living-room door, the doctor and the other Englishman smiled up at her.

"Hel-lo!" said the Englishman in a friendly way. Each time, her mother led her back upstairs to her room, the valanced curtains drawn tight against the cold. "Now it's *time* to go to sleep!" her mother said.

"I can't sleep," Laura said.

"Well, you just lie there and *try*," she said. Usually, she was lenient, spoiled Laura, but tonight she meant business.

Now Laura watched as she padded out of the room, her figure receding, dissolving into the rectangle of light in the bedroom door.

Laura's room was a soft place, of thick rugs, and eiderdowns, and heavy curtains. But still she could hear their voices downstairs, the bark of the men's laughter, the women's low comment.

She wanted to go down. They were having fun down there; in that room there was warmth and laughter and light. She wanted to hear what they were saying. And she wanted to be with her mother, she wanted to be next to her.

Tonight, her inability to sleep was even worse than usual.

She climbed out of bed and made her way slowly down the stairs, her hand sliding on the banister, holding back because she knew they'd be angry.

She stood in the living-room doorway.

Her father caught sight of her, sprang up, and grabbed her tight by the wrist. "Now that's enough!" he said.

"I don't want to go to sleep."

"Well you *must*."

He pulled her out of the room and up the stairs and into her bedroom. "Now you get into that bed," he said. He tucked the covers around her neck and turned to go.

"Don't close the door!" she called.

"Yes," he said firmly.

"I'm afraid of the dark!"

"You are *not* afraid of the dark."

"I am! I am!"

And he shut the door. She began to cry, louder and louder, as loud as she could. She knew he was probably standing there outside the door, listening, trying to decide if the crying was serious. But as she cried, there were no tears. She hammered her fists into the pillow, she kicked her feet, wept until her throat was dry and aching, until she couldn't keep it up anymore, until somehow, exhausted, she finally fell asleep.

She was a child who never slept. She could stay on her feet, keep playing with her eyes drooping from exhaustion, having been up since five in the morning. She refused to give in. It was her "policy," as her father joked, never to nap, even as an infant. She lay there and she tried, but it just wouldn't happen. She wasn't afraid of sleep itself, of losing herself in the dark, but she was afraid of the *act* of falling asleep. She was afraid she would fail. Falling asleep was like diving into the deep water. If you didn't do it just right, it wouldn't work. It was like walking a tightrope. If you misstepped, you would lose your balance and that was it. Just by watching yourself at the moment when you fell off you could fail and stop the process. She was afraid of ruining her chances for sleep by being self-conscious.

Anyway, she was never tired—so much seemed to happen

while she slept; she wanted to run, to explore, to hear what they were saying, to listen.

Because she slept so little, they were always putting her to bed early so she could make up for her lack of sleep the night before. Sometimes they made her go to bed when it wasn't even dark out. How she hated lying there, fresh and alert, eyes wide open, listening to the sound of a lawn mower going on a warm evening, stones rattling against a rake, the push of a shovel against the earth, the murmur of voices on a terrace, the late birds chirping, the cries of other children allowed to stay up.

They tried to put her to bed, but as soon as they shut the door, she began to cry. Minutes would pass and then her mother would suddenly stride through the door.

"Now, I let you stay up an hour later. You go to sleep!"

"I don't want to go to sleep."

"You do what I tell you."

"I don't want to go to sleep. I'm not tired."

"There'll be a punishment . . ." Though there seldom was.

"Nooooo!"

The door clicked shut. Definitely. With finality. Alone. Silence.

She would outwit them. She would scream and scream until they couldn't take it anymore. No one could scream as long as she.

Ten minutes, twenty minutes, half an hour passed. And still she screamed. Her screams wailed up beyond tears, beyond sorrow, until they pierced the gables of the house, were carried across the rooftops into the growing darkness, through the branches of trees, into the windows of neighboring houses, into the dining rooms of neighbors. She cried until at last sleep came, taking her by surprise. And the next morning she couldn't remember falling off.

She loved the morning and the daylight.

In the mornings, her mother braided her hair. She would sit at the dressing table while her mother stood behind her, combing it and plaiting it. They both had the same honey blond hair, fine and flying away into a halo when it was brushed. They looked alike, they had the same wide, heart-shaped faces, the same wide smile. Her mother's voice was American, the vowels round.

Sometimes, her mother would play the piano and sing, the French windows opened wide onto the garden and the grass beyond, the topiary trimmed into the shape of peacocks, and the flowers, pink and yellow and apricot, the colors almost of her mother's hair spun against the light. *"Alouette, gentille alouette . . . ,"* she would sing.

Most of her days her mother spent writing letters home to America. She wrote nearly every day to her own mother, and to her brothers and sisters-in-law. In the morning, she went outside early, waiting at the end of the garden for the postman. Later, she waited by the road for Laura to come home from school. Each day the teacher walked the children home after school—the teacher was a large woman, waddling in front of a long line of them. They followed her like ducklings as she dropped them off one by one at their houses. When Laura reached her house, her mother was always there, and Laura wondered if she had ever left her spot by the road.

Sometimes, Laura found her mother sitting, dreaming, looking out at nothing, into space. "What are you thinking about?" Laura asked.

"Oh, I'm thinking about home," she said. "It's fall now and my papa's going up into the mountain with his dog . . ."

She turned to her. "I wish you could know Everett and my mama and papa. They love you so much and they've only seen you once. I wish you could know my home."

"You should go out, have fun," Laura's father said, "meet people."

"I guess I'm not used to the English," her mother said. "I think you could live next door to them your whole life and never go inside their houses." And when people did come over, Laura saw her always standing in the background, saying little, smiling her wide smile.

"You know, it's important that we entertain," Laura's father said.

Her mother sighed. "Maybe I'm not cut out for the diplomatic life," she said, in her soft, lilting voice. But he laughed at this and hugged her. "Don't be silly!" he cried.

One evening, her father said, "I'd like to invite Timmy Beckworth over, you know, Lord Conroy."

"Is he a *real* lord?" Laura asked.

"Indeed he is. It's one of the oldest titles in the realm."

"How do you know him?" Laura asked.

"I met him through my work. He's in charge of the British effort to rebuild the bombed-out areas."

On the couch, her mother said, "I don't know. Why would he want to come here? I don't know what I'd serve."

"We'll get someone in to help," he said. "We can afford it. . . . I'd like to impress him . . . ," he added softly, almost under his breath.

"I don't feel comfortable having a servant come in," she said. "I'm not that kind of person."

"I don't know why you have this reluctance about servants," he said. "Everybody has help. We have the money. It's part of the budget. It's quite appropriate," he said.

17

She sat there, a worried smile on her face. Then she took a breath, looked at him, smiling eagerly up at him like a child. "I'll manage. I'll make a buffet, maybe something from back home. Don't you think he'd like that? A real American dinner."

"I think he'd appreciate it very much," he said.

She had bought a new dress for the occasion and Laura watched as she slipped it on. "What do you think?" she asked, twirling about in front of Laura's father. The dress had a big print of purple flowers with black leaves. She watched his face.

"It's very nice," he said.

"You don't like it!" she said at once.

"I do!" he said. "I like it very much."

Laura didn't like the dress. The print was too big and dark for her mother's pale skin, the pattern too jagged. She had broad shoulders and the dress made her look awkward.

He was watching her.

"You know," he said, "maybe you should get someone to go shopping with you."

"Why?"

"I don't know. . . . You need so many clothes. . . . What about Barbara Reed? I'll bet she'd love to go with you."

Laura saw her mother look at him. "Barbara Reed? Why her?"

"I don't know . . . she's an actress . . . she knows about things like that . . ."

"Well, so do I." Laura saw her mother's face suddenly flare. She spun quickly around and around in front of the big mirror on the bedroom door. "This dress is just fine . . ."

He stood up and put his arms around her and kissed her.

"Don't be offended. I thought women liked to go shopping with other women."

"I'm perfectly capable of going shopping by myself."

"Don't be mad. Forget about it." He kissed her again, but Laura saw that her mouth was set in a little line, that her body was stiff, that she didn't look at him.

"It'll be something for you to remember," her father said, "meeting a real lord." She was allowed to stay up to meet the lord, and she wore her pink organza dress.

She wondered if the lord would wear a scarlet cloak and a crown. But the lord was a small, thin man with a sunken chest, a big nose, and heavy-lidded eyes. His hair was pale and thinning, and he wore a dinner jacket, not a cloak. He could have been any one of her father's friends, a businessman. He had been nice to Laura, smiling down at her, bending at the waist and shaking her hand, but he didn't seem noble, Laura thought.

Each time the doorbell rang, her father went to answer it and Laura followed. Her mother still hadn't come out of the kitchen.

Dr. Severance arrived, and with him, the Englishwoman, Mrs. Reed. She was wearing a black dress tonight, off the shoulder with a tight skirt.

"Hello, Barbara," said Laura's father. "Good of you to come."

"How are you, Hal?" said Mrs. Reed, extending her long arm. They shook hands and Mrs. Reed smiled at him. Laura saw the pale blue eyes, the dark pink lipstick, the warm smile. The deep, rich perfume seemed to surround her. Mrs. Reed wore black leather gloves that went all the way up her arms,

19

with tiny pearl buttons fastening them at the wrist; and around one wrist, she wore a pearl bracelet.

Mrs. Reed and her father didn't speak again. They stayed on opposite sides of the room.

Her father moved among the guests, big and expansive and friendly, taking each of their hands in his as he greeted them. He was taller than everyone, they seemed so small and pale next to him. When he spoke to someone, he always used the person's first name at the beginning of the sentence— "Louisa, how are you?" and "Cecil, as I was telling you . . ."

And at his elbow, there was always the doctor, the fat, red-faced doctor, with the pale green eyes looking up into his face, waiting for him to finish his sentence. And then Dr. Severance would laugh. Laura could hear him braying from across the room, cutting through all the other conversation.

Even when her father wasn't speaking to the guests directly, Laura noticed they all seemed to be watching him. Their eyes were all upon him, their faces inclined subtly toward him, as if for warmth . . . as if he were the sun. And yet they seemed to be almost laughing at him too, Laura thought. For he was so unlike them, he was so friendly and so warm.

They were jealous of him, she thought. Their family had arrived in England at the end of the war, but even though the war was officially ended, it was with them still. She had driven through the great bombed-out areas of London with her father, acre after acre of ruined buildings; she had seen the English standing in line for rations, even though the war was over. Yet *their* family had everything they needed, good meat and liquor from the PX. The English resented them for this, Laura knew. Sometimes the other children teased her. "Yankee! Yankee! Yankee!" they called her.

Her mother was looking across the room at her. She was coming toward her now. "Time for bed, Laura," she said. "No arguments, please," she whispered. She could see shadows under her mother's eyes. Her voice was unusually firm, so this time Laura didn't argue.

The next morning, at breakfast, her mother sat slumped over the table in her crimson bathrobe. She looked at him. "I'm sorry," she said. "It was awful."

"Come on! It was fine. Nobody noticed the food anyway. They were all too busy talking."

"You should have married someone else . . . ," she said.

"Please! Don't be silly." He stood up, went over to her chair, and kissed her. "Why don't you go back to bed? You're just exhausted."

But she seemed not to have heard him. "The food was terrible. I embarrassed you, didn't I?" she said.

"Of course you didn't. Everyone had a *great* time!" he said.

It was high summer now, "very hot for England," her mother said. The afternoon air stood thick and still. Her mother sat at her desk in the bedroom writing letters. Laura curled around her chair.

"Why don't you take a little nap, honey? It's so hot. All the other children are resting."

"I don't want to take a nap. . . . Where's Daddy?"

"He's at the club, playing tennis."

She slid down the stairs and outside the house. All the way up and down the street, the houses were shuttered against the heat.

21

She set out on her bike. She was supposed to ride only on the sidewalk, but there was no one around to stop her going on the road now.

She pedaled her bike past the house. It was a large house, white brick with a green roof and great, curved windows, separated from the street by a hedge. The house was newly built, and yet it was meant to look old, Laura thought. It looked almost as if no one lived there, for it was so clean and shining and perfect.

All the houses on the street were set back from the road, protected from sight by trees and bushes, neat and shuttered. There were often moving vans parked outside the houses. People were always arriving and departing, foreigners, diplomats, executives who worked in London. The population of the street was constantly changing, whole families coming and going seemingly overnight.

Laura pedaled fast, her hair flying out with the recklessness of it, leaving without permission, riding for the first time alone down the road.

She could see in the distance now the tall poplars which surrounded the tennis club, and the wire fence around the courts. As she came closer, she heard the pop of rackets hitting balls in the heat, the muffled cries of "Damn!" and "Good shot!"

She bicycled around the edge of the courts, looking for him through the lilac bushes among all the players dressed in white. Then she saw him.

His body was arched in a serve, his arms stretched up. He was in his tennis whites, his legs taut. He reached forward, bending at the waist in one liquid motion, and served the ball across the net to Mrs. Reed.

"Well done!" he cried.

Sitting between them, on the bench, his legs spread apart in his tennis shorts, his face red and sweating, the racket lying across his knees, was Dr. Severance.

"Go on, Barbara!" Severance cried. "Give it to 'im!"

Laura watched as Mrs. Reed leapt across the court. She saw Mrs. Reed's white panties showing underneath her tennis dress and she stared, waiting for the panties to show every time she rose up to hit the ball or to send her own serve.

Then her father caught sight of Laura. He stopped playing. His racket dropped to his side. She saw a little flash of anger cross his face.

"Laura!" he said. "What are you doing here? Where's Mommy?"

"She's writing letters. . . . I didn't have anyone to play with."

"You know you're not supposed to come this far alone, Laura . . ." He stopped, his voice cool. "How often do we have to tell you? . . . We're almost through. You wait and I'll take you home."

She sat and watched them, the lively game between them, their graceful bodies.

When they had finished, he walked toward Laura, wiping his brow with his handkerchief. "You remember Mrs. Reed, don't you, Laura?" he said.

"Hello, Laura," said Mrs. Reed, shaking her hand, looking down into her face, smiling.

"Well, you almost got me that time," he said to Mrs. Reed.

"Next time," said Mrs. Reed, with a laugh.

"Do you need a ride home?" he asked.

"I'm fine," said Mrs. Reed. "Tom'll take me home, won't you, Tom?" she said, laughing over her shoulder at the doctor.

"Of course," said Dr. Severance, quickly.

"Okay, Tom, watch yourself," her father said, with a laugh, a graceful, open laugh. Indeed, even for him, he was unusually happy, today, big and rangy.

He reached out his hand to Mrs. Reed. "Good game," he said.

"Does Mrs. Reed live near here?" Laura asked as he loaded her bike into the back of the car.

"A couple of miles away, I believe," he answered, distracted, as if he weren't sure.

As he got in the car, he seemed preoccupied. He started the engine, didn't speak for a while as they drove, and then he said, "So, tell me about school." He was smiling at her pleasantly, evenly, now.

She liked being in the car with him, that was the time when they were closest. Then she had him to herself. He would tell her about his work—or at least as much of it as she could understand. She liked it when he talked about his work with her, for then he spoke to her as if she were an equal.

He was the economics attaché at the American Embassy. "We're trying to help the English make their country strong again, after the war," he told her. "We're lending them money so they can build factories and businesses. We have to make them strong to protect them from the communists."

When she asked him what communists were, he told her a little parable about a man who had a shop in Russia and one who had a shop in England, and how all the money the Russian man made from *his* shop went to the government, but the Englishman was allowed to keep what he earned. He told Laura about his lunches with important people, once even with the prime minister himself.

But he seldom talked about his past. Whereas her mother

24

spoke often of her parents, her father seemed to have no past, no family, no connections. But Laura was insistent.

He had come from "a little town in the States," she knew, where his family had run a chain of theaters. His father and mother had died when he was very young.

"Who looked after you when your mother and father died?" she asked.

"Well, my aunt looked after me for a while, and then I went to live with my uncle."

"Were they nice to you?"

"Oh yes. Very nice. My uncle had made a lot of money, he was a very rich man—the rest of the family didn't have any money. But after a while . . . well, I guess I was kind of a mischievous kid"—he smiled—"and I got in trouble with his old housekeeper. Mrs. Murti. I'll never forget her name. She was kind of a nut. She used to say she was an Indian princess. She said her husband was a maharaja and after he died his sons took away the palace. Used to make me eat pork with applesauce." He shuddered in a mock way. "I still hate pork with applesauce to this day," he said. He looked at Laura and smiled. "Never eat pork with applesauce. It's terrible. . . . Also," he said, smiling, "avoid bread pudding with raisins and rice pudding at all costs. . . . Anyway, I didn't get on too well with Mrs. Murti so they sent me to live in a boarding-house."

"What's a boardinghouse?" she said.

"It's kind of like a little hotel."

"You lived in a hotel by yourself?" she cried. "But you must have been so lonely! Who took care of you?"

"The lady who ran the boardinghouse did. She took in other children as well, kids whose parents had died or something had happened."

"Did you cry?" she asked.

"I don't remember crying very much. There were a couple of other boys staying there too and I guess we kind of had a pact. If you cried, the other kids wouldn't talk to you."

"But why?"

"I don't know." He thought for a moment. "Maybe they didn't want to be reminded."

"Reminded of what?" she asked.

"Oh, reminded of the way they felt, I guess."

He paused, seemed to be reflecting. "Just think of our family as fallen aristocrats," he said suddenly.

"What's a fallen aristocrat?" she asked.

"That's a person from a family that's lost all its money, but still, it's a good family, an old family, an important family," he said.

"But is that true?" she asked. "Are we really fallen aristocrats?"

Her mother stood before her, her face radiant, her wide smile filling it. She took Laura on her knee.

"I have something wonderful to tell you."

"What is it!"

"You're going to have a little brother or sister."

"Are you pregnant?"

"Yes," she said. She patted her stomach. "It's right here, growing inside. Are you happy?"

"Yes," Laura said.

"You'll have to help me take care of it. . . . You're really old enough now to be a big help."

That day, they went out and bought knitting supplies and she taught Laura to knit. Laura made a little blanket for the baby on big needles. The stitches were huge, the sides all stretched out and uneven.

"I can fix that. I'll block it out," said her mother.

Her father arrived home early. He and Laura did the dishes together. They both put on aprons, Laura cleared the table and stood on a chair and washed while he wiped. Her mother wrote her letters to America with a smile on her face.

Her father began to come home late. Often, when she went to bed now he was still not there.

"Where's Daddy?" she asked.

"He has a big project to do," said her mother. "It's very important. A big report."

Laura would lie in the bed in the darkness waiting for him, waiting for the thump of the car door, the little gust of wind that always came upstairs with his arrival. Then he would climb the stairs, look in on her and kiss her good night, and she could feel his cold skin on her face.

Sometimes now, he even worked on Saturdays and Sundays.

"I want Daddy," she said.

"Daddy's under a lot of pressure," her mother said. "We have to understand." Once in a while, he didn't come home at all. "It's easier for him to stay in town, that way he can get in earlier in the morning," she said.

More and more now, her mother sat for hours at a time doing nothing, staring into space. Sometimes, when Laura spoke to her, she didn't even seem to hear.

"Mommy."

There would be no answer. "Mommy, talk to me. Mommy, are you *listening* to me?"

"What, honey?" she would say, and her eyes would shift, focus for a moment on Laura. But then they would wander away and she would seem again to be lost in her own world, sitting utterly still, staring at something in the far distance.

"I miss Daddy," Laura said.

"I know," her mother said. "It's hard."

It was as if all they did was wait—wait for him to come home. They didn't have real dinners anymore, only snacks. They took desultory walks to the park and Laura's mother walked beside her, silently.

Nothing mattered unless he was there. And when her father finally did come home and kiss them, he was like the handsome prince, thought Laura, kissing them all alive.

But now, when he arrived home and went to her to kiss her mother, Laura saw that her back was stiff, she didn't kiss him back. But he didn't seem to notice. He turned around and scooped Laura up in his arms. "Sweetheart, how's my sweetheart!" he cried and kissed her hard on the cheek and scratched her face with his day's growth of beard.

Behind him, her mother's back was turned. She didn't look at him when she served the dinner.

"I'd love some more of that ham," he said.

"Get it yourself," she snapped.

Sometimes, when he was home, he would walk alongside Laura while she rode her bike. But he was often silent and preoccupied. As they went along the road, she looked up at him. His face was closed, his high, domed forehead furrowed with worry.

"What are you thinking about?" Laura asked.

"Oh nothing. Just work," he said. And she wondered what it was about his work that caused him to think so hard.

꒩

One day, when Laura returned from school, her mother was not at the front door to greet her as the teacher dropped her off. She let herself into the house. As she entered, the quiet of the house enfolded her. "Mommy!" she called out. There was no answer.

Before her were the carpeted stairs. She began to climb. At the top she went into their bedroom.

"There you are!" said Laura. Her mother was sitting by the window. She didn't turn or move. Her eyes were fixed on the street outside, unblinking. She wasn't breathing . . . Was she dead? Rooted to the spot, a tree or a stone?

"Mommy . . ." Laura walked around her so she could see her face.

It was wet and gleaming, a sheet of tears lay over it.

"Mommy!"

She didn't move. There was no sound. Her face was still.

"Please, Mommy!" She pulled at her sleeve. "Mommy!"

Slowly, the life seemed to return to her, to push her forward. She reached out, took Laura in her arms, and laid Laura's head upon her chest, stroking her hair. But she said nothing.

Her mother slept all the time now. Her face grew pale and lumpy. She seemed always to wear her crimson wool bathrobe.

Sometimes Laura made her own sandwich for dinner. She played about the house by herself now, while her mother slept upstairs.

One night, when he came home early, her father said, "We've hired a nanny, Hilda, to take care of you." Hilda arrived a few days later, a tall blond woman from Switzerland.

She seemed young, only a few years older than Laura, and spoke with a German accent. Hilda didn't sleep all day, she was thin and athletic, she could *do* things.

Every morning now, Laura went up to her mother's room to be inspected. For a moment then, her mother seemed to come alive. She examined Laura intently as if looking for signs, checking to see if her color was good, that she was washed and clean, her hair tidy. And then, if all was well, she would hug and kiss her, send her on her way. Then she would sink back into the bed, lost in the pillows and covers, her face hidden, sometimes only her hand hanging over the edge of the bed to show that she was there.

Occasionally, she got out of bed. Then she would push her heavy body up into a sitting position, swing her legs across the mattress and onto the floor.

Her legs were huge and round and swollen. They were very pale and in places the skin was cracked. They looked like an elephant's legs.

"What's the matter with your legs?" Laura cried.

"It's just the pregnancy," she said. "It'll go away."

But Laura turned her face to the wall. She couldn't look at them.

After that, whenever her mother got out of bed, she closed her eyes tight so she didn't see the legs.

She stood on the front lawn looking up at her mother's window. All around her the garden was dark, but above the line of the trees the sky was filled with light, the clouds were edged with silver. The moon floated over the house, making it seem very white.

The windows of the house blazed with light. The night breeze ruffled her hair, the skin rose on her arms. She was staring up at the window of her mother's bedroom, which was all lit up. They had forgotten about her, forgotten to put her to bed. Her father had told her to go and play somewhere, even though it was nighttime now. She waited, looking up at the window.

She saw a shadow moving in the window, bending down over something. What were they doing to her mother? Were they hurting her?

The shadow blocked the window and then moved away, revealing the light again. She wanted to go up there, interrupt them, stop them, but her father had said to go away.

Her mother couldn't move now to get away from them. She was too big to move, to even walk now. Hilda had to help her take a bath because her legs were so swollen.

Laura rubbed her arms in the moonlight. She was cold, even though it was summer.

She walked back into the house and climbed the stairs. Her mother's bedroom door was at the top to the right. She had almost reached the top when she saw her father.

"Don't go in there, Laura," her father said. "She's sleeping. She doesn't feel well."

"Be a good girl, Laura," he said softly, warningly, and then he went into the study and shut the door.

Laura sat down on the stairs by the door to her mother's room. She leaned her chin on her hands, watching the door. Always, always, she was resting! Why didn't they want her there? She could rest, she could sleep. She was eight years old. She would make her feel better.

31

≀

Hilda suggested they go for a walk after dinner. It was peculiar that Hilda would want to go for a walk so close to bedtime, but Laura went happily, pedaling her bicycle vigorously along the sidewalk. Hilda was tall and thin, but she had to make long strides to keep up with Laura on her bike.

They went along the pavement, past the houses hidden behind their hedgerows. She saw lights burning in the upstairs windows, golden in the murky evening. Above them, as they went along the road, the trees formed a canopy, darkening the way.

Laura pedaled down to the corner. Then they turned back. As they approached the house again, Laura saw an ambulance parked in front of it. The ambulance's white body glowed in the dusky light. The engine started up; it began to pull away, moving silently, its red light twisting and flashing. And then it disappeared under the canopy of dark trees.

"What's that?" Laura asked.

"They took your mother to the hospital to have the baby," said Hilda. "And they thought it would be better if you didn't see her go."

"Will the baby be born soon?"

"It looks that way," said Hilda, "not long now."

Laura pedaled back to the house and Hilda gave her a snack in the kitchen, sitting opposite her at the table, watching as she put each morsel of food into her mouth. Laura was too thin, they said, she didn't eat, and sometimes Hilda or her mother had to put the food on the fork themselves and feed her.

While they were sitting there, she saw a car pull up

outside the house. Her father climbed out and ran across the grass, leaving the car idling behind him. He came in the back door through the kitchen.

"Hi, sweetie," he called, out of breath, stopping a moment to bend down and kiss her. "Mommy forgot her medicine. She sends you a kiss and says to tell you she'll be home soon." He dashed past her up the stairs.

A few moments later he was down again. In his hand, he carried a little brown bottle of pills.

Her eyes fixed on the pills, the brown glass bottle, the square shape caught in the grasp of his thick hand.

The next morning, she got up very early, even before Hilda. Her father wasn't home yet. She went outside to ride her bicycle. It was already hot.

Laura pedaled, waiting for him.

Soon, she saw the car drive up in front of the house. Laura stopped.

Her father got out of the car, and he was walking toward her slowly, watching her, his face weary and dark and unshaven.

"Sweetheart," he said, softly.

"Did the baby get born? What is it? When's Mommy coming home?"

But he didn't answer. The unexpected silence made her stop.

"When's she coming home?"

He looked at her, as if trying to measure his words.

"I've got something to tell you, sweetheart." He bent down and picked her up. She was getting heavier now, and he seldom carried her.

"What is it? I want to know."

He said nothing, but bore her up the steps, swinging the front door open with his shoulder.

"Tell me!" she asked.

"Sweetheart," he said, drawing her head to his shoulder. Just inside the house, he stopped. "Mommy's gone to heaven, sweetheart."

For a second, she didn't understand and then her mind translated. "She's dead?"

"Yes, sweetheart."

"She's dead?"

"Yes," he stroked her back, her hair.

"Will I never see her again?"

"She's in heaven, sweetheart. You'll see her in heaven."

He bore her up now, up the stairs, onto the second floor. She could feel the points of his collar scratching her face. He carried her into her bedroom and laid her on the bed, then sat down beside her, stroking her while she cried.

"Why did she die?" she asked.

"Things went very wrong with the birth, sweetheart."

"Did she hurt?"

"No, she didn't hurt. She didn't hurt at all."

"Did she bleed?"

"A little, yes. But the important thing now, sweetheart, is that she's at peace. She's happy now . . ."

"But who will look after me?"

"I will. I'll be here for you, and Hilda will take care of us. Everything will be fine . . ."

There was a great darkness around her now, the darkness of his body, her face against his neck, the hot tears coming until her head hurt . . . She yielded to the darkness, she let it cover her, she lost herself in it.

34

When she awoke, he was still there, sitting by the bed, watching her. She didn't know how much time had passed, but she knew that all the time she'd been asleep he hadn't taken his eyes from her, his gaze hadn't shifted.

He reached over and picked her up again and took her in his arms.

"Don't worry, Daddy's going to take care of you," he said, holding her. "Daddy's never going to leave you, I promise you. Just hold tight, just hold tight."

"What happened to the baby?" Laura asked.

"The baby went to Jesus too."

"What was it? What *was* the baby?"

"It was a boy."

A boy. She could have had a brother.

"But there's no pain now," he said, "no sadness now. They're at peace."

At first she cried when he went to work. Hilda held her back as she screamed, her arms stretched out toward him when he pulled away in the car. The first time he went to work, he stopped the car and got out and came back inside the house and stayed behind with her for half a day. Then, the next day, he said, "Sweetheart, I have to work. I have to earn money so we can have a good time. I'll be home tonight early and then we'll have a treat. You call me at the office if you want to, okay? If you get nervous you just give me a call."

Each day, she held onto Hilda crying when he left the house. But after a few days, she didn't cry anymore. She began to forget. She rode her bike, went to school, played.

And as the weeks passed, when she remembered what had happened, she didn't even feel sad now. Her mother's death, her very life, seemed only unreal. She tried to grasp it, comprehend it—one moment her mother had been there and now she was gone, forever. But then her attention shifted, she couldn't concentrate on it anymore.

Sometimes she wondered where her mother was. Was she like the dead bird she found on the sidewalk, its flesh blackened and pulled away from the bones? Maybe she lived in the sunset, wearing her crimson bathrobe.

Occasionally, in school, Laura said the words out loud, "My mother died . . . ," as if trying to make it real. The fact that her mother was dead made her different from other children, set her apart. Other children had mothers. She didn't. But she didn't cry now.

One night, in the middle of the night, something made her come awake. She had heard nothing, there had been no sound, but something had woken her.

She climbed down from her bed and walked out onto the landing. The house was still, nothing moved. Hilda was asleep in the other wing. It was cool and soft all around her. Through the hall window she saw a faint light pushing through the dark, the beginning of dawn. Across the landing, her father's door was open—he always closed it when he went to sleep. She could see a bluish shadow on the rug outside the door. His curtains weren't closed.

She walked toward the room. His bed was undisturbed, the cover flat and perfect and unwrinkled across it. The night before when she was getting ready for bed, he had gone out, to a party, he said, kissing her good-bye and leaving her with Hilda. But now he hadn't come home. Laura stared at the empty room. The window was shut—he always opened the window when he slept. There were no clothes flung upon the chair, no shoes on the floor the way they usually were.

She stood staring at the great, untouched room. And the sight of it filled her suddenly with sadness.

She returned to her own bed. She had just begun to fall asleep when she heard down below the faint sound of the front door opening, the soft jingle of keys, the scuff of feet on the stairs. She sat up.

He was standing in her doorway, his keys in his hand, looking in, wearing his tuxedo, his black tie unknotted.

"Where were you?" Laura asked.

He came across the room and sat down on her bed, leaned over and pulled the covers up around her chin.

"I was out late at a party," he whispered.

"Until morning?" she asked.

"It went on a long time," he said. In the gray light she could see the faint morning stubble on his face. And as he leaned near her, she could smell on his breath cigarette smoke, and the sweet smell of stale alcohol. She could feel his body loose and relaxed. "It's not time to get up yet," he said. "You go back to sleep now."

He leaned down, kissed her, then stood up again. She watched as he trod softly, a tall, lanky figure, across the room.

Laura wondered how many times he had stayed out at night and she hadn't known about it because she was asleep.

When she got up in the morning, the door to his room was shut tight.

"You're going on vacation," he said. It had been several months since her mother had died. "Hilda's going to Switzerland to visit her parents and you're going with her. There's a doctor there we want to examine you for the eczema."

Hilda's family lived in a dark wood house that looked like a cuckoo clock. In Geneva, there was a doctor, a big white room, and, much to her relief, the doctor didn't hurt her, only examined her and said he could offer no alternative course of treatment—the application of zinc ointment seemed the best approach.

When they returned to England, her father met them at the train station. They had been gone for ten days, but it seemed like no time and yet forever.

"How's my honeybunch!" he cried, sweeping her up in his arms, squeezing her hard. "Oh, how I've *missed* you!" he said.

He put her down and took her suitcase.

"I've got a surprise for you. We've moved to a new place, a flat in Hampstead," he said.

"And there's a special friend staying with us, a very nice lady. She's going to help me take care of you."

"Is it Mrs. Reed?" Laura asked.

He stopped. "How did you know?" he asked with a laugh. There was something uneasy in his laugh.

"After your mother died," he said, "Barbara wrote me a note telling me how sorry she was. We grew close and we fell in love. She is going to live with us—we will be married as soon as her divorce is final. But I needed someone to help take care of you now and Hilda will still be coming in every day."

When they arrived at the new flat, it was evening and Mrs. Reed was waiting for them. She was wearing a black turtleneck sweater and beige slacks. "Welcome!" she cried, bending down and kissing Laura and leaving a print of dark pink lipstick on her cheek. "Please call me Barbara now," she said.

That night, Laura slept in the same bedroom as Barbara, in a single bed near her double bed, while her father slept on a cot in the glass-enclosed garden room at the other side of the flat—because they weren't married yet.

The next day, when her father went to work, Barbara said, "Why don't we get all dressed up and go into town?" Barbara wore her navy blue suit and her little hat with the veil, Laura her best coat and straw hat, and they went to tea at Fortnum & Mason on Piccadilly, where they had chestnut pastries.

Barbara bought a television set, and on the children's program there was a contest for who could make the best paper mask. Barbara helped Laura cut out the mask and send it in. She won the contest and her name was spoken on the television.

Barbara spent hours with Laura, cutting costumes out of crepe paper, a fairy costume with wings, a ballerina's tutu. It seemed that each day now, Barbara thought of delightful things to do. She devoted her time entirely to Laura.

"You poor thing, we've got to do something about that eczema," Barbara said, touching Laura's cheek. "Let's try you on an egg-free diet."

At night, sometimes, Laura woke up and Barbara's bed across the room was empty. She would listen for a moment in the darkness. But there was only silence.

She knew that Barbara was in the garden room with her father. Laura pulled the covers over her head—she didn't want to hear anything.

And then in the morning, when Laura opened her eyes,

there was Barbara again, asleep in the double bed as if she'd never left.

How beautiful Barbara was, more beautiful than her mother, Laura thought secretly, with a pang of guilt. When Barbara went out at night with her father, Laura sat and watched her get ready, the transformation of her beautiful face into an extraordinary one. First, the application of foundation to her face and neck, and, if she were going to wear an evening dress, to her chest all the way down to her breasts. Her skin was soft and white and powdery now. Laura touched the corners of her own mouth, cracked and raw from the eczema, seeping and damp. When it was bad, her skin sometimes looked like piecrust. She would never be beautiful like Barbara.

As Barbara watched herself in the mirror, she sucked in her cheeks to make the cheekbones more prominent. After the foundation was applied, she painted a black line around her eyes and on her eyebrows. Then she dabbed powder over the black line to soften it, and over her lips so her lipstick would stay on longer; and then came the dark pink lipstick itself— cyclamen, it was called.

Finally, Chanel No. 5, applied to the pulse points of her wrists, behind the ears, and deep between the breasts.

When it was all complete, Barbara would rise up like a swan from the water, pulling herself toward the mirror, rejoicing in her beauty. And at the bedroom door, Laura's father stood, his gaze caught on her. And Barbara seemed to glow in the light of his love.

And as Laura watched them, sometimes, she remembered the night her mother died, her father rushing back in the car to get the medicine. And for a brief moment, she wondered if the little brown bottle had contained poison. Maybe they had poisoned her mother so they could be together.

But she mustn't think that. It couldn't have happened. She mustn't say anything about it—they'd be angry. She didn't want to make them angry and so she put the thought out of her mind. They were a family now, the three of them. And Barbara seemed to love her.

There were photographs of Barbara from the stage when she had been an actress. She'd had a walk-on part in a movie with Olivia de Havilland; and her hair had been cut short when she tried out for a role in *Joan of Arc*. Laura stared at the photographs. They made Barbara's skin seem even paler and the shadows under her cheekbones even darker, heightened the contrast between her powdery white skin and her dark hair, made her eyes seem more slanting.

Barbara collected movie annuals, and sometimes she and Laura read them together. Laura liked to look at the photographs of the actresses. They always seemed to be wearing dresses with one shoulder bare. She imagined the stories behind the photographs as the men and women clung passionately to one another, or confronted each other. Barbara was like the actresses in the movie annuals, Laura thought, and her love affair with Laura's father was a great romance, like a romance in a film.

"You're so pretty," she said to Barbara. And Barbara smiled fondly at her. "I know what you've been through," she said. "My mother died when I was young too. I understand."

Bit by bit, Barbara told Laura the story of her past. Her mother had been German, her father a soldier in the Allied occupation force in Germany after the First World War. Barbara's mother was very beautiful, she said, she came from a fine family and knew the very best in clothes and jewelry and

41

linens. Her father was a garage mechanic, but he was handsome with his blue eyes and the two of them had fallen in love. Laura understood that somehow Barbara felt her father was beneath her mother. Barbara spoke in clipped, upper-class tones. But sometimes when she was angry, or when she told a joke, Laura could hear a remnant of some former accent, coarse, harsh, which she later understood was North of England. Sometimes Laura noticed that Barbara's Oxford accent became more pronounced—when men were around or when she was nervous.

"I loved my mother," said Barbara, "but my father was very strict, a typical Edwardian father, and they were very unhappy together. We used to spend every holiday in Germany, and we were there when the war broke out. My mother had just had an operation for cancer. My father cabled us and told us to get on the next train. I was only thirteen, and I had to get her out on a stretcher. Luckily, there was a nurse on board who could give her an injection for the pain."

Laura imagined the train carrying Barbara and her mother roaring through the Black Forest, and Barbara heroically bringing her mother to safety. "We just made it," said Barbara. "When she died later, in England, I felt as if it were the end of the world.

"I hated Manchester," Barbara said. "All the houses were exactly the same. They stretched out into the distance into infinity. When you went from one street to another it was like being in a maze. And everywhere, you could smell the factories. The air was so filthy it used to make the curtains yellow—you'd wash them and a day later they'd be yellow again."

When Barbara was fifteen, after her mother died, she had quit school, lied about her age, and gone to fight in the WAAFs, the women's branch of the air force.

42

"I loved the war," Barbara said. "It was like boarding school. I operated a barrage balloon. . . . Oh, the English loved their barrage balloons! They used to be up there in the sky above the city, like fish eggs, great big balloons at the end of long chains.

"I was even injured," Barbara said. "One of the chains cut me up so badly I was in hospital for three days. That's where I got my medal." She kept the medal in her jewelry box along with the jewelry she had inherited from her mother. The wooden box was shellacked to a gleaming finish and cracked with age. The inside was lined with velvet, and there was a secret compartment where Barbara kept her passport and other papers. The box contained her bar pin with the diamond in the center, the cameo shell ring, the charm bracelet of pink gold, a ring with a huge old zircon.

"When the war was over," said Barbara, "I couldn't bear to go back to Manchester, and so I got married." She had married the stooped man with the large, sad eyes. "It was a terrible mistake," Barbara said, looking down. "I did it to escape.

"Your father was my salvation," she said. "I never thought I would have a chance at happiness until I met him."

Sometimes, at night now, when Laura lay in bed, still and quiet, waiting for sleep to come, she would feel her body begin to swell like a balloon. She felt as if she were floating on air. It was not precisely a physical sensation, but rather as if she were on the outside looking down at herself, as she slowly, gently expanded. It wasn't even an uncomfortable feeling, but it was uncontrollable—a slow, quiet swelling, as if her body were about to burst and then diffuse into the surrounding air. The only way to stop it was to get up, switch the light on at once, and break the spell.

How did it happen? The little boy just seemed to appear out of thin air. No one had said anything about Barbara having a child. Life was really quite full of surprises, Laura thought. Who knew what would be around the corner?

He appeared one day, a small figure, perhaps two years younger than she—she was nine now—dressed in short pants and knee socks, a pale blue coat with a velvet collar and a little matching cap, holding on to Barbara's hand. And Laura's father behind them, carrying his little bag.

The boy stood before her, his dark blond hair curled in tendrils against his face, his skin tawny with a deep, red flush upon the cheeks. His eyes were very pale blue, almost slanted, like Barbara's.

"This is Simon, Barbara's little boy," her father said. "He's come to stay with us for the weekend. He's a nice friend for you to play with. I know you'll let him share your toys and make him welcome."

The boy looked directly at her. His eyes were like the palest glass. Laura looked into the eyes and could see nothing there.

"Would you like some lunch?" Barbara asked. She spoke as if she were afraid of him, her own child.

"All right," he said, matter-of-fact.

How beautiful he was, Laura thought. She was nine years old, and she was falling in love again, this time with the son.

He was to sleep in the same room as she and Barbara. He slept in the double bed with his mother, and Laura slept in the small single bed.

In the morning, when the first light touched her eyes, the

first bird chirped outside the window, Laura awoke. It was only five-thirty. She climbed out of bed in the milky light—and crept across the room to view him. Barbara was still asleep. But Simon was sitting up in bed in his pajamas. Laura climbed up on the bed beside him.

Underneath her, she felt something cold and wet.

"You wet your bed!" she cried.

He shrugged. He didn't seem to care.

And she didn't care either.

Simon sprang quickly to the floor. She watched him get dressed, saw his naked body, tawny, thin-loined, the muscles taut, the little penis hanging out.

"Let's go outside," he whispered, "and play." She dressed herself quickly and followed him.

Here at last was someone who slept even less than she.

They went downstairs and out into the garden. The mist hung over the ground and they couldn't see far. The grass beneath their feet was wet with dew. The lawn sloped down behind the house, sheltered by great pine trees and then becoming woodland.

A great privacy seemed to envelop them in the dawn that day, and it felt to Laura as if the whole world belonged to them. They could have done anything together, they could have run away.

The branches of the pine trees hung down as far as the ground, enclosing spaces as big as rooms. They could stand upright and be entirely hidden.

"We could have a house here," he said, pointing to an enclosure. "I will be the man and you will be the woman. I'll go to work in the morning and when I come back you will make supper for me."

"What will I make supper from?"

"Mud and pine needles," he said.

They played until two hours later, when Barbara called to them from the apartment window above for breakfast. But they ignored her. They played all day, stopping only for a snack—meals didn't matter to them, they were but an unwelcome distraction, food meant nothing to them in the intensity of their games. Under the sheltering branches of the pines, they repeated over and over again all the most important moments of life, courtship, marriage, birth. Simon was the younger, but he called all the shots. "This will be the sitting room," he said, pointing to one place sectioned off by a low-hanging branch. Now, as their minds focused on it, the house seemed magically to grow furniture, a bed of pine needles, a fallen log became a couch. Simon went to work in his imaginary car, a black Rover like her father and Barbara's, and returned, carrying his imaginary briefcase, leaving and returning, again and again. One of Laura's dolls became their child, and the game took all day.

Night came, but there was no need for sleep. They wanted only to be together. And because Simon would only be there for the weekend, they were allowed to stay up late. Barbara couldn't force him to do anything he didn't want to anyway. "Perhaps you should go to bed," she said tentatively. But he ignored her and kept on playing.

When Barbara went to kiss Simon, Laura saw that she touched him hesitantly, lightly, as if she were afraid he'd push her away or snap at her. Or as if she didn't really quite know the right way to touch him. And he never kissed her back, he never looked at her.

When Simon refused to eat his dinner, Barbara would look

at Laura's father helplessly, as if she were baffled by Simon, as if *he* would know what to do.

"Would you like a bedtime story, Simon?" Barbara asked, when evening came.

"No, thank you," he answered, his voice cool.

On Sunday, Simon was readied to leave, his little blue coat put on again, his suitcase packed. His face was empty, he didn't seem sad at all. Laura waved feebly after him.

With his going, a light seemed to be extinguished. Now her days were empty, blank. Her father and Barbara were so in love, he was caught by her beauty like a moth dazzled by the light. It was as if they were always on a honeymoon, and she, Laura, felt like a witness to some great love story. And with her skin all red and cracked from the eczema, her scraggly hair bound up in braids, her thin, awkward body, she could never be part of it.

She counted the days until Simon was to return. Weekdays, school, meant nothing now, she waited only for Friday evening, when Barbara would come back with him, Simon and his little bag, his little bag of tricks.

"Simon's father doesn't want him to come to us, so we have to be very nice to him, or he might stop coming," Barbara said, searching Laura's face as if to see whether she would comply. As if she could be anything but nice! As if she wouldn't give every toy she owned to keep Simon there.

"Why does Simon always have to go home on Sundays?" Laura asked her father.

"His father has temporary custody of him, under the separation agreement—you don't really understand what that means. But we're only allowed to have him on weekends."

"Could I go to his house one day to play?" she asked.

"I'm afraid not," he said.

"Why not?"

"I'm afraid his father might not like that."

"But why *wouldn't* his father like it?" she asked.

"Well, his father is a little upset at the moment."

"Why is he upset?"

"He's upset because Barbara left him."

This man, Barbara's husband, was very angry, Laura thought. He was someone who could hurt her. And yet, she thought, he shouldn't be angry at her, Laura. It wasn't her fault that Barbara left him. And in a certain way, even, Simon's father and she were related, connected, because they both loved Simon.

Simon never talked about his father. He lived by the sea somewhere, in Sussex, Laura gathered. His father owned a bookshop there, it seemed, and his father's sister, his Aunt Edna, cared for him when his father worked. But Simon never discussed them. When Laura asked Simon about his father—after all, everyone had fathers—he answered only in monosyllables, indifferently.

"What's he like, your father?" she asked.

"Nothing special," said Simon, busy at his game, tying a piece of string between the garage and the window of their room to make a "telephone" wire. He was a great climber, like a spider. He had actually climbed up onto the roof of the garage, oblivious to the danger. Barbara and her father were out and couldn't stop him.

Simon wouldn't talk about his father. It was almost as if he didn't exist. In fact, Simon didn't seem to pay much attention to Barbara either, one way or another. They seldom spent much time together when he came. He rarely even spoke to Barbara. He seemed to regard Barbara, and his father, all adults in fact, as irrelevant, merely obstacles to his desires and needs, hurdles to be circumvented. None of them were to be trusted or let in. The only person he ever really talked to when he came was Laura. When he arrived, he ran directly toward her, and then they began their games.

He was the most beautiful child she'd ever seen. She felt thin and scraggly next to him. He could have been a girl with his rich dark blond curls. Sometimes, if he were a little tired, he would let her comb his hair. He would lie down on the bed on his stomach and she would sit on the edge of the bed and comb out the curls, wrapping the hair around her fingers, forming it into ringlets, examining the tiny individual strands, platinum and gold and red. She wanted to look like him. She would like to have a little boy like him one day, with his curls, his dusky cheeks, his perfect, straight brown limbs that were always suntanned, even in sunless England.

But Simon was naughty. He lied and he stole. Laura was astonished by the extent of his lying. She herself never lied—her father always said that lying was the worst sin.

"Where were you two this afternoon?" Barbara asked.

"Oh, playing in the garden," Simon said. When, in fact, they had been playing on the Heath. They had been strictly forbidden to go on the Heath by themselves. It was only a few blocks away, but there had been several child murders there in recent years. But Laura and Simon had spent the afternoon there, running on the sloping meadows, playing hide-and-seek in the woods. As long as they were together, they knew they would be safe.

"I called for you in the garden and you didn't come," said Barbara.

"We were over at Rebecca's house," said Simon, which they were not.

That was all they knew about him, the lies he told them.

"I can't find my pen," said her father. "Have any of you kids seen it?"

"*I* haven't," said Simon, when in fact Simon had stolen the pen, a good Parker with a solid gold nib that her father prized, "a very expensive pen," he said.

Simon stole money from the pile of change beside her father's bed, not once, but several times. Laura would watch, holding her breath, as he actually stole from them while they were in the house, as he crept into her father's room in the morning while he slept and took the change from the bedside, walking out undetected. He didn't need the money, for they lavished him with gifts. Any toy almost, that he asked for, was given to him. It was as if he stole for the principle of it. "If you tell anyone I will never come again," he warned Laura. Simon—not come again! She would die—she would never, never do anything to cause that to happen.

"I can't understand it," her father said later. "I thought I had a pound note and some change there. Where could it have gone?"

"I don't know," Simon said.

"You lied to him," Laura said to Simon later.

"So—what does he care? They've got plenty of money."

"But you lied," she went on.

He shrugged, his pale, indifferent eyes scanning the landscape for some other game, some other purpose.

"You're not supposed to lie, Simon. Ever. That's bad," said Laura, instructing him.

"Who says so?" he challenged.

"My father does. God says so." Never lie to me, her father said. He put a great emphasis on this. The worst thing you can do is lie to me.

50

"Hal doesn't know anything," Simon said impatiently. "And God—what can he do?" He laughed.

"*You* don't know," Laura said.

"Well I lied, didn't I? And here I am to tell about it. Nothing's happened to me, has it?"

And confronted with the evidence, Laura was silent.

"Don't tell them *anything*," Simon told her. "Just make that a rule. Tell them nothing about us, understand?" he said. And she was afraid to disobey him.

"Well, what did you kids do today?" her father asked.

"Oh nothing," she said.

Her father and Barbara's requests for information resulted only in cool, indifferent shrugs, or lies.

Lying was Simon's rule of thumb. If he had a chance to lie rather than to tell the truth, he lied. It was a way of keeping them all from him, Laura thought. It was as if he created a whole world, a world of lies, the world he showed to her father and to Barbara. And that world was totally removed from the truth, from who she and Simon really were.

If her father and Barbara didn't know the truth, they could never tell them what to do. They couldn't control them. Perhaps, thought Laura, Simon didn't want her father and Barbara to know anything about them because he thought they weren't to be trusted. Grown-ups were always doing unpredictable things—her mother dying, Barbara leaving Simon, for instance.

And so Laura watched him; she was his witness, his necessary accomplice, audience to all his pranks. It was the principle of the thing, doing something to them, defying them, that was the point. She didn't quite understand why. Perhaps it was because Simon was cross because his mother left him to care for Laura, but he never showed it except in his indifference.

51

They began to speak in their own secret language, "egg language" it was called. The word *egg* was put in front of every vowel sound. Actually, the language was Laura's idea. It was she who explained to Simon what a vowel was. They spoke it as rapidly as they could to make it indecipherable to her father and Barbara. Simon was "Seggimeggon" and she was "Leggauregga."

In winter, Simon discovered a "secret room," perhaps just an oddly shaped closet, or a space left over from when the flat was actually part of the larger house, a passage leading from the hall all the way down to the kitchen, too small for an adult, the perfect size for a child. They made a home in the secret passage, with a flashlight, her old dolls, books. No one could enter. There was no way Simon would let them into his little world, none of them was to be trusted. All of them were the darkest sinners, and he, Simon, wouldn't let them near him. He never, however, seemed to lie to Laura.

How deftly he could move! How quick and quiet he was, like an animal, while she felt herself clumsy and graceless. She had a "trick" ankle, which every once in a while gave way without reason and caused her to stumble suddenly. But Simon's body was centered, coordinated far beyond his years.

Sometimes Laura woke up at night and found him standing by her bed. He had gotten out of the bed he shared with Barbara and moved across the room without a sound—and now he was staring down at her.

"What are you doing?" she asked.

"I want to see if I can move around without waking anyone. I can move quieter than a cat!" he hissed.

He *was* like a cat, slithering into hidden places. He could do everything better than she. He could beat her at checkers, dominoes, all such games. He won every game, although she was the older of the two. He couldn't be beaten. In hide-and-seek he could never be found.

There was something about him that wasn't really human, Laura thought. He was a spirit, a hobgoblin, not quite human, but with a human form. He could outsmart her father and Barbara and any other adult. If he didn't actually know a thing, he could figure it out. And she knew she could trust him. She was the only one he liked, the only one *he* trusted. There was a bond between them, the bond of their being alone, separate from her father and Barbara.

Outside them, strange events were occurring—Laura's mother had died, Simon's mother had left him—but she and Simon never talked about these things, never tried to decipher them, for Simon was uncommunicative, although she would have welcomed some explanation.

But in the midst of all these goings-on—her mother's death, his mother's leaving Simon, events that they couldn't understand—they had one another.

Sometimes, in the afternoon, he asked her to read to him. For some reason he liked this particular quiet activity. Then he became the child, and she was his mother. Then, for a brief moment, he was quiet, motionless, and she was in charge.

She read to him from *The Secret Garden*: " 'I am Colin Craven. Who are you?' 'I am Mary Lennox . . .' "

They had both had the book read to them before. Sometimes, as they sat there propped up against a tree, he recited whole paragraphs ahead of her, as if he were reading the book with her. But he dropped words, transposed sentences.

His handwriting was nearly illegible. She realized that, by some amazing feat, he was memorizing what was read to him, carrying the memory from one reading to the next.

"You can't read, can you?" she said.

"Sort of," he replied, vaguely.

He was seven years old and he couldn't read a word. He was being held back a form at school and Barbara was upset.

"But you can't live without reading!" Laura said.

"Yes, you can," he said, with perfect confidence.

There was something very wrong. In the normal world, you had to read. But he wasn't of that world. He didn't go by the same rules; he was somehow different, like an animal in a way, Laura thought. He had other skills, he lived by his wits. He could do things normal human beings couldn't do.

He could climb better than anyone she knew. Trees seemed to exercise a spell over him. One day, he climbed a great live oak at the foot of the grassy slope behind the house. She watched him as his limbs straddled the branches, outlined like a spider against the winter sky.

"Come on up, Laura! Don't be a scaredy-cat," he yelled from far above.

"I'm afraid!" she cried, rooted there.

"Don't be afraid." His voice echoed in the cold, as he kept climbing, arms and legs spread out, heels dug into the trunk of the tree.

It all happened so quickly, she saw it only for a moment, his body plunging through the air, flopping to the ground like a rag doll, arms and legs bouncing on the earth.

He lay absolutely still. For a moment, she couldn't move. A great cold spread through her body. She screamed. She ran to him—he wasn't moving, wasn't breathing. There was a gash on his forehead. The skin was split; it looked like a piece of fruit cut open, thick and rich with blood vessels traced on the pulsing flesh.

"S-i-i-mon!" She clutched her fist to her mouth.

He was dead. She was afraid to touch him. Something foul about a dead person, like a dead bird, maggots.

She ran to the house for her father—Barbara was out. Hearing her screams, he pushed past her down the stairs. A neighbor, aroused by the noise, came out into the hall, then called an ambulance. In the garden, her father squatted down over Simon's limp form.

Simon regained consciousness in the ambulance. He lay on a stretcher and Laura and her father sat in the back with him.

At the hospital, he didn't cry. She waited in the hallway with her father while they X-rayed him. There was only a mild concussion, the doctor said, and he could be released as soon as the wound was stitched.

As they wheeled him out of the X-ray room, she saw his bandaged head and burst into tears. "Simon . . ."

"Don't cry!" he commanded, annoyed. "Don't be a crybaby! *I* am going to do it without crying."

The doctor was a woman with short, gunmetal gray hair and leathery skin.

"All right, Simon," said the doctor. "I'm going to inject a little painkiller into the skin . . ." Laura watched as the needle penetrated the ripped, wet flesh.

And now as she watched, Simon grew pale, his blue eyes seemed to turn white in his head. He gripped the side of the examining table.

"Attaboy," her father encouraged.

The doctor withdrew the hypodermic and began to sew up the wound with black thread.

"Just a few minutes now and it'll be all over."

When it was finished, Laura's father asked him, "Do you want me to carry you?"

"*No,*" he said. Laura and her father watched him silently.

They were afraid of him. Everyone in the family was afraid of his irritations, infrequent though they were.

Simon eased himself off the examining table and stood up. Suddenly, he went whiter still. He sat down again quickly on a chair.

"Wait a moment, why don't you?" the doctor advised.

Simon sat there, not saying anything. Then he allowed Laura's father to take his arm and he tottered out the door. There would be no aftereffects, the doctor said, except for a scar above the eye.

Suddenly Simon brightened. "Will it last forever?" he asked.

"Probably," said the doctor, "a faint scar."

At night now, when they knew that Barbara and her father would be asleep, he crawled into bed with her and they slept side by side, although it was hard to sleep in the same bed with Simon because he squirmed and tossed, and scratched her calves with his toenails. Somehow, they knew they had to be secret about getting into bed with each other; without knowing why, they sensed that her father and Barbara would disapprove. But there was little danger of their finding out because Simon and she always got up so much earlier than they did. She and Simon didn't kiss, didn't caress one another. Yet it seemed natural and necessary that they sleep together. Here at last was a companion for her nights. Now, the two of them in bed together were in perfect symmetry with her father and Barbara.

"Let's watch each other pee," Simon said. "You watch me and I'll watch you, okay?"

He unzipped his shorts and the stream arched from his penis into the toilet.

56

She wanted to do it like him.

She pulled down her pants, thrust her hips forward to the toilet bowl, but the urine only dribbled down between her legs, wetting her skirt and socks. She shrank back. "I made a mess!" She couldn't help it, suddenly she began to cry.

"Shut up, silly," said Simon. "Just go and change, you idiot."

"But they'll *see*!"

"No, they won't. Just say you spilled something."

"It'll smell!" she cried.

"Don't be revolting, Laura! Go and change. Hurry up!"

And she went and changed, hiding her wet clothes in the laundry basket, hoping they would dry before anyone noticed.

Her father said, "Don't talk about his father with him. Don't talk about the situation."

Laura didn't quite know what he meant by "the situation," or why he didn't want her to talk about it. Anyway, she was closer to Simon than she was to her father—their relationship wasn't subject to adult rules and admonitions.

"Your daddy's evil, a villain, isn't he?" she asked him one day, matter-of-factly.

"Why do you say that?" Simon asked.

"Barbara and my father say he is."

"That's because Barbara left us," he replied calmly.

He seemed to, in some way, understand it all, and yet not to care. It was as if he didn't think it was even worth talking about. But Laura would have liked to have someone to question, to make it clear to her. Why did Barbara leave Simon, her child? Weren't mothers always supposed to be

57

with their children? Was his father so evil that Barbara would leave Simon just to get away from him?

"Why is Simon's father angry at us?" she asked Barbara.

"He's upset because I want to get a divorce."

"But why *did* you leave him and Simon?"

Barbara hesitated. "It's very hard to explain. Simon's father—well—I'm afraid he's a little disturbed. . . . One day, when you're older perhaps, I'll try and explain it to you. But it's very difficult for you to understand now."

What was "disturbed"? Laura wondered. Something sick, dangerous, uncontrollable—and perhaps contagious, something to stay away from.

She sensed they were afraid of Simon's father. She imagined him with an evil leer on his face, a pointed wizard's hat and a black cloak. This man, Simon's father, he might capture her, imprison her. He was so filled with hate he might hurt her, or kill her, even though she was innocent. She tried to imagine where Simon lived. What was it like? What would happen if she went there? Simon's unseen home, his father's house, it fascinated her, it was like an ogre's lair, a forbidden place where strange things occurred.

One Friday, Barbara said Laura could go with her to pick Simon up. "I don't think anyone will mind," she said. "It's a long drive. It'll give Simon something to do to have you there, make the trip easier."

"Will Simon's father be there?" Laura asked.

"No. Only his Aunt Edna. His father always leaves when I come."

They left London at five o'clock, and there was a traffic

jam. For half an hour, they sat on the highway, moving only sporadically.

"Damn!" Barbara swore under her breath. "We're supposed to be there at six. If we're one minute late, they'll criticize me." Laura watched the traffic snarled in front of them. She wanted to get out of the car and pick the other cars up bodily and move them to make way for the Rover. She stared hard at the cars, trying with all the force of her will to make them move.

"Will they still let us have him if we're late?" Laura asked.

"Yes," said Barbara, gritting her teeth at the traffic.

Then the traffic broke, and they were on the way, leaving London behind them.

They were on a great highway. Night was falling. The darkness stretched out on either side of them, and there were seldom any lights now except for the occasional truck or car whooshing by, lighting up the windshield of the Rover for a moment, and then it would be dark again.

Would this Edna try to hurt them? She imagined them getting to the house and there would be a gunshot and screaming and she would cower behind Barbara. And yet she wanted to go, she wanted to see where he lived, to see his room and his toys. She wanted to have more time with him and this would mean she would get to see him sooner. She could feel Barbara next to her, tense at the wheel, her body arched forward as she peered into the dark road. Barbara hadn't spoken.

"Are you scared?" she asked Barbara.

"No," said Barbara, but her voice was small and dry.

"Will his Aunt Edna yell at us?"

Barbara smiled grimly. "No, I don't think so." But Laura was not convinced.

They drove for an hour and a half. Now, through the window of the car, Laura could feel a coolness rising. There was a briny smell, the sea nearby. She strained to look out the window, but there were only great stretches of black on either side.

As they drove on, there appeared on the horizon a phosphorescent glow. "We're near the ocean," Barbara said. "We're almost there."

Laura saw lights in the distance, a town. She saw the vague outline of a round tower on a bluff.

They turned onto a narrow road and there was the ocean now on her right; she could see the waves heaving and falling under the moon. To the left was a wide, flat, sandy stretch, and a string of modest houses, isolated from the town.

"That's the house," said Barbara. She slowed down and stopped the car. There was a small house in the Tudor style, built of white stucco with black beams, like the other houses, with a garage attached to it. In front, there was a garden with a path. It was much smaller than Laura expected, an ordinary house, she thought. She searched the darkness for some sign of Owen. He could be lurking there with a gun.

A dog was barking inside the house. A light went on in front and the door opened and Laura saw a woman's form outlined against it.

That must be Aunt Edna, she thought. Laura sat still, afraid to get out of the car. But Barbara opened the door and climbed out.

"Should I stay here?" Laura asked.

"No, that's all right."

Barbara walked toward the house and Laura followed

behind her. Laura heard a cockney voice—"Come on, Toby"—the woman talking to the yelping dog. Laura could just make out a middle-aged woman with gray hair and glasses.

"Hello, Barbara," said the woman. Her voice was polite, but cool. She held back the little barking dog, who strained to get at them. "Toby, now behave! You naughty boy! *Heel*, Toby!"

"Hello, Edna," said Barbara. Barbara's voice was small, like a child's. "We're a few minutes late. We had trouble getting out of town. Friday night traffic. Awful." Laura could hear a quaver in her voice, as if she were a child explaining herself to a teacher.

The woman picked up the squirming dog.

She peered at Laura. "Is that his daughter?" the woman asked, looking at Laura curiously. There was a hurt, aggrieved tone in her voice.

"Yes, this is Laura. Laura, shake hands," said Barbara. Laura stepped forward, half hiding behind Barbara, and offered her hand.

"How do you do?" said the woman, giving her a cool look. "Come on, Simon. Your mummy's here," she called over her shoulder.

Simon appeared behind her, dressed in his blue coat. He stood still, fixed his eyes on Laura, saying nothing. His Aunt Edna handed Barbara his suitcase.

"Have a nice time now, Simon," she said. She bent down to kiss him, but he paid no attention to her, only looked at Laura.

Edna fussed over the collar of his coat. "Well then," she said to Barbara, "we'll see you on Sunday at six."

"Yes, I'll be on time," said Barbara, like a little girl.

They climbed into the car, Laura and Simon in back. They pulled away, and Laura glanced behind in the rear window and saw the woman standing in the light of the door, watching them.

"I've got some soldiers," Simon said, without preliminaries. "Look. Let's set them up on the seat."

Now, as they drove away from the town, Laura could see in front of her Barbara begin visibly to relax. She shook her shoulders a little as she glanced back in the rearview mirror at the house receding behind her. Barbara switched on the radio and the car was filled with a big-band tune. In the back, Simon set up the soldiers on the seat. There were foot soldiers, soldiers on horseback, and generals. As usual, Simon controlled the game, an empire and a war so complex and so elaborate that only he and Laura could understand it.

Simon wasn't coming at Christmas—"Under the terms of the separation agreement, his father has the right to have him," Barbara said. On Christmas morning, Laura awoke to see that it was cold and gray outside. The house was so quiet and empty without him. Who would she talk to? She went downstairs and found her father and Barbara were there. Their smiles seemed strained, as if they were trying to be cheerful for her.

Underneath the Christmas tree, amid all the packages from America, from her grandmother and grandfather in Everett, was parked a little red electric car in which you could actually ride. It was almost life-size, the perfect size for a child. It had chrome fenders and lights that worked, and there was a great green satin ribbon tied around it.

"It has a motor that runs," her father said. "You can really drive it."

She touched the shiny red body with her fingertips. There was a bucket seat upholstered in real black leather, and a dashboard that lit up too.

"Shall we take it outside and try it?" he asked.

They wheeled the car outside and he showed her how to start it up—it had its own ignition key—"You can only drive it in the driveway now and on the sidewalk," he warned.

"It's for you *and* Simon," he said. "He couldn't come today, but when he comes it's his Christmas present too. It's very expensive, for the two of you to share. Don't forget now."

"I won't forget," she said. How could he think she wouldn't share it with Simon? She couldn't *wait* for him to come!

When, finally, Simon did come, after Christmas, they drove the little red car all the way around the block, past the big houses set back from the street, where no one seemed to live. Without a curb to stop its progress, it could go six miles an hour steadily.

"You're not to take it on the road," her father warned again. Of course, they did take it on the road, once they got away from the house. It was a stupid rule because there were few cars on their quiet suburban street and the little car didn't go very fast. The car was the most expensive, elaborate toy any child in their neighborhood had ever seen—but then, her father got paid with "the American dollar" and somehow that was worth more. They lived better than anyone else. There was a brand-new piano for her to take lessons on, a life-size doll had appeared at her birthday. Whatever she and Simon wanted, her father and Barbara gave them.

Now the car was one more thing that set them apart.

She was not like the other children—she was American, and she was newly arrived. She didn't have a real mother, or brothers or sisters. She had a stepmother who didn't look like other mothers, who was so beautiful that sometimes on the street people stared at her as they walked past.

But when Simon was here she was almost normal, they were suddenly like other children, a family.

Besides, Simon could fight. Once Laura got into an argument with another girl about who really won World War II. The English wouldn't have won without the Americans, said Laura, and then the girl said Americans were stupid, loud, and vulgar.

"That's the girl who called Americans stupid," she said to Simon, pointing her out on the street.

"Pardon me, but did you say to my sister that Americans are stupid?" Simon asked the girl.

"What if I did?" said she, folding her arms firmly across her chest. She was taller and older than them both, a boyish, wiry girl with a sharp voice.

"No one talks like that to my *sister!*" Simon lowered his head and raised his fists. He had called her "sister"—she had never heard him do that before. She loved hearing him say the word. "Sister." A *normal* thing, to be a sister. He had said that word, given language to the fact that he loved her. If one was a sister, that meant that someone, a brother, or a sister, was protecting you, would never let you down, would love you through all time. Now she had a brother.

If they said it enough, it would become true. Besides, none of the other children needed to know the actual truth. It wasn't the sort of thing the other children talked about—they were too busy.

Now Simon went at the girl, tackling her. They tore at each other. The girl was a wiry fighter; she dribbled, sucking in her saliva as she tackled him. Simon's face was bright red. Simon was a good fighter too—but the girl was bigger, and finally it was a standoff.

64

They stopped fighting, both of them trembling, crying, their faces streaked with dirt and tears.

"This is my brother," Laura announced from there on, whenever the opportunity presented itself. Once, meeting her teacher in the street by accident, she said, "This is my brother, Simon."

"Well, hello, Simon," said the teacher, bending down and shaking his hand. "I didn't know you had a brother, Laura," she said, doubtfully.

"He's away sometimes," said Laura.

"Oh, I see," said the teacher, doubting her, curious.

Secretly, Laura wanted to marry him. They weren't related, they didn't have the same blood. Even then, she understood that, legally, they could marry. But she never said to him, "When we grow up, we could get married." Because she was afraid—that the very idea of it would violate some boundary they had observed even though they were children, the boundary of being brother and sister. For even though they played house and were husband and wife, even though they peed together, slept together in the same bed in mimicry of a married couple, these things were done safely in the imaginary world of play. When they grew up they would no longer be able to do them.

At night, as she fell asleep sometimes, she imagined herself grown up and pregnant, and Simon her husband. They drove a car, a black Rover like her father and Barbara, and Simon came and went from work. They had a house. When the time came to have the baby, he took her to the hospital. Next, she saw a tableau, the baby born, all swaddled in white, and she was leaning down over the baby, just like in the pictures of the Queen and the newly born Princess Anne. But Laura didn't tell Simon about these dreams. Somehow, she was afraid that they would trouble him, would make him think too much, would jar his perfect self-confidence. They might make him run away, stop playing with her. She would never do anything that might make that happen.

And she knew that she would always love him.

What *is* a brother? she wondered. Your own flesh and blood, your own image. And yet, of course, he wasn't really her brother.

One autumn evening, during the week, when Simon was not with them, she approached the living room, where her father and Barbara were sitting. She had had her dinner in the kitchen with Hilda and she was dressed for bed. They were going out later and having a cocktail now before they left.

She could see them sitting at the far end of the room near the window. It was evening, and the branches of the trees outside pushed against the glass, the shapes of the leaves outlined by the light from the room. A fire crackled in the grate. Barbara was sitting on a banquette by the fire. Laura could see only her profile. She was wearing her black, off-the-shoulder dress; her shoulders were full and round; there was a deep line between her breasts. Her father was standing behind her, holding his drink.

As Laura stood by the door unseen by them, they paused in their talk; for a moment they were silent.

Her father glanced at Barbara over his shoulder. Then he said, "Parkinson called. He's spoken to Owen's solicitor." He stopped, watched her. "The only way Owen will go through with it is if we let him have Simon."

He waited, watching her again.

Barbara was very still.

66

She looked up at him. "He wants to punish me to the end, doesn't he?"

"We were worried it would come to this," he said. "We knew it might happen when we got to this point."

She was silent, not looking at him.

He kept his eyes upon her. "We're going to have to make a decision."

She said nothing.

"Parkinson says we can go ahead with the divorce and then sue for custody later."

Suddenly she looked up at him. "What am I supposed to do? Go back to him? . . . Is that what everybody wants? Is that what the world wants from me! He's *sick*!" Barbara gave a little shudder and clutched her arms around her body as if she were cold. "Just the thought of him makes me physically *ill*!"

He sighed. "It's a rotten system."

Barbara seemed not to hear him, but stared straight ahead.

Then she said, "They've already taken him from me, a long time ago. Right from the start, they wouldn't let me have him, him and that sick sister of his." Laura could hear Barbara's voice curl with scorn, the North of England intonation coming through it. "Even when he was a baby, *they* were the ones who always held him! *They* were the ones who encouraged me to go up to London to work. They wouldn't let me be his mother. I was just a vehicle for them so they could have their own baby! That's what I was. Sick, both of them!"

She looked up at him, almost imploringly. "They took him away from me from the moment he was born."

"I know," he said.

"I shouldn't have gone through with the pregnancy. I shouldn't have kept the baby, but *he* made me. Having a baby made him feel like a *man*!" Laura saw her shudder again.

"We'll fight it," he said. "We'll fight it with everything we've got."

He rested his hand on her shoulder, but she pushed him away. Laura saw the tree behind them in the window. She saw the leaves moving and shifting in the dark, the branches scratching at the windowpane. The only sound was the fire crackling and spitting in the grate.

Laura stepped into the room. "Are they going to take Simon away?" she asked.

Barbara heard her, and turned quickly away toward the window.

"Laura! You should be in bed. You shouldn't be listening to this, sweetheart," her father said. He sounded angry. "This is grown-up business."

"But, I couldn't help it. Are they going to take him away?"

He looked at Barbara. "Come, let me take you up to bed," he said to Laura.

"But what about Simon?"

"I'll try and explain."

She followed him along the hallway to her room. He motioned to her to get in bed, and she climbed under the covers while he perched on the edge.

"They can't take him away! That's not fair!" Laura said.

"I know, sweetheart. We know that."

"Don't children *belong* with their mothers! Aren't they supposed to be with them?" she cried.

"It's something you can't understand," he said. "We're not absolutely sure what's going to happen in the end."

"But you're not going to let him go!"

"Of course not. We're going to fight for him. We're going to fight as hard as we can, with every tool we have. And they

68

won't take him away completely. Even if his father gets him, he'll still come to visit us, just like before."

"But why don't we just *kidnap* him!" she asked.

"We can't do that. I have a job. I'm a diplomat."

"But *why* won't they let him come and live with us?"

"It's all grown-up stuff. It's too much for you to understand."

"But I *want* him to."

"I know you do, sweetheart," he said, "I know you do. We're trying our best, fighting every way we know how . . ."

"But why are they taking him away from us?"

"Let me try and explain," he said, putting her on his lap. "When your mother died, Barbara saw us all alone and needing someone to take care of us and she felt very sorry for us. She understood how you felt because her own mother had died. So she came to live with us . . ."

She didn't believe him. Barbara didn't leave her husband just to take care of her, Laura. She left because she wanted to be with him. And yet Laura sensed she mustn't question what he said. It might make him angry.

"But what about Simon?"

"His father was very angry . . . ," he continued, as if he hadn't heard her question. She held her breath impatiently, tried not to interrupt.

"Barbara had been terribly unhappy with him," he said, "in ways—ways you can't possibly understand. He's a very disturbed man. She couldn't go back to him. I'm afraid she'd—kill herself—if she went back to him."

Kill herself? Would there be blood? Would Barbara be all white?

"Barbara wants to divorce him so she can marry me and take care of you. Now, we want that, don't we?"

69

"Yes," said Laura, uncertain where her reply would lead.

"We want Barbara to be with us, right?"

"Yes—"

"Anyway, to obtain a divorce, Barbara may have to agree to give up Simon. At least for a while until we can fight it in the courts."

Here, Laura sensed, was the nub of it.

"That means she's going to give up Simon so you can get married?" Laura repeated.

He hesitated, hearing his own meaning come back to him, as if he didn't like the sound of it quite. "Well, yes . . . , something like that. Temporarily, at least, until we can get him back. You can't really understand now. When you're older, you'll understand. . . . You see, the English courts are very antiquated. They always favor the husband in cases like this. And then on top of that, Simon's father is telling all sorts of lies about Barbara."

"What lies?" she asked.

"Lies that are too disgusting even to tell you. Lies you couldn't even understand."

On Friday in the late afternoon Simon arrived as usual. It was still light out. "Let's go to the Heath," he whispered, though they were not supposed to play alone there, especially at this hour.

"We're just going out in the garden," Simon said to Barbara.

"But it's dark—and cold," said Barbara.

"We'll be all right," said Simon, and Barbara said nothing; perhaps she had given up telling them what to do.

When they reached the Heath, thick cumulus clouds had

begun to gather. The wind was rising; the other children and their nannies were going home, their shouts and cries receding in the wind as they moved across the breast of the Heath.

It was getting dark, the wind shifting among the spindly trees.

They were alone now. All around them, the Heath sloped up into low hills with pockets of woodland, and paths leading into the trees. The Heath seemed to go on forever, even though they were in the middle of the city. There was no sign of other human beings, no buildings visible.

A stream flowed down from the woods, over a dam, then a waterwheel, and into an artificial lake. The wind ruffled the gleaming gray surface of the lake, and at the edge, ducks and geese huddled together.

"We're the only ones here!" Laura cried.

"It's all right," he said, his voice blown away from her.

In a short time it would be completely dark. Laura wrapped her scarf tight around her head. Simon ran alongside her, his coat flapping open. He wore only short pants and knee socks, but he seemed not to feel the cold. His curly hair whipped around his head, his cheeks were a dark tawny red, his knees chapped and raw with the cold.

He walked to the lake, to the water's edge, poking in the sand with a stick.

"Do you know Barbara is going to give you up so she can marry my father?" Laura asked.

He didn't answer. He was bent over the sand, digging at something.

"I know," he finally said.

"How do you know?" she asked, stomping her feet on the ground in the cold.

He shrugged. "My father told me."

"They're giving you up," she said again. She hoped he would say something more. She hoped he would fight. She hoped he would have an idea.

"I know," he said. Still not looking at her, he was scraping away at the wet sand.

"Your shoes are going to get soaking wet," said Laura, watching him for a reaction. "Well, don't you care? Don't you care that they're giving you up?" she asked.

"She already gave me up," he said, not seeming to care.

He stood up, began moving toward the ducks and geese again, the wind sweeping in great gusts around him.

"But don't you want to be with us?" she asked.

He didn't answer.

"Do you?" she said.

He still said nothing.

He shrugged. His back was to her.

She didn't believe that he didn't care. She trailed behind him along the sand. "But what about *me*, Simon?" she asked. "You want to be with me, don't you?"

He continued along around the boggy shore; he was pointing his stick at the ducks and geese and they were backing away from him irritably.

"Be careful," Laura said. "They can be nasty." She came up behind him. "Don't you care about being with me?" she asked him.

His eyes were a very bright blue now against his rosy cheeks. "We'll still see each other," he said.

"Yes," Laura answered, "but we won't be together *permanently, all* the time. Like a real brother and sister."

"Nothing'll change then, will it?" he said. She could hardly hear him in the cold and the wind.

His arms were outstretched now and he moved toward the

birds, his coat swirling around him. The birds backed away, clucking.

"Simon!" she admonished him. "Don't! They can attack!"

She stood there. The wind was sharp, like a knife on her face. She pulled her scarf tighter, shivering and sniffing.

"Say something," she asked him. "Do you *want* to be with him? With your father?"

"It doesn't matter." At the edge of the gray water, a goose stretched out its neck, hissed at him, and he hissed back.

She knew he didn't mean it. He couldn't mean it. Somewhere, she knew, he had to want to be with her, it *did* matter to him.

One afternoon, when she came home from school, she found Barbara and her father there, home earlier than usual. Barbara was dressed up in her suit and her father wore a white carnation in his buttonhole. They looked at her and smiled. "Barbara and I got married today," her father said.

"You got married!"

"Yes, we went to the registry office in town. Just the two of us."

"But you didn't invite me," she said.

"We didn't want to make a big fuss, darling," said Barbara. "It was a very quick thing." She drew Laura to her and kissed her. "I know you're disappointed, but we didn't think it was appropriate to have a big wedding." She meant, perhaps, because she had just gotten divorced, because she had given Simon up.

"You didn't wear a wedding dress?"

"No, just my blue suit," Barbara said, pointing to the suit

73

she wore. "You didn't miss anything, really. It was so simple. We had Daddy's secretary as a witness."

Somehow, Laura thought that you had to wear a white gown to be married, to have a ceremony. She was disappointed that they hadn't invited her.

Her father continued to sleep in the garden room while they looked for a new place to live; though often now, in the morning when Laura woke up in the bedroom she shared with Barbara, Barbara wasn't there.

Her father began to type. He typed, it seemed, day and night in the garden room, pounding away at the little Remington portable. He sat at a card table with the little red typewriter in front of him, wearing a cardigan, for it was cold here. His whole body was arched over the machine, typing, typing. He typed quicker than anyone she knew, his fingers on the keys sounded like the rat-a-tat of a machine gun. His body seemed sometimes to overwhelm the typewriter; she thought it would fly off the table under the force of his hands.

"What are you doing?" Laura asked.

"We're trying to get Simon to come and live with us and I'm typing up some things for the lawyers, to help them."

At night, when she went to bed, she could hear it, the dull pounding of the typewriter at the other end of the flat, the sound drumming against the walls.

The pounding went on into the night, it filled her dreams and her sleep. When she woke up in the morning, she heard it, for sometimes he got up early to do his work.

"Will you play a game with me?" she asked him in the evenings, after dinner, while he sat at the card table typing.

"I can't, sweetie. I've got to do this," he said, not even stopping.

"Why do you have to type all those things?" she asked.

"It's very important that we give the lawyers all the help we can," he said. "You're going to have to understand and let me work."

Laura wasn't quite clear what he was doing. But she saw his body bent over the typewriter, his knit brow, the ferocity of his pounding, and she knew that it was something dire that required that he be continually at it. There was no letup.

They began to go to court. Every morning they got dressed in their dark suits, Barbara in her navy blue suit but now with a high-necked white blouse, her father carrying his briefcase loaded with documents. He didn't go to work during those days. At night, they came home very tired, their faces somber, and Barbara often went right to bed, having her dinner brought to her by Hilda on a tray. Laura was good, and silent, because she knew they were fighting for Simon and she didn't want to distract them. And if she were bad, somehow news of it might reach the judge and affect his decision.

Laura trod about the house like an animal in the woods, afraid to cause a sound. She played quietly in the corner of the room, pretending to read, straining to hear what was being said, some clue.

She waited patiently now, not saying anything, for Simon to come. She was good, she went to bed and lay awake in the dark for hours, not wanting to disturb them. When Friday came and Barbara and her father went to get him after court, she waited by the window, looking down onto the street for the car.

It was six o'clock. They'd said they would be home by

seven, but maybe they would be early. She knelt on the wooden bench by the window.

Outside, the air was dull and cold. It was a quiet street, there were few cars.

Her knees hurt digging into the wood.

Hilda came up behind her. "You want supper, Laura?" she asked.

"I want to wait until Simon comes."

"They might be late. It might be a long time," said Hilda.

"I don't care. I want to wait for Simon."

She dug her knees in harder into the wood. Her stomach gurgled from hunger, her mouth tasted sour.

If she didn't eat, if she endured the hunger, if her knees hurt enough from digging into the wood, if she offered up this pain and hunger to God, He would make Simon come.

At seven, they still hadn't arrived. She went downstairs and took the little red car out of the garage so it would be ready for him. She climbed in the car and began to ride, up and down on the sidewalk. It was dark and cold now, there were no other children in the street. The car would be there for him, so he could ride the moment he came.

Hilda called to her from the window. "It's dark out, you better come in!" But Laura ignored her.

Then she saw the black Rover, its headlights on, driving down the road. She could make out the shapes of her father and Barbara in the front seat.

As the car grew closer, she strained to see in the backseat. Simon wasn't there.

The car stopped, they began to climb out. She ran toward them.

"Where is he!"

Her father didn't answer her. "Darling," he said to Barbara, "you go in and rest."

"Where's Simon?" she said again.

She saw Barbara's face, white and tearstained. Barbara moved slowly toward the flat as if her body were suddenly very heavy. She wore her court clothes, her dark suit and high heels.

"Where's Simon?" Laura asked.

"Just a minute, Laura," he said. "Let me help Barbara."

Laura ran behind them, hopping from one foot to the other.

"I'll explain in a moment," he said.

They climbed the stairs, entered the flat. He deposited Barbara in the bedroom.

"Please!" Laura said. "Please tell me!"

He went into the living room, sank down onto the couch, sighed. "I'm afraid I've got some bad news," he said.

"What news?" she cried.

"I'm afraid Simon isn't coming to us anymore."

"Isn't coming! Why not?"

"He doesn't want to."

"He doesn't want to! Why?!" She sat down on the couch next to him.

"Well, it seems that Simon's father has been telling his lies even to Simon himself now." His voice took heat, the words came quickly. "He's made Simon think his mommy's bad."

He paused, took a breath. "He's told Simon that we bought the little red car just for you, that it wasn't his car at all."

"But that's not true!" she cried. "I want to call him! I can tell him that!"

"He's told Simon that we think of *you* as our real child, that we love you more than him."

"But . . ."

"Today, when we went to pick Simon up and Barbara went

inside to get him, he suddenly got very upset and started crying. When he saw her, he just began to scream. He said he didn't want to go with her. He clung to his Aunt Edna. Barbara tried to pull him away, but he just held on to his aunt, crying and saying he didn't want to come."

"He said he didn't want to come! I don't believe that."

"Well, I'm afraid he did. Barbara's afraid that seeing him will only upset him. She thinks the whole situation is tearing him apart. She thinks it would be better if we stay away for a while until he's older."

"I don't believe Simon said that! I don't believe it."

He wasn't coming again. She tried to understand.

"I'm afraid it's true," he said.

"But are you going to try again and get him?" she asked.

"I don't think so. I think we're going to leave him be for a while, until things settle."

"But *I* could go! Simon loves me."

"I know he does. But it's better for now just to leave things alone. We don't want to upset him any more."

She started to cry. "I'll miss him . . ."

"I know . . . I know," her father said. He pulled his handkerchief out, began to wipe her tears. "Listen, let's go in the kitchen and make some hot chocolate."

"I don't want hot chocolate."

He drew her to him, paused.

"There's one more thing. I don't think we should talk about Simon to Barbara anymore. She's very upset. It's been really terrible for her and she's suffering a lot. I think we should just not mention him to her. Would you mind, sweetheart?"

"I—I won't," she said. But not to even talk about him, not to mention him?

It was dark now, the apartment was quiet, the lights out.

78

They walked along the dim hallway to the bedroom. Barbara lay on the bed, fully dressed under the bedspread. Her dark hair was untidy, there was a Kleenex box beside her. Her face was puffy, she had been crying again. The room smelled of her perfume. It was everywhere Barbara had been, that fragrance, suffusing the draperies, the towels, the bedding, her clothing. Laura went up to her. Barbara's face was swollen. The sight of her sorrow frightened Laura.

She could feel her father's eyes upon her.

But how could she give Simon up? How could she give up her own son?

She remembered what he'd said, but now she couldn't help herself. "*I* could call him," she said to Barbara. "I could explain it to him."

Barbara looked at her. It was a direct stare, a furious, angry look.

Laura stepped back from the bed.

Then Barbara looked away. She sank back into the pillows and closed her eyes.

She kept her eyes shut, as if she had a terrible headache. Laura felt her father's touch on her shoulder; she turned and he beckoned her to come away.

THREE

Barbara took to her bed, lying there for hours on end, sometimes venturing out for a short time for meals, and then returning again for the rest of the day. She seldom spoke to Laura now, or to anyone, and Hilda ran the house again, just as she had when Laura's mother was alive.

Barbara hardly ever left the house now and Laura thought of green plants and the way they turned pale if the sunlight never reached them.

"Is Barbara sick?" Laura asked.

"It's not a physical sickness, honey," her father said. "But all the things that have happened in the last few months"—he didn't say Simon's name—"they've been very hard for her. We just have to let her get better on her own time."

It was as if there had never been a Simon. No one mentioned him, his name was never spoken, it was as if he had been killed by silence. His memory had faded and scattered like dust.

Laura played with the red car on the sidewalk outside the house. In her mind sometimes, she pretended that Simon was with her. As she rode along, her lips moved in silent conversation with him. Sometimes the conversation grew lively. "No, Simon!" she would say, out loud, then look around to see if anyone had seen her talking to herself.

At night, as she lay in bed, she re-created him in her mind. She did it very carefully and slowly, allowing his face to become flesh gradually, building it with all her will, making his hair grow from nothing. She closed her eyes tight and then he became real, flesh and blood, hers again, with her, right here. She played out whole scenarios, entire games with him in her mind, a creature she constructed from memory. She imagined riding in the car with him, she imagined him settling scores with other children who had hurt her. "I'll tell my brother on you!" she said in the dead of night. She imagined him sleeping at her side, there. She tried to smell him.

If she concentrated hard enough, she could retain him there with her for long periods of time. But then, gradually, the image diffused into the thin air, and he was gone.

"How would you like to go to America for the summer?" her father said. Simon had been gone for a month now. "Your grandmother wants me to let you come live with her for a while. Ruth's death was such an awful blow for her—it would make her so happy. It won't hurt you to spend the summer in America. You'll go on the plane by yourself—won't that be fun? All by yourself. Like a big girl." He smiled down at her. She was ten now.

"We'll come and get you at the end of the summer," he said. He saw her face, she must have looked worried. "The time will go very fast—and we'll write letters all the time."

"But what will happen if I fall out of the plane?" she asked.

"You won't fall out of the plane!" He laughed.

"But what if I *did*?" she asked.

"You *won't*."

"Then what would happen if someone *else* fell out of the plane?"

"Well, I suppose at that height, they would freeze to death first," he said.

They were sending her away because she reminded them of Simon, Laura decided. She reminded them of the fact that he wasn't there. She was being sent away as a sacrifice, so that Barbara could get well.

Her father drove her to the airport and he was allowed to escort her onto the plane. The words PAN AMERICAN CLIPPER were written in giant letters on the side.

She was dressed in a new coat, but it was too short for her long, thin legs. She wore a straw hat to match the coat, black patent-leather shoes, and carried a straw handbag.

Her hair had been permed for the occasion and now it stood out on either side of her head, the ends crimped and frizzy.

Her father bent down and kissed her good-bye. "You be a good girl now," he said.

Then the propellers burst into motion, there was a great wind; the plane shook and rumbled and moved down the runway. It lifted off into the sky, and now she was alone.

They had packed a bag for her with books to read and coloring books and crayons, but Laura played with them only fitfully. Sometimes, when she wasn't busy, a sweet-smelling stewardess with bright lipstick stood against the seat in front and talked to her.

Outside the cabin window, night appeared, and the other passengers settled down to sleep. It was a long flight, eight hours in all. Her father had traced it for her in the atlas, across the North Atlantic and Newfoundland, then down over the city of Boston in the United States. She didn't sleep; she sat the whole night staring out at the cloud formations floating by the plane like islands in the sky.

At Idlewild, when she climbed out of the plane, she paused at the top of the ramp, dazzled by the sun, the wide open space, the brilliant, humid air, the roar of planes landing and taking off.

A figure was running toward her across the tarmac, a middle-aged woman in a dark blue dress with a white collar and pale blue hair.

"Honey!" She pulled Laura to her tightly. Her breasts were wide and soft and warm.

She remembered her grandmother only dimly. She touched her grandmother's hair; it was very fine, like gossamer silk. It had a blue rinse in it. Her grandmother had large eyes, a heart-shaped face, a thin mouth, like Laura's.

She hustled Laura into a cab, and they drove along the choked expressway into New York. There, at the railroad station, they took a train south.

Her grandmother had brought a hamper of food, sandwiches, a thermos of chocolate milk.

"You're so thin, honey," she said. "Are they feeding you okay? We've got to fatten you up."

The journey took all day. They traveled for free because Laura's grandfather was an engineer on the railroad. The train rode up through mountains covered in evergreen, along great gorges, rivers rushing and fuming beneath.

At nightfall, they arrived in Everett.

There, in the shadows of the depot, as they climbed down from the train, Laura saw a man waiting for them. He came forward into the light, a tall, broad figure, wearing overalls and a stovepipe cap with a brim. He was watching them silently.

"There's Grandpa!" said her grandmother.

He had sandy hair and a thin mouth and blue eyes. He didn't smile, he didn't stoop to kiss Laura. For a moment, he looked down at her. Laura didn't understand. Then he touched her on the top of her head.

"Hello, Laura," he said, without smiling. He turned away and took the bags.

"Don't mind Grandpa," her grandmother whispered. "He's never gotten over your mother's death. . . . She was his favorite. He's still in a state of shock."

They walked in the dark down the road toward the house, following him as he carried a suitcase in each hand.

All around her, Laura heard the silence of the mountain as it loomed over the little town, she smelled the sweet summer air of the country, heard crickets calling in the dark.

The house was built directly on the railroad track; it was white frame with a lattice trim and a front porch that faced the tracks. Across from it, the mountain stood, a great, dark body, hanging over the village.

Inside, the house was low-ceilinged, with thin walls covered with wallpaper in a pattern of waving ferns. There was a gun rack with her grandfather's rifles laid across it. And clocks—a brass clock under a glass dome, a cuckoo clock, a grandfather clock with a sun and a moon in the face that turned. A big television set was enclosed in a gleaming cabinet with doors that shut across the screen, and a lace doily on top.

That first night, her grandmother put her to bed in the room across the landing from her, in a big, dark bed made in the shape of a sleigh. The room was stuffed with furniture, chests of drawers and wardrobes, piled high with boxes filled with clothes, and mementos wrapped in tissue paper. The air was thick with the scent of Noxzema and mothballs.

"I'm hot," said Laura. "Will you open the window?"

"Grandma doesn't like to open the window at night, honey," she said. "The night air carries disease, honey."

Laura lay there in the strange room with its great, dark wardrobe and chests of drawers, her body sticking to the sheet with sweat. Even though it was summer, there was a flannel bottom sheet on the bed and no top sheet, only a patchwork quilt.

She tried to fall asleep, but it seemed that every time she was about to drift off, a train came by. A great white light filled the room. Suddenly, the roar of the engine shattered the silence. The house shook and trembled and rattled all around her. She could feel the walls vibrating on their foundations.

Laura felt a movement near her. She looked over, and in the thick gray air she saw the shape of her grandmother's body. She came nearer to the bed, dressed in her wide, white nightgown.

"You awake, honey?" her grandmother whispered.

"I can't sleep."

"I know. Want Grandma to lie down with you?"

"Yes."

She lay down on the bed next to her, put her arm around Laura, and stroked her forehead. "So many new things," said her grandmother. "It's hard for a little girl. Grandma will lie with you until you go to sleep."

"Will you hold my hand?"

"Grandma will hold your hand. . . . You're going to have lots of fun, you'll see. There are so many nice children for you to play with."

Laura closed her eyes and tried to sleep. She could feel the skin of her grandmother's hand, rough and chapped, almost like sandpaper. She ran her thumb along the little ridges of flesh.

What was the connection between here and there? She had gotten on a plane and now, here she was, in another world, in a little village in another country. It was like England, in that they spoke English here, but with a strange accent. Would she ever see her father and Barbara again? Were they happy now that she was gone and they didn't have to be reminded? She wondered about Simon. What was he doing? He was so many thousands of miles away. Did he ever think of her? Did he miss her? Were they keeping him a prisoner? Were they mean to him? But she didn't know how she would ever get in touch with him to help him.

It seemed as if she lay for many hours, in the dark, thinking of her father and Barbara, thinking of Simon, while her grandmother slept, snoring lightly now beside her.

In the morning, when she woke, her grandmother had gone from her side. When Laura appeared in the kitchen, her grandmother made eggs for her in a special way, well done but still soft, sandwiched between two pieces of toast, then all cut up in child-sized pieces so she would eat them. (Her eczema was gone now and she could eat eggs.)

Laura saw at once that her grandparents were poorer than her father and Barbara. Nothing in the house was wasted or thrown away. Her grandmother saved string in a glass jar. Newspapers were kept for wrapping and storing, pieces of aluminum foil were reused, old clothes too worn to be passed down were cut up for quilts. Her grandmother made all her long-distance calls on the pay phone at the drugstore to save the tax. She scrubbed the laundry herself on a scrubbing board. Her hands were chapped and rough from the house-work. Her hobby was collecting salt and pepper shakers, which stood in a veneered cherry-wood cabinet in the dining room and which she got from promotions on the backs of cereal and detergent boxes. There were salt and pepper shakers in every conceivable shape and form, little houses, trains, cocker spaniels, mushrooms.

Every morning, her grandmother rose at 6:00 A.M., before anyone else, and in the thick summer evenings she sat in the rocker on the front porch dozing and greeting her neighbors and they sat and gossiped together in the darkness. As Laura played on the sidewalk in front of the house, she could hear voices coming from front porches all the way up and down the street. Her grandmother never said bad things about people, but when someone told her a piece of gossip, she listened carefully and then she said, "My! My, oh my . . ."

On that first Sunday, they went to church. Her grand-mother pointed out the organ pipes she and her grandfather had donated in honor of her mother, Ruth. Her grandmother sang the hymns in a high, warbling soprano. She sang out of tune, and Laura giggled into her hymnbook.

After church, they drove up to the graveyard at the top of a hill overlooking the town, the car raising the dust on the dirt road along the way.

"Your family—my family—the de Crecys, used to own all the land around here," her grandmother said, as they drove up the side of the hill, which looked out over blue mountains and the smoky valley beneath. "It was given to my great-grandfather as a land grant for service in the Revolutionary militia. It was all farmland until the railroad came along and built the town." They reached the graveyard and stopped the car. There were other people there tending their family plots.

It was silent in the dusty morning but for the sound of the dry wind sifting across the hillside, and the plucking of weeds from the earth.

As they walked through the cemetery, Laura saw the name de Crecy everywhere. Some of the graves were very old, from the eighteen hundreds, and the lettering on these was crude and childlike, softened by wind and water. There was Levi De Crecy, and Josiah De Crecy and Abraham and Emma and Jedidiah . . .

All these people were related to her. Somehow, Laura had thought she had been born a stranger, but these were her people, the same flesh and blood.

And yet she was different from them. She had been raised from infancy in a foreign country. Her father was a diplomat, these were farmers and railroad workers. She was like them, and yet not like them, English, not American.

They came to a gleaming granite stone on which were carved the words "Ruth Hallem Fiske, 1921–1953, wife and mother." Somehow, she imagined that her mother had not been buried anywhere, but that she had simply disappeared when she died. She used to think of her living somehow in the sunset, in her crimson robe. She would look up and see the red clouds spread across the sky and imagine that her mother was there. But now she saw that the grave was relatively new, she could still see the faint outline of the mound where it hadn't sunk completely into the earth. She had thought of her mother's death as happening long ago. But now she realized that her death had been recent.

Her grandparents bent down over the grave, pulling up the weeds, straightening the faded plastic flowers. As her grandmother worked, she wiped the tears from her eyes.

Laura stared at the grave—*that* was her mother, right

there, whatever was left of her. She had a sudden impulse to get down on her hands and knees and dig at the earth, to uncover the coffin, open it, to lay eyes upon her. What would there be? A skeleton.

It was forbidden. She was frightened by what she would find, and yet she longed to see her mother, above all, to know her.

Then Laura thought of something. What about the baby? There had been a baby, a boy.

Where had they buried the baby?

"Grandma," she asked. "What about the baby? What happened to the baby?"

For a moment, her grandmother looked puzzled. "The baby?" she said, as if she didn't know what Laura meant.

"The baby she was having when she died."

She stared at Laura. "Honey, I don't know," she said. "I don't know where they buried the baby." She looked distraught for a moment. "I imagine the hospital took care of that."

"But why didn't they bury the baby with its mother?"

"I don't know, honey," she said. And she turned away and began to cry into a handkerchief.

Laura went up to her and touched her shoulder. She hadn't meant to upset her. She wanted to know, that was all.

"Tell me about my mother," Laura asked. "What was she like?"

"She was a sweet, wonderful girl," her grandmother said, and then she stopped and her eyes filled with tears.

Laura waited for her to go on, for she had told her nothing.

"But what was she *like?*" Laura asked.

"She was just—just a perfect girl," said her grandmother.

"But was she ever bad? I mean naughty, as a child?"

"No. Not that I can ever remember," she said. She wasn't going to say anything real, Laura realized. "I don't remember her ever misbehaving," her grandmother said. "She was always a great help to us, to your grandpa and me."

"Tell me about when she got married to my father."

"Well, they met when she was in nursing school in Washington. Hal had no family of his own, except his aunt and his uncle, whom he never saw. He was orphaned very young. He was just devoted to her. We were like a family to him. Then they went to live abroad." She wiped the tears from her eyes as if this was the greatest tragedy that had ever befallen her. "It nearly broke my heart when she left."

"Why did she die?" Laura asked.

"Oh, honey, it's too sad to talk about."

"But why *did* she die?"

Her grandmother was quiet a moment, her lips pursed, as if she didn't want to talk, but now it was as if she couldn't help the words coming out.

"If she hadn't gone to England, she wouldn't have died. If she'd been here, she would have survived—she would have had the right medical care. Doc Baldwin said so." Dr. Baldwin had delivered Laura in the hospital in Cumberland, and he had delivered her mother. As Laura listened to her grandmother's words she felt the dawning of a new idea. Her grandmother believed that her father was somehow responsible for her mother's death. There was something about her father's conduct that her grandmother disapproved of. Perhaps because of Barbara. Perhaps her grandmother believed that her father should never have married again.

᠌

The town, being in a valley, was stifling hot that August. The mountains all around enclosed the heat, trapping the moisture. Some days the heat seemed to squat down over the town, crushing it, and then nothing seemed to move, except the insects buzzing in the dry gardens.

At night, she slid out of bed and walked across the landing to their door. "I can't sleep, Mama." (She called her that for "Mother" now.)

Her grandmother sat up, dazed from sleep, and began to climb down from the bed.

"You're spoiling her," her grandfather said from the bed.

"She's had a hard time, Dell. Let her be."

Her grandfather was angry at her, Laura knew. He didn't like her because she wasn't a good girl like her mother. She knew her grandmother was spoiling her, but she seemed to feel it was necessary.

She and her grandmother lay side by side, Laura's eyes wide open, waiting for sleep to come. She had kicked off the quilt in the stifling night.

Lying in that bed, in that room, her mother's china doll with its ragged dress sitting on the dark wood bureau, Laura thought, My mother is here, somehow she is here, but it is all locked away.

Every night, all night long, she went into their room.

"That child needs a spanking," said her grandfather, his voice muffled in the pillow.

"Now, Dell, she needs me," said her grandmother, getting out of bed for the third time that night to help her go to sleep.

But what if she didn't make it? What if she was con-

91

demned to remain awake the whole night? The night seemed to stretch before Laura forever, eight hours, more time than her mind could encompass—what would she *do* through all those hours if she couldn't sleep?

"Will you stay awake with me until I fall asleep, Mama?"

"Mama will stay awake until you fall asleep . . ."

"I can't sleep, Mama . . ."

"Try, honey."

"I just can't."

Laura lay still for a moment.

"It's not working," she said.

"I'll stroke your head."

Her rough hand stroked Laura's forehead. Laura tried to pay attention to going to sleep, tried to concentrate on the hand.

Laura looked over at her. "I'm still not asleep."

"You *will* be. Just lie still, honey."

Laura lay quiet, stiff and tense, concentrating hard.

"It's not happening."

"Count sheep, honey. Count them jumping over the fence. One—two—three—"

She began to count, but at ten she stopped. "Promise you won't go to sleep until I do?" Laura asked.

"I promise. Keep on counting now."

She kept on counting, and she could feel her body begin to relax, she was being swept away in the cold water. Then, suddenly, there was a spasm in her legs. Her limbs jerked involuntarily as if she'd had an electric shock, and she woke up.

She looked over at her grandmother. Her eyes were closed.

"You're asleep!" she accused.

"No, honey, I'm still awake."

And her grandmother lay on her back and held her hand, trying to catch some rest, but not to sleep, while she waited for sleep to come to Laura.

Laura knew she was being spoiled. She knew that she was being a brat.

She pushed her grandmother.

She refused to sleep. She would eat only walnut or butterscotch ice cream and peanut-butter fudge. She ordered her grandmother around.

On Sunday mornings, when they got ready for church, Laura sat on the bed in her underpants and undershirt while her grandmother brought her her clothes to wear, her dress, freshly ironed and starched, her white gloves, and her straw hat. Her grandmother laid the dress out on the bed, smoothing the material.

"I don't *want* that one!" Laura said. "Get me the yellow one!" She pushed the dress aside, crushing it under her fist, and watched the reaction. Her grandmother stared at her blankly a moment. Then, silently, mulelike, she went to the big dark wardrobe and fetched the other dress. Watching her, Laura hated the meek, obedient look of her soft back.

At night, after dinner, when Laura saw that her grandmother had fallen asleep on the couch, she tugged at her arm and woke her. "I want ice cream," Laura said. And sighing, her grandmother rose up and took her to the drugstore. She let her choose any flavor she wanted from the selection displayed in the pictures above the counter, and sat there while Laura ate sometimes two different servings, never hurrying her.

"We have servants at home," Laura said.

"Is that so, honey?" said her grandmother, accepting it, believing it, simply because Laura said it.

Laura hated her sometimes. She hated her for doing everything she wanted. She hated her for obeying her. She hated her for letting her be a brat.

And yet somehow, her grandmother seemed to feel it was necessary to spoil her.

Her grandmother took her calling at the house of the funeral parlor director. There was a girl her age there, Irma, "someone for you to play with," said her grandmother.

"Do you ever see the dead bodies?" Laura asked the girl when they were alone.

"It's nothing," said Irma. "Just people asleep, that's all. They're in there," she said, showing Laura the door that closed off the mortuary. It was only a few feet from her own room. "It's always locked," said Irma.

One August evening, while they played in the street outside Irma's house, the heat broke, and suddenly it began to rain. The rain beat down with a violence, ribbons of water streaking over them like a waterfall. The water swept along the red paving stones, made a river rushing beneath their feet. They screamed and splashed, their hair clinging to their foreheads. From all the way up and down the street they could hear the cries of other children dancing in the rain.

But as Laura played, something made her glance up.

A figure stood motionless on the porch of Irma's house, behind a thick veil of rain, a vague form permeating the wet. It was Irma's mother. Laura wondered how long she had been standing there, with her eyes fixed on her.

Laura kept on playing, and when they had finished, they

went inside to dry off. Mrs. Schiller put milk and cookies down on the kitchen table before them, and Laura sat there feeling cool now and clean and soft, eating the cookies and drinking down the cold milk.

"How are you enjoying your stay, Laura?" Mrs. Schiller asked.

"Fine, thank you."

"And how's Hal?"

Laura paused a moment—this woman knew her father. Her father and her mother and this woman had had a life before she even came into the world.

Mrs. Schiller looked at her. "You know," she said, "your mother was my best friend. We went to high school together."

Suddenly, Laura stared at this figure who, until now, had been merely in the background. She had on a tailored dress, her hair was freshly set. She might have been about thirty-five, Laura thought. There was something almost pretty about her, although as the wife of the funeral director, she had to wear that proper dress, with its long hem and the sleeves that covered her arms. Her mother would have been the same age, she thought. She would have been like her. She looked at Mrs. Schiller and saw her own mother, intelligent and soft. If Mrs. Schiller was her mother's best friend, she would have known all her secrets, Laura thought. She would have known if she was bad.

Laura sensed a crack in the wall of secrecy. "What was she *like*?" she asked.

Mrs. Schiller looked at her with intelligent eyes, as if gauging her maturity, how much she should tell Laura. The prosperity of the funeral parlor business, the guaranteed business over which the family had a monopoly, made the Schillers one of the town's leading families.

"Well, of course, I was just heartbroken when your mother died," Mrs. Schiller said at last, her voice careful. Laura realized that whenever anyone spoke of her mother, they tended to use the same kinds of words, empty words that gave no real information.

"No. I mean what was she *like?*" Laura asked.

Mrs. Schiller hesitated again, as if thinking carefully.

"Oh, she was a lovely person," she said.

That told her nothing.

"What did she like to *do?*" Laura asked.

"She loved music. She was very talented at music."

Laura was angry. Why didn't anyone tell her anything substantial? There must be more to Ruth than that—perhaps something bad, some fault. Wasn't she ever bad when she was little? There was so much they couldn't, or wouldn't, tell her.

Letters came from her father and Barbara, written on thin airmail stationery. "We miss you, sweetheart, very much," her father wrote. "Last week we went to the Queen's garden party at Buckingham Palace," Barbara wrote. "The Queen's very pretty though she's absolutely tiny, much smaller than you'd think. We love you, darling . . ." They must be happier now. They were having fun. Perhaps it was easier for them without a small child.

The summer was ending, and Laura waited vaguely for them to arrive.

"When are they coming for me?" she asked.

"I don't know, honey," her grandmother said. And Laura tried not to ask too many times because she didn't want to hurt her. But she imagined it wouldn't be long now.

"There's a letter from your dad," her grandmother said one

day. She held the airmail envelope in her hand, and Laura recognized her father's formal, slanting script upon it.

"You're going to stay here a little while longer," said her grandmother. She looked at her and smiled. "You're doing so well, we thought it would be nice for you to stay awhile."

"Oh," said Laura. She wondered whose idea it was for her to stay. Was it her father's or was it her grandmother's? Maybe her father and Barbara wanted to get rid of her? Perhaps because they were still upset about Simon and she reminded them of him? Or maybe they just wanted to have a good time alone. Then they could go to parties without being hampered by a child.

Well, she didn't mind staying—she was having fun here. Her grandmother spoiled her, she gave her almost anything she wanted. She took her into Cumberland to buy toys and clothes in secret, so her grandfather wouldn't know she was spending the money. They had better television here than in England. There was the "Armstrong Circle Theatre" and the soap operas, and Howdy Doody and Lawrence Welk. Sometimes, she sat for hours in the darkened house in front of the television.

"I'm going to enroll you in school here," said her grandmother.

"But when *will* they come?" Laura asked, her voice casual.

"I don't know, honey. But you'll be just fine here with me." And she drew her to her, squeezing Laura against her soft chest.

She enrolled Laura in school. Laura listened to the other children and soon she acquired an American accent, an accent with a Maryland twang. She became part of the life of the town, her grandmother's child now.

Sometimes, as she sat watching television, or as she played in the yard behind the house, very quietly a memory would intrude on her and the image of Simon would flit silently across her brain.

Where was he? she wondered. Still with his father, in the ogre's lair? Was he still alive? He was so far, far away, too far away now to ever be reunited with her. Did Simon ever think of her? she wondered. Maybe he *was* happy. She imagined him playing with that concentrated air of his. He played so intensely, you couldn't distract him sometimes. He could play for hours and hours, and got very annoyed if you tried to interrupt him. Maybe he was happy now, absorbed in his games.

Had he believed his father about the little red car? That it wasn't really meant for both of them? That *she* was her father and Barbara's real child, not Simon. Laura wanted to explain it to him. She would have *given* him the entire car for himself, just to keep him with her. She thought of trying to write a letter to him. But she didn't know his address. She couldn't ask her father or Barbara for it. They would get upset. She knew they didn't want her to contact him. It hurt them to remember. They wanted her to forget. And maybe they thought that if they did contact each other they would say bad things about her father and Barbara—about Barbara leaving Simon. About the fact that her father and Barbara got married so soon after her mother died.

She wondered if Simon had ever tried to write to her. Of course, he couldn't write very well, but perhaps now he had learned. If he wrote to her, would Barbara and her father send her the letter? She thought not.

They wanted to forget, they wanted his memory to go away. They didn't want anyone to know what Barbara had done. And she couldn't go against her father and Barbara. If she displeased them, they would punish her.

One hot afternoon, skipping rope in the dusty street, she looked up and saw a child, a boy, scratching at something in the dust. The boy looked up at her. It was him. Simon. She let the rope fall to her side. She stared at the child—the dark blond curly hair, the slanting blue eyes. He was playing right there. He'd found a way to come to her. Now he was playing, not looking at her—he wanted to take her by surprise.

But perhaps it was Simon's ghost, inside another body.

And then, quickly, the child's features reformed. It wasn't him. It was someone else. It was the Allbright boy, the neighbor's boy.

Going into Cumberland with her grandmother to shop, she saw a boy, tawny-limbed, curly haired, holding his mother's hand—it was him! She opened her mouth to call out, but the boy's features dissolved into the face of a stranger, and the boy and his mother passed them by.

Laura never told anyone about these visions of hers. They were just a part of her, frequent, brief, her secret self. For the merest second, a silence descending around her, all other sights and sounds vanishing, and there he would be. And then, just as quickly as it had come, the vision would pass.

Sometimes, when she was playing, she pretended Simon was there with her, at her side. She realized Simon probably wanted to play different games than the games they had once played together. She was a girl, of course, and he was a boy. It wouldn't matter. They would simply be together, side by side, each one playing his or her own game. They would be brother and sister. They would have a perfect, magical understanding, they wouldn't even need to talk. And her grandmother, *she* would be their mother! Her grandmother, who loved her without any questions, who would give her anything. She had room to love another child, especially a child that she, Laura, loved. Laura's brother. If she told her grandmother to look after him, her grandmother would do what she said. She would accept him and love him.

"You know, I have a brother," Laura said. She was sitting in the kitchen watching as her grandmother made peanut butter fudge.

"You do?" her grandmother said. She didn't even look up, but smiled at the childish fantasy.

"Yes. His name is Simon."

"Simon?"

"He's Barbara's child."

"Now, honey, don't be making up things."

"But it's true. He's two years younger than me. He used to come to see us in London."

She stopped her churning. A shocked look passed over her face. Laura knew she was bad, talking about Simon, but something made her do it. Her grandmother's stunned expression pleased her.

"I didn't know Barbara had a child," she said. "My, oh my," she said. That was what her grandmother always said when she was truly surprised by something. Now she couldn't help herself. Laura knew her surprise had gotten the better of her natural discretion, and she had forgotten herself.

Her grandmother looked at her, struggling with the meaning of it. "That's funny. Hal never told me there was a son."

"Barbara had to give him up to his father, so she could marry my father."

"Well, isn't that something." She shook her head. Why

had no one told her about Simon? Laura wondered. Were they ashamed? Did they not want to tell her that Barbara had another husband? But by not telling her about Simon, they made him not important, they made him nothing. They were acting as if he didn't exist. Laura felt a flash of anger—didn't they love him, even if Barbara *had* to give him up? Didn't they care about him at all? Well, this was her revenge, mentioning him. They were trying to pretend he didn't exist, and telling her grandmother about him was one way of keeping him alive.

On weekends and holidays the cousins came, ten of them in all, of all ages.

There were family dinners of dry fried chicken, mostly wings, tomatoes from the garden, and white bread, and then the cousins escaped—later, when Laura remembered that time, it was the sound of the screen door banging as the cousins fled the house that stayed in her mind. They ran wild in a pack. In the warm weather, they hardly ever wore shoes, and when evening came, her grandmother lined them up, sometimes four or five of them at once, on the edge of the bathtub and scrubbed their blackened feet with a scrubbing brush and Ajax.

In the evening, the adults fell asleep in front of the television set. One by one they dropped off. First her grandmother, then her grandfather, and then the others, until the room was filled with still and sleeping forms, except for the children, who played until late into the night, the television chirping cheerily on. At last, the adults roused themselves from their evening nap and slowly spread out across the house to their beds on couches, on mattresses, on the floors. There was always room for another cousin or an aunt or an uncle, no one was ever turned away. Usually Laura shared a bed with

101

another child, or two, and they talked and played until long after the grown-ups were asleep. Falling asleep was no problem when the cousins were there, because there was always someone willing to stay up with her. There was no more loneliness now, and her grandmother could return to her marriage bed.

Laura was finding her place among them, the cousins, the uncles. She was one of them. She could see her face in their faces, their big, round, blue eyes, their thin, wide mouths, their honey-blond hair.

Over a year passed. One day, returning from school, Laura found her grandmother lying on the couch, holding in her hand another of the airmail letters. Her arm was covering her face, she seemed devastated, as if there had been a death or a terrible illness.

"What's the matter, Mama?"

"They're coming for you," she said.

"They're coming for me?" she repeated, not understanding.

"Yes. In two weeks. Your daddy's being transferred to the States."

Laura sat down on the couch next to her.

"But . . . what about you?" Laura asked.

"We'll still see each other. You'll come and stay here on vacations and Mama will come up to see you."

"But I don't want to go," Laura said.

"You have to go, honey."

Laura remembered how unhappy they had been, how . . . ill Barbara had been.

"I don't want to go. I won't go."

"You have to, honey. I'm afraid you have to go," she said.

"Your daddy's your legal parent. We have to do what he says," and Laura realized that she had no choice, that it was the law.

They came to get her on a dun-colored day. Laura remembered watching for them from the window, the beige Ford pulling up, the tall, loping figure of her father getting out of the car, then Barbara, wearing a white dress with a tight skirt and high heels, and dark glasses. They walked across the cracked pavement toward her. She couldn't hear them through the glass, but she could see them, moving silently toward her, like marionettes.

Her father stood in the doorway, his head nearly touching the top of the door. "Laura!" he cried, scooping her up. Barbara bent down to kiss her, a cloud of the Chanel around her, and murmured "Darling" in her low English voice.

Her grandmother wanted them to stay to lunch. "Gee, we'd love to!" he cried, full of enthusiasm. "But it's a five-hour drive to Washington and I hate to drive on those mountain roads in the dark. But we'll be coming back soon, won't we, Laura? We'll see Grandma again very soon."

And then they were nudging her out to the car, and suddenly tears exploded in her eyes. Her grandmother crouched down on the sidewalk. She held her and wiped her face with the hem of her dress. "Mama will always love you," she said. "Remember, no matter where you are, Mama will always be with you."

The car door slammed, Laura heard the sound of her father throttling the engine. And then they were gliding away along the railroad tracks, up onto the mountain road, and as she twisted around in the backseat, she saw her grandmother standing in the middle of the street, waving to her and crying at the same time.

FOUR

When Laura remembered the years that followed, she thought of Barbara as a bird, a bird desperately plunging into dust and dirt, throwing up leaves into the air, flying frantically from nest to nest carrying its twigs in its beak, perching for a moment on each newfound nest, dipping and bowing, building and rebuilding and unbuilding again and again.

That day, in 1956, when she was eleven and they came to get her, they drove to Washington, D.C., where her father and Barbara had rented an apartment. Barbara spent the fall decorating and buying furniture for it. At Christmas, the apartment was "finished," Barbara said.

"The city is no place to raise children," she said. "I really think we should look for a place in the country."

In the spring, they moved to Virginia, to a white colonial they got "for a steal," said Barbara, because it needed "work." Barbara began to fix the house up. She painted and plastered, designed kitchen cabinets from old barn wood she had salvaged. To save money, she bought carpet remnants and cut them up with scissors, until she couldn't cut anymore. She dressed only in jeans and workshirts now, her hair tied back in a kerchief, her hands callused and paint-stained. She had put on weight, but still Laura thought she was beautiful, the extra weight gave her a ripe, healthy glow.

Her father had a desk job in Washington now, and commuted two hours each way, leaving at seven in the morning and returning at eight at night.

By winter, the house was "finished," and Barbara had found a place in St. James Parish. "It's a divorce sale," she said. "The couple wants out, quick. It's going for nothing. We can get twice as much for this place as we paid for it, and buy that one. We're *crazy* not to do it!" Laura liked the new house, also a white colonial, but a little bigger than the last, prettily set in a garden with a root cellar. Barbara got to work on the house. She extended the living room into the porch and knocked down walls to enlarge the kitchen.

But after a few months, when that house was "done," Barbara said, "This place is just too expensive to heat." She had seen "a great house over in Talcottville. The new highway is being built right in front of it. The price is incredible!" And so they moved again, to another white colonial, but larger, with a little conical tower on the roof, set on a hilltop. It was an old house too and Laura didn't understand why it was cheaper to heat. "It has a better heating system," said Barbara. Once perhaps, it had been the house of a landowning family, commanding from its height a view of rolling hills. Now it looked down over a great gash of orange earth, and trucks and bulldozers, where the new highway was being dug. All day long, the rumble of the road-building machinery filled the air. Laura sat for many hours in the window seat, watching as they moved the orange earth, smoothed it out, and spread the asphalt.

They stayed there for five months. Until Barbara found something "better," a house in a lower tax district.

And so it went, every few months they moved. Each house was a little farther away from Washington than the last, usually in some isolated stretch of countryside. And yet the houses were always in the same general region, as if Barbara were like some migrating bird, thought Laura, who had mysteriously fixed on this area as the one to which she must always return.

Barbara began calling the moving around "a business." "I don't go to work like other people," she said, "but I make money for the family this way." Barbara hated most domestic activities. She hated sewing and cooking, usually serving dinner grudgingly, burned or underdone, but she loved to renovate. The houses were in a perpetual state of flux, a crucial article of plumbing was always missing, the doorknob lacking on some important door. They were always empty and echoing because they couldn't afford to furnish them. And, because they moved so often, they traveled light, tending to discard things as they roamed, taking only the biggest pieces of furniture, the couch and the easy chairs with the blue-and-white floral pattern, and Barbara's antique four-poster bed with the beige-pink silk spread. These furnishings provided a thread of continuity wherever they went, placed in each successive location in a slightly different arrangement. Sometimes, when Laura entered a room, she had a disconcerting moment of déjà vu. The navy-blue-and-white floral pattern on the couch would strike her memory, would infuse her with its familiarity. She would feel a sudden jolt, the ceiling of the room would suddenly seem to lower itself, or jump higher. The walls moved closer together—or, suddenly, farther apart. For a moment Laura thought she was in the house before

106

this—but it wasn't that house. It was a different one, it was a new house.

"We're moving! Isn't it exciting!" Barbara said. And when Laura didn't clean up her room, Barbara threatened, "Next time we move, I'm not going to do your room first. I always do it first, but since you don't seem to care about it and leave it in such a mess, in the future I just won't bother." It was as if she took it as a matter of course that there *would* be another move, that this was only a temporary resting place.

And at the end of every moving day, they had a drink. They sat amid the boxes and cartons, surrounded by mess and upheaval, the ice tinkling in their glasses, surveying the fruits of their labors, on their faces an expression of calm and satisfaction. And Laura realized they were *happy*. "We could put asphalt on that driveway. It would save the car," or "We've got to get someone to fix that fence," Barbara said. "Good idea," said Laura's father, and "You're absolutely right." "Fixing up the house" would preoccupy them for months now.

At each new school, Laura studied the other children, watched the way they dressed, the shoes they wore, the proper way to be, listened to the slang they used, and learned to imitate them. She didn't protest the moving, because somehow she knew that this frantic nest building of Barbara's, incessant, extending into the evening hours, was necessary for her.

"I just have to get this house done!" Barbara would cry. She abandoned all her other hobbies, she didn't shop for clothes anymore, an old interest of hers. They never took vacations. Her only friend was the real-estate agent who called up periodically, "I've got just the thing for you! You've got to come and see it!"

Occasionally, they were forced to see other people. A

workman arrived, or a neighbor to pay his respects to the newcomers. Then Barbara sucked in her cheeks, her English accent became stronger. And if the person was a man, she looked wide-eyed at him, her voice became soft and sweet, like a little girl's. "Always let men think they're smarter than you are," she said to Laura.

Sometimes they were invited to a neighbor's house for dinner. Then Barbara dressed up, became beautiful again the way she had been, and Laura saw her father watching her. It was as if then Barbara were summoning up some memory of her former self. But they had few friends and they didn't seem to mind. They had almost no contact with relatives, they rarely saw her grandmother.

"Why don't we visit Mama?" Laura asked.

"It's a long drive," said her father. "And besides, the place makes me depressed. . . . Anyway, we've got too much work to do around the house!"

It was just the three of them, no roots, no ties, but drifting, wandering from place to place, alone together, a little family of three always in the middle of the countryside, protected by the vacant fields, cut off from all.

On weekends and holidays, Laura helped Barbara with her chores. One day, when Laura was twelve and they were living in the house overlooking the new highway, she and Barbara were working in the room that was supposed to be the living room. The room had a parquet floor and big bay windows. It was large and beautiful and empty because although her father made a good enough salary, they couldn't afford to completely furnish a house this size.

Laura was helping Barbara scrape the door frames and

baseboards "back to the original pine," as Barbara put it. Laura didn't understand what was so great about pine that it should warrant all these hours of labor, herself crouched low and awkward on the floor scraping the paint off the wood. She knew they would never use this room because they couldn't afford to furnish it. But she wanted to please Barbara, because Barbara had a vision of how the room would "work," and she wanted to help her fulfill it. Laura didn't question Barbara because she didn't want to make her angry. Why force her to see something she didn't want to see? Laura wanted her to be happy and she liked being with her. While they worked, Barbara was cheerful and companionable.

At eleven, they stopped for coffee. Laura was allowed a cup, a half teaspoon of instant mixed with hot milk. At one o'clock, Barbara made tomato-and-onion sandwiches for lunch, Laura's favorite. Then they turned on the television and watched soap operas. Barbara scheduled her day as if it were a regular job. She kept workmen's hours. At two, on the dot, Barbara was up again and ready to go.

Now Laura's arm ached from the awkward way she held the paint scraper and her knees were sore from kneeling.

Barbara stood above her on the ladder. Her face was red with the effort of scraping and smudged with dust.

"There's something I want to ask you," Laura said.

"Yes." Barbara sneezed from the dust.

Laura paused, but then she took a breath. They had been happy and companionable that afternoon and perhaps Barbara wouldn't mind her question. She kept her voice even.

"What happened to Simon?" Laura asked.

Above her, Barbara stopped working. She stood poised a

moment at the top of the stepladder, paint scraper in hand. Then she climbed down and sat on a chair.

Barbara pressed her hand to her chest. "When you ask me that question, Laura, it's like a knife twisting in my heart."

"I'm sorry," Laura said. She didn't want to hurt her. She was afraid Barbara would cry. Her father would be angry if she made Barbara cry.

Barbara sat still in the flat, gray light of the autumn afternoon, staring down at the floor.

Then she turned and her eyes focused on Laura again. "I think this end's finished," she said. "Maybe we should get started on the other end, okay?"

Laura didn't ask Barbara about Simon again.

When Laura was thirteen, they alighted for a while in a white clapboard farmhouse that stood on eleven acres of land. It had been a working farm not long before, but they got it for a good price when the farmer went bankrupt. There were no other dwellings visible from its windows, only fields and then distant mountains. On autumn weekends, people from Washington came and stayed in the estates at the end of the long driveways. Laura's father and Barbara had been invited to parties at the estates on a couple of occasions, but they never returned invitations.

They had begun to drink now, more than before, Laura noticed. Their serious drinking began when her father came home from work—they prided themselves on never drinking before five, except for a beer at lunch on weekends. When he was home, her father watched the clock until the big hand hit the stroke of five exactly. "Five more minutes!" he would cry, and then he broke out the vodka and tonic. By nine o'clock at night now, Laura noticed that their words were slurred.

One Saturday night, after dinner, Laura sat reading in the living room. The pine floor was bare, for they had no rug. A hard yellow light filled the room from the shadeless fixture on the ceiling. The tall, curtainless windows looked out onto dark fields, the deserted countryside beyond. They had been talking about their plans for the house and Laura had been only half-listening to them when she became aware suddenly of a long silence. She heard the tinkling of ice cubes in glass. Her father was standing at the mantel—the fireplace didn't work because the chimney was bricked up. He was holding his glass, standing stiffly. Barbara sat in the armchair, dressed in her jeans, still wearing her apron. She too held a glass. She was looking out into the room, on her face an expression Laura hadn't seen before, an odd, fixed smile.

"I'm lonely," said Barbara, suddenly.

"Well then, let's have some people over!" her father cried gaily.

"We can't," said Barbara. "How can we have people over in this mess?"

"They won't care," he said. "All they care about is the hospitality."

"But *I* care," said Barbara.

She looked at him, on her face a sullen expression now. "It's all your fault," she said.

"*What's* my fault?" he asked.

"You know," she said, the smile returning, holding her head stiffly. "You *know*," she said, taking another sip of her drink, her voice low and throaty, the North of England tone in it.

"Darling, I'm afraid I don't," he said, sounding exasperated. But yet he wasn't really angry at her, Laura thought, it was as if he simply thought this was the proper feeling to express at this moment, it was a kind of imitation of what he thought was normal. He could never be truly angry at her because he was too scared of making her unhappy.

"Come, have another one," he said. He walked over to Barbara and put his arm around her; Barbara pushed him away with her elbow, her face still fixed in the half smile.

"Leave me alone," said Barbara. She stood up, walked to the sideboard, and poured herself another vodka and tonic.

"People would love to come over," he said.

"No, they wouldn't." She was silent again for a moment. "Nobody likes me," she said.

"Now that's silly!"

"I'm worthless," said Barbara.

"Oh, darling, I can't let you talk like that."

"Yes, I am. I'm stupid," said Barbara, and suddenly now, she began to cry, dabbing at her face with a Kleenex.

"Maybe you should go upstairs," her father said to Laura. "Let me handle this."

From her room upstairs, Laura could hear their voices batting back and forth down below.

They were coming up the stairs now.

Laura went out onto the landing. He was pushing Barbara up the stairs. She was struggling upward, holding on to the banisters.

Every few steps she stopped, standing there, refusing to move.

"Attagirl," he said, "only a few more steps now. Attagirl."

"Mommy overdid it a little," he said. Laura had called Barbara "Mommy" now for some time. "You can call me

112

Mummy if you want," she had said, and Laura had begun to do it, but calling her "Mommy" in the American way. She had no other mother now and Laura had taken the suggestion as a gesture of affection. But in her mind she still saw her as Barbara.

Now, standing on the stairs, Laura's father said, "She'll be fine in the morning."

Barbara looked up at Laura, grinned. "Laura," she said. "There she is! There's Laura," said Barbara, as he gave her another push up the stairs. "Hel-lo, Laura," said Barbara, leaning toward her as they passed her on the landing. She kissed Laura's cheek. Laura didn't return the kiss, she was afraid to touch her.

The next night, after dinner, when they had been drinking, they put a record on in the living room, "Moonlight Serenade." Barbara made him dance with her, and they moved about the room, avoiding the furniture, Laura's father self-conscious and grinning, gripping his pipe between his teeth, Barbara laughing. Then he put *South Pacific* on and sang "Some Enchanted Evening" in a mock baritone to Barbara along with Ezio Pinza, and Laura, watching them, laughed, relieved that they were happy now.

Laura returned home from school through the fields and the low, deserted hills. She walked up the driveway, the rain falling softly on her face. Entering the house, she heard the hum and rumble of the washing machine, almost like a musical theme on these late winter afternoons. Barbara was bent over the ironing board, her back to her. Laura approached, put her arms around her, laid her head a moment on her shoulder.

"Do you love me?" Laura asked.

"Of course I love you!" Barbara cried, straightening up and turning around, hugging Laura, their breasts touching.

Sometimes, in the silence of a sleepy Sunday afternoon, Laura asked her father the same question, "Do you love me?"

"How can you ask such a thing!" he cried.

Every day now, they seemed more alone. It was as if an invisible circle were being drawn around them, wider and wider, stretching out across the fields. They were all alone in the world now, a little family in the middle of nowhere, their silences growing longer.

"You're not listening to me!" Barbara said to Laura's father.

"I *am* listening to you," he said. "You said we should put a second bathroom in. It would increase the value of the house."

"You don't care," said Barbara.

"I do care," he said. "Of course I care."

One rainy day in early spring, when her father and Barbara had driven to the supermarket to do the weekly shopping, Laura emerged from her room into the upstairs hallway and her eye was caught by the attic door.

She walked over to it, opened it. A rush of warm air came at her from above, the close atmosphere of a shuttered room. There was the smell of raw wood, the sweetish odor of rotting paper.

Laura had almost never gone up there before.

She climbed the attic stairs, and at the top she stood still

114

for a moment. The attic ran the full width of the house. It had two windows, one facing east, the other west, both nailed shut. Through the windows, Laura could see the fields, the soft rain falling on them, an expanse of gray mist rising up.

She switched on the light. Stretching into the recesses of the attic were bits of old, discarded furniture, and boxes and suitcases and trunks, everything covered in dust. These suitcases and trunks were familiar objects to Laura, they packed and unpacked them so often.

Her father and Barbara had never told her not to come up here. But now, as Laura stood in the attic, she had the sense that they wouldn't want her to be here.

She saw a small, cream-colored leather suitcase near her on the floor. She knelt down, opened the clasp, and peered inside. There was a pile of old photographs, brown and cracked with age, lying loose. She began to sift through them. They were pictures of people she vaguely recognized as great-grandparents and great-aunts, women with their hair pulled back, wearing high-necked bustle dresses, some of them with their mouths curiously concave, perhaps where they lacked teeth; men with walrus mustaches and morning coats.

One of the pictures was of a boy of about eight. The boy had horn-rimmed glasses, a high, domed forehead, soft brown hair, a sensual mouth; he was wearing a starched collar and britches. It was her father. What a beautiful child he was, Laura thought. How could anybody put a boy like that in a boardinghouse?

"Do you remember your father," she had asked him, "before he died?"

"Not much," he said. "I really don't remember much."

Once, they had driven north, to upstate New York, to the little town where he had been born. "Just think of us as fallen aristocrats," he used to say. Yet they came to a sleepy town, and the house where he grew up had been far less grand than she had expected, a small green house with asphalt siding. This was not the house of aristocrats, she thought. His old aunt, the woman who had given him up, was living there now—the uncle had died.

"Why are we going to see her? She gave you up," Laura asked as they stopped the car in front of the house.

"She's an old lady now," he said. "And she feels very guilty—she couldn't handle a small child." The aunt was in her seventies. Her hair was in tight curls; she was tall and thin with a loop of flesh hanging down from each bare arm. She had seemed pathetically eager to see them.

"Oh my Lord, this can't be Laura!" she exclaimed. Laura said nothing, only stared at her. She was the woman who had sent him away. Laura would never forgive her, she could never like her.

The woman had baked a cake for them and she brought it out into the living room on a platter. It was delicious looking with thick, moist chocolate icing.

"Isn't that nice, Laura?" her father said.

"Let me cut you a slice," said the old woman.

"No, thank you," said Laura. She wouldn't eat the cake. She would punish the woman for giving him away.

"No? I made it especially for you."

Laura shook her head. "I don't want any."

"She must not be feeling well," said her father.

Now, in the attic, in an old wooden trunk, she found more family photographs. A picture of Barbara as a baby, a fat, dimpled child with thick black curls and pale slanting eyes, photographed against a diorama of the River Rhine. Across the photograph was inscribed something in German script. Barbara was German, she remembered. The enemy.

There was a brittle black-and-white snapshot of Barbara in her WAAF uniform, smiling in front of a barrackslike building. Another photo of Laura sitting on the grass in front of the flat in Hampstead with Barbara, and all Laura's dolls lined up in a row.

They had never gone back to England. Barbara disliked flying. "I hate England," she always said. "I could never live there again. Not after living here. What would I do without all my appliances?" She laughed.

Did this mean they would never go back to see Simon? Laura wondered. That they would never try to see him again?

She continued rummaging through the boxes and suitcases. Each of the suitcases had a green-and-white label from the Holland America Line attached to it. Mr. and Mrs. Harold J. Fiske, Jr., Destination: Southampton, July, 1948. Mr. and Mrs. Harold J. Fiske, Jr., Destination: New York, September 10, 1956. Like the chapter headings in a book, Laura thought. Two Mrs. Harold Fiskes, Laura thought, Ruth, then Barbara . . .

Suddenly, from down below, there was the thump of a car door closing. Laura went to the window. They had come back from their shopping.

She watched as, methodically, they began to unload the groceries. Almost the only time they went out was when they drove to the supermarket on the outskirts of the town twenty miles away once a week.

They had reduced the loading and unloading of the groceries almost to a science. It seemed to give them an odd kind of pleasure, carefully arranging perishables, then paper goods together for more efficient unloading.

Quickly, she shut off the attic light.

But at the top of the staircase, she paused. There hadn't been any photographs of Simon. Had they never taken any pictures of him? Or had they destroyed them? Why weren't there any pictures of Simon?

The next Sunday, when they retired to their room to take a nap, she returned to the attic.

In a big cardboard box, she found photo albums filled with old postcards, someone's collection. There were pictures of maidens in flower gardens, Pyramus and Thisbe, and Diana with her bow surrounded by cupids and garlands, each postcard a little story. There was a tin can filled with buttons. Some were made of mother-of-pearl or silver, others studded with garnets and rhinestones. Laura ran her fingers through them, they were like jewels.

In another box, she found typed manuscripts, full of charts and graphs, the paper yellowing at the edges. "The Post-War Recovery Effort in Great Britain," by Harold J. Fiske, Jr., said one; and another thick manuscript, "Industrialization in Western Europe, the Outlook for the 1950's," again by Harold J. Fiske, Jr. At the bottom of the box, there were expired passports, her father's and Barbara's. They both looked thinner, her father like a boy almost, Barbara so beautiful, with her short hair, her thick, dark lips. Here was Laura's old passport. The picture showed a thin child, with a heart-shaped face, untidy hair, her front teeth missing. There was something about the face that was exhausted, Laura thought.

She opened a suitcase and two tiny white moths fluttered into the air. There were only old clothes, sweaters, a raincoat lining. Nothing interesting.

She kept going. She was looking for something and she knew what it was; she was looking for clues, clues about what had happened to Simon and to her mother, to Ruth.

In an old briefcase, she came across another batch of family photographs. There was a cardboard folder with a border of gold scrollwork. She opened it and saw a sepia-stained photograph of a young woman. The woman had a heart-shaped face, a wide smile, her hair was pulled up in thick rolls around her face. It was her mother, Ruth. Dimly, she remembered having seen a photograph like it before, in her grandmother's house.

Laura stood up and moved into the light, where she could study it. She was shocked. Ruth was pretty. Somehow, Laura had never known she was pretty.

She stared at the photograph and now the image came at her with stunning force. She, Laura, looked just like Ruth; it could be a picture of Laura herself only a few years from now.

Here she was, the living, breathing image of Ruth, moving among them.

She closed the folder and carefully replaced the photograph where she had found it. She wanted to remember exactly where she put it, so that she could return and study it again.

With reluctance, she switched off the attic light. She would like to stay here for hours, with these old photographs and documents. It was cozy here, peaceful and quiet, and they were like a story unfolding before her eyes, a story that had gripped her with its intensity, a story that she couldn't put down.

FIVE

Later, when Laura thought of her father, she saw him next to her in the driver's seat of a car. That was when she felt closest to him, most at peace with him. It was when he was softest, most open with her. It was on these rides with him that she got her education about the world, when he discussed his work with her and the larger foreign policy issues that affected it. "You're a very bright girl," he would say, when she asked some question, or made an appropriate comment.

On one of these rides in the car, when she saw that he was in a good mood and there was no tension in his body, she asked him, "Do I look like my mother?"

He turned to her, his eyes rested on her face a moment. "Why, yes," he said, his voice sounding surprised. "You *do* look like her. It's funny, now that you're older, you're beginning to look like her more and more."

Maybe that was why he was so open and relaxed with her when they were in the car, Laura thought, why he confided in her then. Because when they were driving in the car he couldn't see her face.

One Saturday, Laura drove with him to Agway to buy a

lawn mower—why was a man of his interests spending his Saturday driving twenty miles to buy a lawn mower? Why wasn't he like other fathers? Why didn't he have hobbies, play tennis anymore, have friends?

"Can we stop somewhere?" Laura asked.

"We ought to be getting home," he said. "There's work to do."

"Please," she said.

On the highway ahead of them, there was a diner, and he pulled off the road into the parking lot.

Inside the diner, he ordered coffee and Laura ordered a butterscotch sundae.

"Tell me about when Ruth died," Laura said.

Opposite her, sitting at the Formica table, he became very still suddenly.

She had trapped him. He had to answer her now. It was her *job* to ask him about her mother. She couldn't help herself.

"I really want to know," she said quietly, as forcefully as she could. But she was careful not to let her voice betray too much emotion because then he might censor himself, if he thought that what he might say would have too great an effect upon her.

He sat very still, as if preparing his words. Laura waited.

As she waited, sitting there in the diner, the memory came back to her again, of that summer night, the high wind in the trees, the sky filled with light, almost like daylight, the rectangle of light in her mother's window.

He cleared his throat. "Well," he began, as if searching his memory. Laura didn't move. If she moved or said anything, it might interfere with his concentration. The diner smelled of cigarette smoke.

He took a breath. "Well," he said, "looking back, the

121

situation was terrible to begin with. She had a rough pregnancy, she was very sick, headaches, all swollen up, it just wasn't good. We had a family doctor, Tom Severance, I used to play tennis with him—"

"I remember him," said Laura. "I used to go to him for my eczema. I hated him."

"I don't know why you didn't like him," he said. "I guess kids naturally don't like doctors. But he was the best doctor around."

He paused again. "Well," he said. "She went into labor in the afternoon. It was about five o'clock. We had Hilda, that was your nanny, take you for a walk so you wouldn't have to see her leave in the ambulance. You won't remember—"

"I remember," said Laura.

He looked at her, surprised. "You do?" he asked. The fact that she remembered seemed to unsettle him in some way, and yet at the same time, Laura thought, he seemed proud of her good memory, almost amazed by it.

"The ambulance came around six, I think it was—," he said.

"Yes," said Laura, "and then you came back. You'd forgotten her medicine and you came back just after I got home with Hilda. I saw you and I asked where you were going and you said, 'I forgot your mother's medicine . . .' What happened then?" Laura asked.

"I went back to the hospital," he said. "At about ten o'clock that night, Severance came out and suggested I go home and get a couple of hours' sleep, because nothing would happen till morning. So I went home and had a drink. We only lived five minutes from the hospital, and of course all I would be doing was sitting in a waiting room. I lay down on the bed and I was just drifting off to sleep when the phone rang . . ."

He stopped, bent his face down toward the ashtray, and stubbed out his cigarette. He swallowed.

The door of the diner opened, letting in a gust of cold air. Laura didn't take her gaze from him, she didn't want him to follow her eyes and be distracted.

"Then?" Laura prompted.

"Then . . ." He sighed, collecting himself. He went on. "The call was from the doctor. The baby had died on the way down, and she had taken a bad turn. Gone into convulsions on the delivery table. She was bleeding badly, and they weren't having any success in stopping it. She was still conscious though. He asked me if I wanted to come—"

He stopped, took a drag on his cigarette.

"I tried to think it through. And I realized that if she saw me now, she would know something was wrong. She would know she was dying and she'd only be frightened. I'd just said good-bye to her a little while before and she knew I was going back to the house. If I returned so soon she would know she was in trouble. . . ."

He hesitated. "So I decided not to go back and see her."

"You mean you knew she was going to die and you didn't want to say good-bye to her?" Laura asked.

"I didn't want to frighten her. Maybe I was wrong." He looked away. "I wanted to do the best thing for her."

The best thing for her? But how could he have not said good-bye? How could he have not wanted to see her one last time?

She saw that there were tears in his eyes. She had never seen him cry before. Perhaps he did love her, perhaps her death really was awful for him. Now the sight of his tears frightened her.

"So," he continued, "I didn't go to see her that last time. I decided not to go. I did it for her," he said softly. "She died shortly afterwards."

He wiped his eyes. She was afraid of his tears, afraid to go on. But there was something she had to know.

"What about the baby?" Laura said.

"The baby was born dead," he answered.

"What sex was it?" Laura asked, although she knew the answer. Maybe if she asked the question again he would accidentally reveal more information.

"I don't remember," he said. "It was a long time ago."

"You don't remember!" How could he not remember? She waited, giving him more time, so he could save face.

"You said the baby was a boy," she said.

"Did I?" he asked. "Then it must have been a boy."

How could he not remember? The sex of his own child.

"Where did they bury the baby?" Laura wanted to know.

He looked at her a moment, startled. Then he seemed to be thinking, his brow furrowed.

"You know, I don't know," he said.

"You don't know?"

"I guess things were . . . in such an uproar . . . everyone was so upset. They took care of it . . ."

Laura was silent, watching him. He wasn't there now, he looked past her, preoccupied.

Laura didn't dare ask more now. She was afraid he would really cry.

But driving back with him along the highway, she realized she had to take advantage of this last moment of intimacy before it was shattered by their arrival home. If she didn't ask

124

now, there might not be a chance to ask him for a very long time.

She looked over at him; he was driving silently, thinking.

"Were you in love with Barbara before Ruth died?" she asked.

He turned his head to her, let out a little laugh.

"Whatever makes you ask such a question!"

"I don't know. Because you got married so soon afterwards," Laura said.

"It was a year. And I wanted someone to help take care of you." But, Laura wondered, if he and Barbara loved each other so much now, how could they *not* have loved each other before her mother died? She remembered Barbara arriving down below that night, the sad, stooped man, Barbara pale and fragrant and beautiful.

Now, sitting in the car, her father didn't seem angry at her for asking the question. She decided to push on.

"What about Simon?" Laura asked. "What happened to Simon?"

She expected him to say he didn't know. She thought he would try to deflect the question.

Instead, he answered, "Simon is fine."

So, Laura thought with surprise, he isn't dead. And they knew about him.

"From time to time," he said, "we have him watched. We employ a firm of private detectives in London who look out for him. They talk to his teachers and his neighbors. He is apparently happy and doing well."

Private detectives, Laura thought. She didn't know anyone else whose family members had each other followed by private detectives.

He had said Simon was happy. Had Simon forgotten about her so quickly?

"Does he have a new mother?" Laura asked.

"His aunt, his father's sister, takes care of him," he said. "I'm sure she does a good job."

There was a note of finality in his voice. That door was closed now, Laura realized.

That summer, Laura looked out from her window at the road in front of the house, hoping someone would pass by, but the road was quiet and empty. Coming from the flagstone terrace at the side of the house, she could hear the voices of her father and Barbara, the steady drone of their conversation. Barbara had built this terrace herself, as if to cut a human mark on the rough farmland. She had leveled the ground, lugging the heavy stones with her bare hands. The terrace faced toward the fields, the line of sight unbroken by any human sign, except for a weather-beaten hayrick with great gaps between the slats. Like everything Barbara built, the terrace had a kind of impermanence, perhaps because, although Barbara was skilled at many things, gardening, painting, and minor carpentry, she wasn't a professional.

Now Laura could hear below her in the night, the tinkling of ice on glass. That sound always signaled tension to her, her father and Barbara sitting silently, pondering. And then there was the sound of Barbara chewing at dinner. She chewed like a cat, thought Laura, and listening to it, Laura thought of a cat tearing the flesh off a mouse.

She heard Barbara's voice coming from down below. "You know, we could convert that barn into an apartment. It could be a great source of income," she said.

Silence again, the tinkling of the ice. They had begun to offer Laura wine at dinner but she always refused it. She didn't like the taste.

Laura came out of her room into the hallway. She didn't want to go down to the terrace, where they were. She was bored tonight. The boredom was almost a physical sensation; she wanted to bash her body against the walls, the way the moths and mosquitoes hurled themselves against the screen windows.

She opened the attic door, began to climb the steps. It was August now and the hot air hit her in the face. The heat nearly threw her back down the steps. But she kept on going.

At the top of the stairs, she pulled the light cord; the bare bulb glared in her eyes. The sweat ran down her forehead.

She stood in the close attic. Her breath came in short, shallow gasps. She couldn't open the windows. It was suffocating. How still it was. And yet she could feel the stillness teeming with life, the mice panting silently in the corners, waiting for her to get out, the boxes and trunks and suitcases all around her bursting with their stories.

It would be hard to work here tonight in the heat.

She had gone through most of the suitcases and boxes already, she knew their contents by heart.

She saw a small suitcase in the corner of the attic, one she hadn't explored before. The suitcase was exactly square, about two feet wide and a foot deep, made of beige leather with a tweed pattern stamped on it. The leather was scuffed and worn at the edges, the brass corners and locks rusted. Years ago, when people traveled with a large number of boxes and trunks, the suitcase must have been designed for some purpose that was obsolete now.

She flipped the clasps open and looked inside. There was a

pile of documents bound in blue, folded over, some tied with pink ribbons, others with red ribbons.

She wiped the sweat from her mouth with her fist, and untied one of the folders bound in red. She opened it and the paper rattled in her hands. The paper was onionskin and there was a watermark coming through. The pages were neatly typed and some of the words were underlined in red.

On the first page it said:

HIGH COURT OF JUSTICE

(Probate, Divorce and Admiralty Division)

Affidavit of Morgan Towner in Support of Respondent, Owen Frederick Reed's Application for custody of Simon Basil Reed, June 10, 1954.

Laura turned the page and read: "I, Morgan Towner, state as follows: I am a private detective. My place of business is the Squire Detective Agency, 31 Bradley Street, London, S.W.1. I am over the age of 21 years and I am not party to the within specified action. In the matter of the custody action filed by Mrs. Owen Reed, Case Number 10-27-B-lh, I was employed by the Respondent, Owen Reed, to follow Plaintiff. At the time, I was in possession of a photograph of Mrs. Reed, as well as a complete physical description . . .

"Between June 1, 1951, and September 18, 1953, I had the occasion to observe a series of meetings between Mrs. Reed and Mr. Harold Fiske, Jr., employed as an Economics attaché at the American Embassy in London . . .

"June 1, 1951, 10:00 hours: I followed Mrs. Reed to Paddington station, where she met Mr. Fiske. They boarded a train bound for Sedley Green. Upon arrival at Sedley Green, they registered at the Lily Pad Inn, in a double room, under the name of Mr. and Mrs. Williams. After luncheon in the dining room of the inn, they retired to their room until 17:00 hours, when they then proceeded to a boat rental establishment, Alf's Canoe and Sailboat. I observed them from my own boat on the River Thames, kissing and embracing. At 19:00 hours, they returned to the Lily Pad Inn, where they had dinner in the dining room, retiring at 22:00 hours to their room. The following morning, at 7:00 hours they checked out . . ."

It continued. Laura read the words in a daze, "subjects observed holding hands across the table . . . December 12, 1952 . . . entered the Hotel Forbes in Chelsea, registered under the name of Mr. and Mrs. Eagle . . . January 4, 1952, observed dining at Le Champignon, at 39 Aldwood Street . . ."

And so it went, date after date, the times and places of all their meetings. The rattling of the paper in Laura's hand was the only sound in the attic, she hardly breathed.

Here it all was, clear as could be. Her mother had not died until the summer of 1953, and all this, the affair between her father and Barbara, had happened before that time. He had lied to her. But she'd known it all along. She'd known it since that very first night when she was just a child and stood at the top of the stairs and saw Barbara entering the house on Cambridge Road.

For a brief moment, an image flashed before Laura of her father and Barbara making love, him on top of Barbara, concentrated on her, fixed on her. Her father vulnerable, under the power of another being, Barbara's power, a power so great he couldn't help himself.

She felt sick. She made the image go away.

And all the time they were together, they had thought they were alone. But someone was watching them. This man Owen, he knew about them, all along.

Laura's throat was dry, she needed a glass of water.

But there was more, the folders tied in pink ribbon.

She untied one of the folders, and began to read. "Affidavit of Barbara Downs Reed in Support of Application for Custody of Simon Basil Reed, June 10, 1954 . . ."

She turned the page: "My name is Barbara Downs Reed. I reside at 13 Fleming Road, Hampstead, N.W.3. I was legally married to Owen Reed on March 11, 1945. I hereby swear that the contents of this affidavit are true to the best of my knowledge, so help me . . .

"During the course of my marriage to the Respondent, I was subjected to repeated mental and physical abuse. When we were first married, Respondent neglected to inform me that he was a homosexual. During the course of our marriage, he denied me my due marital rights. . . . During sexual intercourse, he masturbated rather than complete the normal sexual act . . ."

Laura stopped. It was disgusting. She couldn't read it. She remembered Owen Reed that night, standing in the entryway with Barbara and Ruth and Hal, stooped and dark-haired, smiling, a little nervous. And when she couldn't sleep and came downstairs, he had been nice to her, friendly.

But he was someone who could hurt you.

Laura sank to the floor, grasping the folder in her hand. The sweat trickled down her back and her armpits. She sat staring out the little attic window at the hot, dark fields.

Somewhere below, they were sitting on the terrace.

He had lied to her. She had asked, "Were you in love with Barbara before Ruth died?" and he had said no.

Laura stood up. She clutched at a beam, sat down quickly again, afraid she was going to faint.

If she told them she knew, they would turn on her. The thought of talking about their love affair, about sex, with them made her squirm.

She bent down and closed the suitcase, then pulled the cord and switched the light off. She climbed down the stairs to the second floor, shutting the door behind her.

On the second floor of the house, it was suddenly cooler. A faint breeze had penetrated the thick heat. Laura stood a moment inhaling the fresh air. She could feel the sweat evaporating from her face. She heard the sound of the TV going now in Barbara's room.

She walked along the hall toward it. Barbara was lying in her four-poster bed, Laura's father seated beside her in the wing chair with his drink. Bob Hope was on. The windows were open wide, and outside, the elm trees were in full summer leaf. A harvest moon stood over the flat fields, and the long, dry grass was still.

Barbara looked up as Laura entered.

"Hi," Barbara said.

"Hi, sweetie," her father said. They continued watching the television, and Laura sat with them for a while and watched Bob Hope with his dead-penny eyes.

The next morning, her father set off to shoot pigeons. He wasn't a hunter, in fact, his only sport was tennis, which he had stopped playing when he came to America. Now he lit his pipe, took up a gun, and asked Laura to go with him.

"Why do you hate pigeons so much?" Laura asked.

"Because, just after the war in England, sometimes pigeon

was the only meat you could get. I had too much pigeon pie, I guess. One day I was eating it and I bit into a piece of buckshot. I've hated pigeons ever since."

He was a man who should have lived in cities, Laura thought. He was walking beside her, dressed in khaki pants and a white shirt, a tall man.

They cut across the driveway. Before they moved here, the driveway had been only a rutted road used by the farmer who lived in the house. But Barbara and he had made it into a real driveway, suitable for a gracious dwelling. They had spread the gravel over the earth themselves. Barbara had dug a circular flower bed in the center. She built a retaining wall of brick around the flower bed, carting the brick and topsoil herself. When it was finished, the little flower bed seemed lost in the center of the yard, and now all the flowers had shriveled up in the dry, hot summer. This had been a working farmhouse and it wasn't meant to have a circular flower bed in the center of the driveway, which had been carved out wide enough to accommodate hay machines and plows and trucks. Now there were gullies where the rain and wind had begun to erode the gravel.

They turned into the barnyard. Insects buzzed in the hot silence. An old plow was embedded in dried mud and rotting out with rust.

"Let's sit here," he said, lowering himself to the ground and propping himself against the wall of the barn.

The pigeons were lined up on the roof above them. "Wait a minute," he said. He relit his pipe, puffed on it, shaking out the match and laying it carefully on the dry clay—fire was a danger at this time of year.

"Let's see if we can get one of those bastards."

Pipe in mouth, an unlikely sportsman, he raised the

132

shotgun and aimed. Quickly, the pigeon under scrutiny winged up into the air.

"Damn," he said.

"There's one." She pointed to a pigeon sitting high up on a cupola.

"Okay, let's get 'im," he said.

He fired and the shot echoed through the air. The bird exploded in a flurry of feathers and flopped to the ground. He stood up, loped across the barnyard, fetched a shovel, and scooped the dead bird up, throwing it in the garbage can.

"Not bad," he said, sitting back down again beside her.

He sat contemplating the barn roof and his next target, his gun in hand.

"I know about you and Barbara before my mother died," Laura said.

Next to her, she could feel him grow suddenly still.

"I read about it in those papers in the attic from Barbara's divorce," she said.

There was a long pause. He sat without moving, staring at the ground. Then he said, "It must be very hard for you. Do you want to talk about it?"

"Yes."

They got up and walked along the rutted path that led across the barnyard, through another gate, down to the pond. The clay was cracked from the heat. He picked up a stick and beat it against the grass on the side of the path. She watched the stick.

As they came to the pond, a snapping turtle plopped into the water, breaking the silence.

"Is there anything you don't understand?" he asked. He asked it rationally, as if it were his fatherly job to educate her.

"No. Not really," she said.

Laura knew he meant the sex, the technical side of it. In the fashion of the times, he had to be sure she got the scientific facts right. She was thirteen. She understood that part of it, she thought.

It was the rest she didn't understand.

"Did you love Ruth?" She was very careful to make her voice neutral, as noncommittal as possible.

"I loved her very much," he said. "She was an outstanding person, a remarkable person."

"Why did you fall in love with Barbara then?"

He paused, as if thinking, gazing out at the still pond.

"There are different kinds of love," he said. "One day you'll understand what I mean."

"But what was *wrong* with Ruth?" Perhaps if she continued questioning him, she would understand better.

He stopped and turned to her, and this time his voice was excited, almost as if he were reproving her.

"There was *nothing* wrong with Ruth!" he said. "Nothing whatsoever."

"But there must have been," she said, "or you wouldn't have fallen in love with Barbara."

"No. Not true," he answered.

He continued walking around the pond. Above them, the sky was a flat, unrelenting blue.

He seemed to think for a while, and then he said, "I'll try and explain." He paused. "Ruth and I," he began, "we both came from small towns. I went into the Foreign Service. The Foreign Service changed me, and maybe Ruth didn't change as much. She wasn't happy. She missed her family, your grandmother, very much. She wasn't comfortable living in a foreign country. In the diplomatic service, a wife is important, has to entertain and so on. She was never comfortable with that."

So, thought Laura, he wanted something better. He wanted someone more glamorous.

"Was it because Barbara was prettier?" Laura asked.

"Of course not," he said. "That's ridiculous. People change. They change at different rates. I changed, but Ruth didn't. But I always loved her. Always."

He paused, his face set.

"We had ended it, you know, before Ruth died," he said.

Had they really, she wondered? She wondered if he were lying about that too. She remembered Ruth's sorrow when she was pregnant.

"We realized we couldn't go on," he said. "It was very hard—Barbara was bitterly unhappy with her husband. But we felt it was the right thing to do. I loved Ruth—and I loved you . . . and—"

"And then she went and died on you," Laura said, finishing the sentence.

"It was a tragedy. It wasn't ever meant to happen. When Ruth died, Barbara heard the news and wrote me a letter telling me how sorry she was. I needed someone to take care of you and she was willing to love you and raise you as her own."

Barbara left Simon so she could be with him, that was the truth, Laura thought. She didn't leave Simon in order to take care of me. Yet he made it sound like something she should be grateful for.

"I used to think you and Barbara murdered her," Laura said.

He stopped, startled. "Whatever made you think a thing like that!"

"Because you and Barbara loved each other so much. I thought that you wanted to get rid of her. I remember when you came back that night she went to the hospital to get her medicine, I thought there was poison in the bottle."

He looked off into the distance at the scrubby hills, the big elm in the middle of the field with its brittle leaves, the heat waves rising. "Well, that shows how much it affected you," he said, his voice grim.

"Are you going to tell Barbara I know?" she asked.

"Not if you don't want me to."

But she knew he would tell Barbara.

"I don't understand how Barbara could have given up Simon," she said. "I don't understand how a mother could give up her baby. Why hasn't Barbara ever gone to see him?"

"She's waiting for the right time. Waiting until he's older and will understand, and then she'll go and see him."

"When will that be?" Laura asked.

"I don't know. When he's a teenager perhaps. But not for a while."

"In a couple of years?"

"I don't know. We'll have to see. . . . But meanwhile, I can promise you, she thinks about him every day of her life. Every day of her life, she suffers."

Laura waited, watching him.

"I don't see how you could have loved Ruth and Barbara at the same time," she said.

"Well, I did. Maybe one day you'll be able to understand."

"Were you glad when Ruth died?"

"Of course not!"

"But it meant you could marry Barbara."

"Yes," he said, "it meant that."

"Then you *must* have been glad," Laura said.

"Nothing could be further from the truth," he replied.

♪

After dinner was eaten and cleared away and the dishwasher was churning in the kitchen, Barbara went to bed and turned the TV on. When Laura climbed the stairs and entered Barbara's room, Barbara was lying in her bed in the darkness. The light from the television screen shifted and moved across her face. Her father was sitting in his accustomed place by the bed. At Barbara's side, on the table, were her vodka and tonic, her bottle of aspirin, a glass of water with bubbles in it.

Barbara's face was swollen, she was wiping her eyes. She had been crying.

Laura sat down on the hard-backed chair near the window.

Barbara looked at her. For a moment she said nothing. Then she said to Laura, "You don't understand."

"But . . . ," said Laura.

"No. You don't," said Barbara. "It was something we couldn't help. You can't understand that now. But one day, you'll understand . . ." She spoke with certainty, looking out across the sheets to where Laura's father sat watching her.

SIX

One spring day, after Laura had become a writer and moved to New York, she got a phone call from Hal.

"I'm coming to New York," he said. "I want to see you about something."

"Fine. What's it about?" she asked.

"I'll tell you when I get there," he said, mysteriously.

He had never before come to New York just to see her. Usually, he combined his visits with some kind of business.

"I'll take you out to lunch," he said. "Pick a good place."

She made a reservation at a restaurant in the basement of a town house in the West Village.

She was twenty-seven now and she was living in the loft. Her grandfather had died three years before and after she got out of college, her grandmother had given her the small amount of money it had cost to buy the loft. "It's your inheritance, honey," she said. "The money your mother would have gotten. Take it now when you need it."

When Laura entered the restaurant to meet Hal that day, he was already waiting for her. He stood up from the table and they kissed. It had been six months since she'd seen him. He had had a cataract operation recently and gone back to work earlier than he was supposed to. Now he looked aged, pale and drawn. He was wearing special glasses with thick lenses and his eyes seemed to swim at her from behind them, as if he were in a perpetual state of tears. She looked at him and thought, He could die. She was distant from him, wary always, and yet the thought of him getting old, dying, worried her, made her sad.

The waiter came.

"What are you drinking?" he asked.

"I don't drink at lunch," she said. "I'll have a club soda." If she had a dollar for every time they had this exchange, his asking her to drink with him and her turning him down, Laura thought, she would be rich. In truth, she did sometimes drink at lunch—but not with him. If she drank with him, it would be saying his drinking was okay. These days, she didn't even bother to call home after six anymore because it was impossible to have a rational conversation with them. And the next day, they usually didn't remember what they'd said anyway.

"How *are* you?" Laura asked.

"Ahh! I'm ready to give up the rat race," he said. "I'm ready to retire."

"Retire?" What would happen to him without his work to distract him? she wondered. Then he would have to think.

"You know, ever since we got back to the States, I haven't liked the job very much," he said. "They've offered me early retirement. It's a very good deal, financially, and I'm thinking of taking them up on it."

His career had never been the same since he'd been transferred back from England. She had asked him once why they'd transferred him. "Oh, some people didn't approve of

139

my marriage to your mother," he said, "some of the embassy wives—they had nothing better to do with their time than gossip. Anyway, my superiors thought it would be better if I moved."

She understood that there had been a scandal of some kind—he'd given up his career to marry Barbara.

"You know," he said now, "I've always wanted to write a book—my thoughts on the Foreign Service." He smiled, mocking himself a little. "It would give me a chance to get some stuff off my chest. And your mother hates the winters. We're thinking of going south maybe."

Laura's antennae quivered. They were getting ready to move again and looking for an excuse. Retiring was an almost inarguable one.

"Where to?" she asked.

"We're thinking of South Carolina. We're going to take a week down there and look for a house, something your mother could fix up. Maybe a place by the beach."

"But you *hate* the beach!" He had fair skin like she did, he couldn't take the sun.

"I know. But your mother likes it. Anyway, it would be an investment." There was a note of apology in his voice. He looked at her quickly, to see whether she was going to criticize him.

"Do you know anyone there?" she asked.

"No," he said.

She didn't pursue it. They were in a restaurant, she wasn't going to make a scene. Besides, nothing she said would change them—they *had* to keep moving. She wondered what would happen when they got old and didn't have the strength anymore.

"So what's this thing you've got to talk to me about?" she

asked. Her manner toward him was cool. She was angry, she supposed, but she suppressed it. Perhaps out of love, or out of some need to protect him. And she was still afraid of him a little. He was, after all, her father.

He paused, took a sip of his vodka. ("Vodka doesn't leave an odor on your breath," he once told her. Of course, after he had recommended it, she never touched vodka.)

The spring sunlight filtered in between the thick curtains. Through the window, she could see the legs of people passing by on the sidewalk next to them.

Then he said, "I feel like killing myself."

She looked at him. He wasn't a man to utter such thoughts. He had always kept his sorrows to himself, never betraying weakness or pain. He was the boy who hadn't minded the boardinghouse, who hadn't cried. He was the gracious comforter of others, Barbara's caretaker.

"What?" she said.

He cleared his throat. "As you know, I was in England a month ago for the government."

"Yes?"

"Well, when I was there, I tried to see Simon."

"You did!" For years, they hadn't mentioned Simon's name and it was incredible now to hear it. She thought of Simon often, but in silence and isolation. Sometimes it seemed that she was the only one who ever thought of him, who even remembered him. There were times now when she wondered if it hadn't all been a dream, if he had even existed. Who was he? Someone she had concocted in her childish imagination? An imaginary friend? They wanted her to forget he had ever existed, she thought.

She waited for her father to speak, amazed. He took a sip of his vodka.

"I'm going to tell you something now," he said, "and I'm going to ask you not to tell your mother about it."

"Okay," she said, quickly. She would give any assurance, just so he would keep going.

"Do I have your word of honor?"

"Yes!"

"It's very, very important that you not tell her about this."

"Okay!" she said, impatiently.

His mouth set in a line. "I'm afraid it would destroy her." He stayed quiet for what seemed a very long time, as if wording what he was going to say in advance.

"As you know," he began, "the events surrounding your mother's divorce and our marriage were very"—he paused, looking for the right word—"painful. Things were done, because of the legal system, that caused great grief to your mother and me."

She hung on his words, waiting.

"Obviously, the most painful thing of all was the separation from Simon." He used the passive tense, as if it were all far removed from him.

"Our plan from the beginning had been to wait until Simon was older and then to try and explain things to him, when he could understand . . ." He cleared his throat, then continued.

"When Simon was twenty-one, Barbara wrote him a letter. That was four years ago. In the letter, she tried to explain to him what had happened. She had waited until he came of age, thinking that as an adult he might understand. She explained that she and his father had been unhappy together, that she wanted to keep him, but that the court had made her give him up."

A letter? They'd never told her anything about a letter.

142

Their capacity for secrecy surprised her. She imagined Barbara writing the letter. She would have had to have been drunk, of course. She would have staged it in some melodramatic way, probably after a night of drinking. Laura could picture the scene. Barbara would be sitting at her desk. There would be that look of manic glee on her face, of subdued hilarity she wore sometimes when she was drunk. But then, inevitably, she would have cried, cried out of real sorrow and incomprehension, cried because she would have wanted Hal to think she was a good person, that she wasn't all bad and unfeeling. He would have tried to stop her writing the letter because it was causing her pain, because of the wounds it opened.

"There was never any response to the letter," Hal said now. "We waited and waited and nothing came.

"Anyway, when I was in England, I decided to try and see Simon," he said. "I called his father."

"You called his father?" For a moment, it all came together, became real. There had been a father, there had been a Simon. Now the two old adversaries, talking on the phone.

"Yes," said Hal. "I called him." He stopped talking, as if the words were hard to come by. He waited, then swallowed. There was another pause, then, "It seems that Simon has become—a criminal."

He said the word *criminal* in an almost clinical way, as if the very idea were completely foreign to him. He said it carefully, keeping the idea at a distance.

"A criminal?" she asked.

Laura could hear the tinkling of silverware. She smelled the fresh linens. The voices of the other diners were muted by the thick carpeting, the heavy brocade draperies of the restaurant.

143

"He's been in prison," Hal said.

"Prison!"

The idea of prison was as remote from the family as— typhoid, or the plague. Laura tried to picture Simon now— beautiful, he would have to be, but older, of course, a man, in a prison cell, in prison clothes.

"What did he *do?*" she asked.

Now a veil seemed to cross Hal's face, to shadow it. She knew he was going to tell a lie.

"Something serious, very serious," he said. "I don't know what it was." His eyes avoided hers. He had pulled back—he could only trust her so far. But he had to unburden himself— it was too much to bear alone, and he couldn't tell Barbara about it. If he told Barbara about Simon being in prison, then what they had done to him would become fixed between them forever—and this was the final result. And there was always the fear that if things got too bad, if the guilt became too great to bear, she'd up and leave him and everything would break apart.

But he could only go so far with Laura, because he was afraid. If he didn't talk about it, then it would go away. Which, of course, was the story of his life.

"Where is he now?" she asked.

"He seems to have completely disappeared. His father hasn't heard from him for a couple of years. He's just—gone. He may be—dead."

He leaned toward her anxiously. "Promise me you'll never tell your mother. It would kill her."

"I promise," she said, her voice dry and angry. Protecting her like a child. Maybe if she faced up to things it would heal the sickness. If someone popped the sore, the sickness would ooze out, the wound would dry.

"Well, what did his father say?" Laura asked. "Has *he* tried to find him?"

"Yes, he has," said Hal. "He said he's been in contact with the police." He paused. "Nobody knows where he is."

"Is there anything we could do?" said Laura. "Maybe we should hire someone?" She remembered the private detectives who had watched Simon when he was a boy, who had talked to the neighbors and his teachers.

"I discussed it with his father, making further efforts. I think he's done everything that could be done." He sat back, looked at her.

"So that's that?" she asked, wonderingly.

"I guess so." He looked down at the table, shook his head, not seeing her now.

"It must have been strange talking to his father after all this time," she ventured. He'd opened up to her, given her permission to talk about it. Maybe he'd reveal more. "Was he civil?" she asked.

"Naturally, it was—well, somewhat uncomfortable," he said. "That was to be expected." He spoke in proper tones, keeping it distant from himself. "He was a little cool, naturally," he went on. There he was, pretending to understand everything, to be above it all, above sorrow and anger.

He took some more of his drink.

Then he looked at Laura.

"At the end of the conversation, he said—" He stopped, staring into the room, unable to finish.

"What did he say?" she asked.

For a moment, he didn't answer. He glanced out the window, frowning.

"At the end of our conversation, he said to me, 'Well, what did you and Barbara expect?' "

Now he looked at Laura as if for her reaction. He wanted her, she realized, to comfort him.

She felt like saying, Well, what *did* you expect? But she didn't dare.

"Naturally," he said, carefully, properly, "his words made me very upset. But"—he shook his head again, looking down at the table—"one has to go on."

But what *did* you expect? she thought. Then she thought, Maybe Simon's father and I are hidden allies, allied against Hal and Barbara.

"Well." He sighed deeply, taking a sip of his drink. "I guess that's that."

That's that? The end? Somewhere, she'd always believed that Simon would come back. Somewhere, she'd believed that her life couldn't really end without seeing him again, without some kind of closure. But now—he'd disappeared into a void. Even his own father had lost touch with him. Now she'd never see him again. Gone now. Forever. It wasn't fair. She'd wanted to tell him that the red car was his too. Funny, how things from childhood, a little red car, stick with you, she thought. You can be twenty-seven, sleeping with men and then, but that's what's real.

But *she'd* never tried to find him, had she? She was as bad as they were. Afraid he'd reject her, turn his back on her. Afraid of their anger, afraid of hurting them.

What kind of crime had it been? It must have been serious, violent, or they wouldn't have put him in jail. Armed robbery, maybe. Murder? She tried to imagine the child she knew doing that. She remembered him—cool, daring—indifferent to everyone. Everyone, except her.

The waiter was standing in front of them with his notepad.

"What'll you have?" Hal said now.

He was going to close it down now, she thought. She wanted to yell at him. See what you've done! See! Don't you care! Don't you give a shit!

Instead, she answered him coolly. "I'm not very hungry." She ordered a salad.

"Well," said Hal, looking up at her. "How's your work going?"

"Fine," she said, enraged.

He knew she was angry, knew the cause of it. He would ignore it, try to distract her.

"I read those clips you sent me. That piece in *World* was good. I was very proud." He smiled. He always followed her work closely.

"What're you up to next?" he asked, sipping his vodka.

"I'm doing a piece on Michael Harrington . . . the antipoverty activist . . ."

"Sounds interesting," he said. "And how's your social life?" he asked. "Any new beaus?"

"No one special," she said, looking at him across the table.

SEVEN

She had met him at a Holiday Inn in Detroit where a group of Vietnam Veterans Against the War was holding a conference. One of the magazines she worked for had sent her to Detroit to cover it.

"You know Ben Michaels," someone said.

She saw a man with a beard and steel-rimmed glasses, and sandy brown hair, a thin, wiry man, wearing a blue workshirt. The man smiled at her with a particularly warm smile.

"I know your byline," she said. He was a contributing editor at another magazine, covering the conference.

During the course of the day, she watched him as he interviewed the veterans. He sat very close to them with his spiral notebook, seeming to envelop them with his intensity.

At lunch, in the dining room of the Holiday Inn, she sat at a long table with him, some of the veterans, and a couple of other journalists. He gulped his food down hastily, as if food meant nothing to him and what mattered was the work at hand, or as if he were afraid someone would come and steal the food from him. When he finished eating, he sat tilting his chair back on its legs, listening to what the others had to

148

say, a faint, polite smile on his face. When, occasionally, his opinion was solicited or he interjected a comment, he seemed to know more than any of the other journalists about what was going on. And she could tell the veterans liked him. He was neither servile nor patronizing with them, the way some of the journalists were, but respectful, equal.

In the afternoon, as they listened to the veterans' speeches, she saw him sometimes pause and look around the room, as if seeking someone out, and when his glance fell upon her, he would smile that particularly warm smile, a smile that seemed to envelop her.

By ten o'clock that night, Laura was exhausted by the veterans' stories, of atrocities committed against women and children, of whole battalions refusing to fight. Her voice was hoarse, her eyes stung from the smoke in the room, and she decided she'd gleaned enough material for her piece. But as she left to go to bed, Ben Michaels was still talking to the veterans, bent over his notebook.

In the morning, when she saw him again, she asked how late he'd stayed up. "Till four," he said. "I got a couple of hours' sleep at dawn." She felt guilty that he seemed more committed than she, that he had more stamina.

Most of the journalists were taking the same flight back to New York, and in the line boarding the plane, she and Michaels seemed to fall in place next to one another, and they sat together on the journey home.

He sat by the window, the brilliant light coming in behind him, and turned the full beam of his attention upon her. His smile, from behind his glasses and beard, was warm. They ordered a drink.

"Tell me about yourself," he said—magic words, and when she spoke, he seemed to listen with close attention.

He'd seen one of her articles. "Good piece," he said, and she was flattered because it came from him.

He told her he had studied classics. "I was going to teach," he said, "but then I got interested in politics."

"Do you have a family?" she asked, wanting to know if he was married.

"I'm married and I've got a son," he said. "He's nine months old and he's just about to start walking. I travel so much I'm afraid I'm going to miss his first steps."

"What does your wife do?"

"She's a poet. She's very good. She's had some things published in little magazines. But she's kind of slowed down lately—it's hard with the baby."

The conference had been draining. The passion of the veterans was contagious. They talked about the veterans' stories. They had been initiated into an experience it would be difficult to explain to others, she thought. They were somehow isolated together by it. She'd often experienced that feeling when she covered a story, an intense involvement, as if she were *becoming* the people she was writing about. No one else could quite understand what they'd seen, she thought. He wouldn't be able to share this experience with his wife in quite the same way they had shared it.

The plane lunch came. Again, he ate quickly. He turned and saw her watching him and he laughed. "They say Yeats was an incredibly fast eater. His children were terrified of him. I came from a household of brothers—you had to eat fast or someone else would grab your food."

When the plane landed at La Guardia, as soon as it had taxied to the terminal, he stood up from his seat. He pushed into the line in the aisle and stood tapping his foot, waiting for the door to open. When he saw her looking at him, he smiled again, as if apologizing for his aggressiveness. It was a sweet smile, as if he wanted to disguise his restless energy.

They shared a cab into Manhattan from La Guardia, and as she dropped him off at his building in Chelsea, he looked at her and said, "Let's have lunch sometime," and she said, "Great."

"We'll talk soon," he said.

When his piece on the veterans appeared a month later, she called him to tell him she liked it. His article was very good, she said, and she'd learned from it.

"It's very nice of you to call," he said. "Maybe we should have lunch," and they made a date for the following week, at a coffee shop he suggested near his magazine. It was a narrow space with small Formica tables, torn vinyl chairs, grease-slicked windows. The food was terrible.

At lunch, again he questioned her closely about herself. He seemed interested in everything about her. They talked about writing and journalism. She asked his opinion of an article on the veterans' conference written by a mutual acquaintance. "Did you see his piece?" she said.

"Yes." He shook his head slowly, then smiled, a rueful, dismissive smile. The smile was enough. He obviously didn't like the man's article. It was an indirect way of criticizing the man, and somehow it was more effective. But his standards were high, and she couldn't help agreeing with him.

At the end of lunch, he said, "We should do this again."

In the days that followed, she found herself thinking about him. He was older than she by four years. People talked about his articles. One evening some friends of hers spoke admiringly of a piece he had written on McGovern, not realizing she knew him.

His image began to invade her work. Sometimes, as she sat at her table writing, she would pause without realizing it and see his face in her mind, remember something he had said. She tried to shake the image loose—but then it only reappeared again.

A week later, he called her to get the phone number of one of the veterans and they made another date for lunch.

"Tell me about your family," he said when they met. "Do you have brothers and sisters?"

"I have one brother," she said, "a brother I haven't seen for years."

Usually, she never mentioned Simon. If someone asked her about brothers and sisters, she said she was an only child. It was almost as if she had forgotten about Simon, though actually she hadn't. She simply didn't regard him as part of her conscious life. If she mentioned Simon, she would have to explain him, and Hal and Barbara had always told her not to talk about family business. And besides, who would be interested in the story?

"I loved him," she said now. "Then, when his parents— his father and my stepmother, were divorced, the courts gave his father custody of him. I guess my stepmother thought it would be easier not to try and fight for him—he'd been through a lot."

Ben listened attentively, seriously, for a long time without interrupting.

"Have you ever thought of trying to find him?" he asked.

"Yes. But I never have."

"Why?"

"Because—I don't even know where to begin. Besides, on some level I guess I don't want to rock the boat. I don't want to hurt my parents."

"Maybe you should try," he said.

"I don't know," she said. And she clammed up. The impossibility of going to a strange country and trying to find Simon overwhelmed her. She didn't even know where to begin. Going back to England, arriving at his father's doorstep—no doubt his father hated her the way he hated Barbara and Hal. She was still afraid of the ogre, like a child. Besides, Simon probably hated her too, hated her because Hal and Barbara had kept her for their own and given him up.

She changed the subject.

"Tell me about your family," she said.

"My father's a lawyer on Wall Street," he said. "We don't have much contact. We disagree on political things." She guessed his family was rich, but that he probably wouldn't take money from them.

There were four brothers in all. "We used to sit around the dinner table and he'd give us quizzes on, say, the presidential primary. And we'd all compete like crazy."

He could have gotten a well-paying job on a newspaper any day, but he chose instead to work for relatively low wages at the magazine, which gave him more freedom and enabled him to delve into subjects in depth. She noticed he was thrifty, always choosing to walk rather than take public transportation. He had suggested they eat lunch again in the same dingy coffee shop, and he seemed always to wear a uniform of jeans and a denim workshirt.

When she left him that day, she defined it—she was becoming attracted to him, and he was married. It would be better to stay away. But there was nothing to worry about,

nothing had happened between them. And he hadn't given her
the least little signal—other than his warmth and interest—
that he wanted her sexually. In fact, that was one reason she
liked him, because he seemed so devoted to his family, an
honorable person. She couldn't give up seeing him, she
couldn't give up his friendship, his warmth.

He began to phone her now in the most friendly way.
"Busy?" he would ask. "Lunch?" And she would hurry to meet
him.

Their lunches grew longer. She realized they always stayed
in the coffee shop until the last possible moment, until 3:15,
when the afternoon was already beginning to wane. Everything
she did or said or wore he seemed to notice and to find
interesting. "You have a new haircut," he'd say. Or, "That's
a nice blouse." The personal remark in the middle of a
conversation about work would startle her, she was surprised
that he noticed these things, but she was pleased.

He asked her to read his articles in progress—he wanted
her opinion, flattering. Of course, the pieces were always
excellent.

"Why don't you do something for us?" he said, suggesting
she write for his magazine. It would be a step up for her career.
The magazine he worked for was thick with pages and
combined the literary and the popular. It had a widely male
audience, and very few women writers worked for it. She said
she'd love to write for it. She'd begun her career writing for
marginal publications. She had supported herself doing stories
for women's magazines too, sometimes under pseudonyms, on
such subjects as "What do you do when he says good-bye?"
Now, through Ben, she was beginning to expand her horizons.

One day, as she watched out the window of the coffee shop

for him, she saw him crossing the street. As he came toward her, his body seemed to her suddenly to be filled with light. He seemed almost to be borne upward by the light, a man walking briskly, freshly, expectantly, a little smile on his face, toward her.

As he sat down opposite her and they began talking, her eyes fell to his chest. The material of his shirt was stretched tight across it, and she could see the tiny imprint of his nipples. She imagined unbuttoning the shirt, touching his chest, running her tongue across his nipples.

Then, in the middle of the conversation, he looked at her and smiled. His glance seemed to penetrate her for a moment. He had hazel-colored eyes with flecks of amber in them; his smile was warm and kind and engulfing. It was a smile that should not have been between an ordinary man and woman, she realized. It was a smile that went beyond the boundary, the allowable. But perhaps he didn't know it.

That night, she dreamed about him. In the dream, she came upon him on a dark street. He took her in his arms and pushed her up against a wall, lifted her skirt, and they made love while her legs were wrapped around him.

In her sleep, her body moved with the orgasm and it woke her up. As she came awake, her pelvis was rocking, her eyes fluttering in the morning light. But she didn't want to wake up, she wanted to hang on to the orgasm, and she tried to keep herself in the dream until it was over.

In the morning, she knew she was in trouble.

Shortly after, he called her. "Lisa and I would like you to come to brunch on Sunday," he said.

But she had dreamed of making love to him, she had stepped across the line. She would be uncomfortable with the

155

wife, for she had made love to him in her dreams. But she was curious. She wondered what his wife was like.

When she arrived at the apartment, his wife, Lisa, greeted her warmly. "Laura," she said, "I've heard so much about you!" So, Laura thought, he had talked about her. That meant he didn't think there was anything wrong with their relationship. He saw her just as a good, new friend. His wife was beautiful, Laura thought. She had long, curly blond hair, her complexion was pale and delicate, heightened by her flushed cheeks and the violet shadows around her eyes. Her posture was erect, almost too stiff. She was a real beauty, but she didn't take care of herself. She was overweight, her hair was unwashed, and she wore an old cotton blouse and jeans that were too big for her.

As Laura stepped into the apartment, she was shocked. There was hardly any furniture, just the bare necessities—a dining table and chairs but no armchairs. The floors and walls were bare. Perhaps they were hard up for money.

A child of about a year old was sitting on the floor, pushing a red plastic fire truck. "This is Jesse," Lisa said. The child was the spitting image of Lisa, he had the same blond curly hair and the same pale delicate skin.

Laura crouched down on the floor to talk to the boy. "Hello, Jesse," she said, "hello." He shrank away and moved toward his mother, staring up at her as if he hated and feared her.

She could smell the child's dirty diapers in the air. There was chaos everywhere, the baby's toys were scattered all over the floor.

All through the meal, the child cried and whined. "He needs a nap," said Lisa, "but he just won't nap. He's a terrible sleeper."

156

Ben seemed oblivious to the situation in the house, unaware of the chaos and filth. He was attentive to Lisa, preparing the brunch, frying the eggs.

Lisa had the same kind of sweet attention he did, Laura noticed. Perhaps they'd learned it from each other, that style, she thought—and then she caught herself and realized she was being mean.

"I envy you," Lisa said to her, "with your career. Being able to do all that work. I mean I don't regret Jesse. He's the best thing that's ever happened to me. But it must be wonderful to be able to do so much."

On the floor, Jesse was fussing, crying indiscriminately. "Here, have this," Lisa tried, offering him his bottle, but he pulled away. "Want some coffee cake, Jesse?" The boy took it, threw it on the floor.

He started to cry louder. Lisa picked him up and began to rock him, but he kept fussing. His nose was running, his thumb was in his mouth. He lay in his mother's arms, watching Laura.

"This is my favorite age," said Lisa, holding the baby to her chest. She was lying, Laura thought. It was horrible.

Now Ben took him from Lisa. He held the child gently to him, the boy's head on his shoulder. He began to sing to him, his eyes looking out to the distance, while he patted the boy on the back. "Daniel, Daniel in the lion's den . . ." His voice was unexpected. A pure, sweet tenor, a voice she wouldn't have expected for a man who was as aggressive, as hurried, as tough as he. She sat, listening to the voice, the high, sweet tenor, and for a moment the baby seemed soothed by the song.

At the end of the brunch, Ben and Lisa saw her to the door. As they said good-bye, Ben put his arm around Lisa. Lisa kissed Laura, but Ben only took her hand.

Walking away from the house that day, she felt sorry for his wife. It seemed such a struggle with the child, yet she was trying valiantly. But how could he love someone like that? A woman who was so sloppy? Who didn't take care of herself, who seemed hardly able to cope? And yet he *did* seem to love her. Strangely, that made Laura drawn to him even more—he was devoted to her, devoted to the boy. He was a good man, a good father.

It was dangerous, the whole thing. She knew the consequences of breaking up a family, of taking a man from his wife and child. She had been such a child, thin, covered in eczema. She'd loved a child whose family had been broken. And now, as she walked along, it came to her again, the secret image, the boy, Simon, the pale-eyed boy.

But she couldn't help it. She didn't *want* to help it.

And walking away from them, the feeling bore her up. There were no words for it, it surrounded her, rose up beneath her, a wave sweeping her along.

One day, a week later, Lisa called and suggested they have lunch.

The call took her aback. Was she suspicious? Did she want to co-opt the opposition with her sweetness? Check her out? Laura didn't want to go—but she couldn't very well refuse. Lisa was Ben's wife, her friend's wife.

Lisa was late. Laura was always on time and she had to wait half an hour. When Lisa arrived she was out of breath. "I'm sorry, I had to get Jesse down for his nap." She was wearing a full, Mexican cotton top. She smiled her smile, so like Ben's. During lunch, she talked mostly about Jesse. "He's just wonderful," she cried, smiling radiantly.

"I brought something for you to read," Lisa said. She reached into the canvas bag she was carrying and took out a manila folder and handed it to Laura. Inside was a sheaf of typewritten pages, her poetry. Lisa seemed to want to be her friend.

"Thank you," said Laura, "I can't wait to read them."

Lisa, with her sweetness, her smile, seemed almost to be pleading with her. Pleading with her not to take her husband away, pleading with Laura to be her friend.

She, Laura, had all the cards on her side. She was thin, she was effective. The other woman was worn down by child rearing, she was overweight, she was overwhelmed.

Laura took the poems home. They were depressing little pieces, a woman contemplates the man she loves and "the space between us"; a woman dreams of drowning. Laura thought they were hackneyed, full of flat, unredeemed depression. But the next day she called Lisa and said, "They're really great. You ought to do more."

"All I need is time," Lisa said.

Lisa asked her to have lunch again. They wouldn't have been friends if it hadn't been for Ben. Laura didn't have a child, she had work that took her to far-off places. She felt as if she were in control of her life, she could manage, whereas Lisa seemed barely to be hanging on. Lisa's parents lived on the Upper West Side, and she was always taking Jesse up there so they could help her with him. Once more, Lisa came late to lunch, which annoyed Laura.

Laura visited their apartment again; the three of them went to a concert, a movie. Laura was a colleague, a nice person—why couldn't they all be friends? She could be Lisa's friend too. In a funny way, Laura was becoming part of the family.

Why was she doing it? She wanted to be with him, to be part of his life. She could see more of him this way. And in some way, she knew, she enjoyed the spectacle of this fragile woman, a woman overweight, messy, out of control. Yes, she wanted to beat her, beat her in the sense of winning—and of hurting her too.

She stopped herself. What was happening? She wasn't an evil person, a cruel person who broke up families, who took men from their wives. She had never been involved in anything like this before. But she couldn't help herself.

She could feel herself stretching out, growing, extending into space, taking flight like a bird, becoming beautiful in the face of Lisa's misfortune, beautiful in Ben's eyes. Becoming Barbara.

Whenever the three of them were together, Ben was demonstrative to Lisa. As they said good-bye to Laura, he put his arm around Lisa. It all seemed too sweet—they were in love and happy, despite the chaos.

Yet, when it came time for Laura to leave him, to go home from the restaurant or from their place, he always walked her to the subway or the bus, staying with her until the last possible minute. But when they said good-bye, he never kissed her, he seemed almost to be avoiding touching her.

And yet Laura could feel him now looking out beyond Lisa, toward her, perhaps without his even realizing it.

One day at lunch, he suddenly began to talk about Lisa. "She's been depressed lately," he said. "I think it's because she isn't writing and it's hard for her to cope with the baby and run the house. And I'm away so much.

"I feel so bad for her," he said.

Laura waited, wondering what would come next.

He shook his head. "She has no confidence in herself. You know, she's always been second best. She has an older sister who's been very successful, a doctor. The parents always favored the sister. When Lisa was a little girl and she came into the room, they'd say, 'Oh, it's only little Lisa.' "

Laura listened sympathetically, not commenting. Yet part of her was glad he was opening up, was glad to hear him say that Lisa was in trouble; she was happy that he was being even mildly critical of his wife.

Then he said suddenly, in a strangled voice, "I love my wife. I have a good marriage. And I love, above all, my son."

"I know," she said.

"I really do," he said.

He suddenly stopped. He looked directly at her and for a moment, his eyes rested on her. She looked back at him, the air between them was charged.

Then, abruptly, he shifted his glance away.

"So tell me," he asked, "how did that article go?"

"I think they liked it," she said. "They're going to run it in June."

Their conversation had nothing to do with what was going on between them, it was only words jiggling in space outside them.

A couple of weeks later, in December, Laura was asked to do an article in Paris on the international student movement. The assignment was a perk. The magazine had received a grant to devote a whole issue to the subject. In leaner times, Laura's payments had often been delayed. Now there was money, and they were sending her to Paris.

When she told Ben about the trip, he said he had to fly to Europe too. He was going to Israel to do a piece on the Yom Kippur War, and he'd have to stop over in Paris anyway. "We might as well fly together," he said, "I've got some contacts in Paris, some old friends from the movement, they could really help you out." He'd stay overnight and introduce her to them, ease the way for her.

The whole thing was forced, of course, though she didn't say that. He presented it with a certain logic—he had to leave at the same time, why not fly together?

"I hear you're going to Paris. Isn't that wonderful!" Lisa said when Laura saw her. Lisa's face was all lit up with that peculiar radiance of hers, the eyes a little damp, the cheeks flushed. Laura wondered if she meant it, but then why shouldn't she? Nothing had gone on between them.

Just before they were to leave for Paris, Laura dropped by at Ben and Lisa's apartment. When she arrived, Lisa had just left to take Jesse to her parents' place uptown, and Ben asked Laura to go to the store with him on an errand.

There had just been rain. Ben and Laura walked slowly through the tall yellow buildings of the housing project that abutted his apartment building. They were absorbed in their conversation, talking about their schedule, the student leaders they would contact in Paris.

But as they were going along, some instinct made Laura turn around. There was Lisa, walking behind them. She was walking determinedly, with her peculiar, stiff posture, her head jutting out to the side. She was wearing a parka, and baggy drawstring pants. Her hair was long and unkempt. Had she heard what they were saying? Laura went over the conversation in her mind—there was nothing personal. Why should there be? Nothing had happened between her and Ben. They had been talking innocently enough about work, and about the schedule.

Ben turned and saw her. His voice caught in surprise. "Lisa! I didn't know you were there!"

Lisa smiled at them. Ben stood still, waiting for her to catch up. As she came closer, Laura saw the tears in her eyes. She was trying to keep them back. Ben saw the tears too.

"What's the *matter*?" he asked.

"Oh, I'm just going through a lot of things!" she said, and she smiled at him in that sweet way they both had.

The three of them walked together to the store, Ben with his arm around Lisa's shoulders. Nothing more was said about the tears.

But that image of Lisa walking determinedly along the path toward them, the Cyclone fence on either side, her head at that peculiar sharp angle to her body, stayed in Laura's mind, the image of Lisa's tears rolling silently down her cheeks.

On the day they were to leave for Paris, Lisa and Jesse came to the airport to say good-bye. But when they got to Kennedy, they discovered the plane had been delayed for two hours because of bad weather over the Atlantic. "Maybe we should all get some dinner," Ben said.

They settled in at the airport restaurant. "You're going to have a wonderful time," Lisa said, smiling.

"You should have come with us," said Ben.

"No, it would be too hard on Jesse," said Lisa. He was twenty months old now, busy pouring salt and pepper in piles on the table. "Change is hard on babies this age."

So, thought Laura, Lisa *had* been invited to come to Paris. But she'd said no. Perhaps it was because of Jesse. But perhaps she didn't come because she knew Ben didn't want her. And instead of being angry and confronting him, Lisa had sensed his unspoken, perhaps still unconscious wish—and she had obeyed it.

Now, in the restaurant at Kennedy, Jesse was toddling over to another table in his blue snowsuit. Ben got up and brought him back, whereupon he reached across the table and grabbed a glass of water, spilling it all over Ben's jeans.

Ben handed him back to Lisa and tried to wipe the water off with a napkin.

"Hey, Jesse—look!" said Laura. "Look at the camera." She held the camera out to show him, but he only glanced at it and reached across the table for Ben's food.

"Can I hold you?" Laura asked. But he shrank from her, clutching Lisa, staring at Laura as if he was terrified of her. He didn't like her, it was obvious.

He was a beautiful child. But whenever Laura was in the apartment, he seemed to be screaming. "He's up all night," Lisa would say. "I don't know what to do. Last night he was up from four-thirty on . . ."

The announcement to board came over the loudspeaker. They all walked together to the gate, Ben holding Jesse in his arms. Laura watched as he kissed Lisa good-bye. He held her, kissing her on the lips tenderly. Laura felt a stab of anger. Why was he making such a phony show? He just wanted to look good to himself, she thought.

"Bye-bye, Jesse," said Ben, taking the boy in his arms again, then handing him back to Lisa. "Bye-bye."

Now Jesse waved dumbly at Ben. Then Ben started to move away, and the boy began to cry.

As Ben and Laura walked toward the plane, his cries grew in intensity, they seemed to tear out of his body, they became sobs of unfathomable grief. As they looked back, he was stretching out his arms to Ben supplicatingly, shaking and trembling.

Ben stepped back to the gate, his face distraught. He grabbed Jesse and held him tight, as if he would never see him again. "Don't, baby, don't," he cried. "Please!"

Laura stood impatiently in the stream of passengers boarding the plane. People were bumping into her while Ben was trying to comfort Jesse. Jesse had locked his arms tight around Ben's neck now, and Lisa was trying to pull him away, but he only reached out his arms toward Ben beseechingly. "Daaaaaaad . . . ," he cried. "Noooo . . ."

"Come on, Jesse," said Lisa. "Daddy be home soon. He'll be home soon."

At last, Ben yanked himself away. Lisa stood with Jesse in her arms at the gate. "Wave bye-bye daddy, wave bye-bye," she said, but Jesse continued to scream, his face red and wet with tears, his lower lip trembling, passengers and well-wishers staring at him.

Watching them, Laura wondered if Jesse would remember this, if he would always carry this image of them in his mind forever, a screen memory as they call it, of his father leaving with her on the plane.

Even as they entered the cabin of the plane, they could still hear Jesse's cries, his distraught, desperate wailing. Laura wondered if Lisa was lingering at the gate just so they could hear him.

They handed the stewardesses their boarding passes. Ben was preoccupied. They found their seats in the back of the plane—it was a late flight so they had three seats across to themselves and they were alone.

The plane took off, flying out over the Atlantic, its lights reflected in the black water.

They lay back in their seats, looking out. Beneath them, Laura imagined the uninhabited reaches of the North, reindeer moving against the storms, but here in the plane, it was like a cocoon.

During the flight, they hardly talked. They didn't touch. Sometimes Ben would look across at her from his seat and smile, and when he slept, she could see the same light smile on his face.

When the plane landed at Orly, there was a long search by

customs. They probably fit some profile—Ben had a beard, and they could have been students.

In the taxi, he didn't touch her. Perhaps he was afraid, even here in this foreign city, that someone they knew would see them.

Paris was gray and bleak, and although Laura had never been there, she had little interest in what she saw. From the cab window it seemed an impersonal city, a city full of monuments. She was conscious only of Ben, of wanting to preserve this American entity, transported across thousands of miles.

At the hotel, they had rolls and fruit and coffee with hot milk, and then they went upstairs. It was a small place on a back street. They'd requested two single rooms, of course.

In the dark winter afternoon, they climbed the stairs behind the proprietress. She opened the doors to both rooms, and Ben tipped her. They watched her walk down the hall away from them. There was a pale gray light. Each room was small and neat with a high double bed and a feather quilt over it. The floors were bare but for a small Oriental rug by each bed.

Laura walked into her room and Ben went into his, carrying his bag, as if signaling even in this backwater hotel in a foreign country that there was nothing going on between them. She left the door to her room open.

Laura turned and saw him standing in the doorway of her room. He was still wearing his blue parka. He smiled. It was that kindly smile that so attracted her, and yet at times made her so peculiarly angry—because it denied the aggression she knew he had in him, because he loved Lisa. Because he was betraying Lisa. Then she saw hesitation in his face. But nothing he thought mattered, because it was going to happen anyway.

He closed the door behind him. The sunless early winter light flooded the room. The window looked out on a narrow street below, and a big limestone house opposite with a red tile roof.

Ben walked across her room. There were voices coming from downstairs, the proprietress talking on the phone, the sound of someone pushing a cleaning cart in the hall. He walked over to Laura, took his parka off, and then he put his arms around her. She could feel the roughness of his wool sweater, his body wiry and tense.

The first time it was quick, half in their clothes, no time to really undress, and then the second time she saw the hair on his barrel chest, his strong but rather thin arms, his hands small but tough and wiry. She could feel her own nakedness as a revelation through his eyes. Her breasts were perfect, round and full, she wasn't too thin anymore.

And she felt a kind of cruelty, in reducing him, his properness, in making him like a boy underneath her hands, seeing him lying there, his head tossing from side to side as she touched him, sucked him. He'd tried to stay away from her, tried to be moral, to keep his family together, but she'd made it all dissolve, made all his strength, his good intentions, melt away. And she knew she was beautiful, more beautiful than she'd ever been, her skin was rosy, her body perfect and clean. As she mastered him, as she grew radiant, the name lurked in her mind, shadowy, unspoken. She could feel the name even as the light changed in front of her eyes, as the center of her gravity shifted and swirled.

When they finished, it was dark. They slept for a while and then woke up hungry.

"Let's eat here," he said. "We better not go out, someone could see us."

"No one's going to see us here!" She laughed.

"I know," he said. "But let's just stay here anyway."

"For goodness's sake!" she said. Whoever would see them here?

They went downstairs to the deserted dining room and the proprietress gave them soup and bread.

There was snow that night, building up gradually on the tile roof across the way. They made love again until they were sore, and then they fell into a deep, exhausted sleep.

In the night, with the snow and cold outside, Laura turned in her sleep and discovered him next to her, his body fitted against hers; it almost took her by surprise. Half asleep, they made love; it was like floating, as if there was no gravity, as if there were no up or down anymore, but only turning.

The next morning, they were scheduled to meet the students. Ben had a contact, an old friend with whom he'd gone to graduate school. The man was Lisa's friend too, and they had to pretend to him there was nothing between them. Sitting there with Ben, in the reasonable light of the students' apartment, Laura wondered if the man could tell from their faces that they had made love, from their bright eyes and their flushed cheeks. She could hardly pay attention to what the students were saying, she could only think about Ben over in the other chair, appearing to be completely absorbed in what they were saying.

After they left the students, Laura didn't want to work on the story, she didn't want to follow up leads, to seek people out. She only wanted to go back to their hotel and make love.

In the hotel lobby, Ben bought some postcards. "I'm just going to send these to Jesse and Lisa," he said and sat down to

168

write them in an armchair in the corner. Laura could tell he was trying to hide what he was writing from her. He had fucked her and now he was turning his attention to Lisa. The hypocrisy of it! He was writing to Lisa and Jesse when he had been here making love to her all night.

Laura buried herself in the *Herald Tribune*.

When he put his postcards in the mailbox, she was cold and silent.

On their way upstairs, at the turning of the landing, he put his arm around her and tried to draw her close, but she moved ahead of him up the stairs. He followed her into her room.

"Okay, what's the matter?" he asked.

She didn't answer.

"Look, what do you want me to do?" he said. "Not write to them? You think I should forget about them?"

"I don't know."

"I'm not a monster."

"I know, but it's so hypocritical! The whole thing . . ."

He didn't say anything. He began to kiss her neck, running his tongue along the skin.

"Leave me alone. I hate you!" she said.

And as he began to fuck her she said the words, "I hate you, I hate you!" and she could feel the black hate rising up inside her, but still the sex was good, even better than before.

At the airport, before he was to fly to Jerusalem, they had one final cup of coffee. "I love Lisa," he said. "I do love her. I've loved her since I was twenty years old."

Laura was silent. She felt the loathing for Lisa rise up in her. How could he love her?—she was dirty, she was disorganized. But she didn't dare say anything. He would just close up to protect Lisa.

"Look, you know we can't go on," he said. "These things just happen. We'll put it behind us. I'm sorry, Laura."

He kissed her good-bye. Then he kissed her again, at first almost formally, and then, desperately, and then he tore himself away.

When she returned to the hotel, she climbed into bed and pulled the covers over her head. In the darkness it was all the easier to think about him.

Two weeks later, when they both had returned to New York, she waited for him to call her, but he didn't. She phoned him.

"Can we have lunch?" she asked.

"Meet me at the magazine," he said. He was always thinking. If they met openly, their relationship would appear more innocent to those around them.

It was closing day at the magazine, there were editors and writers running about. When she got off the elevator, her eyes met Ben's immediately. He was sitting at his desk facing the elevator. She knew he had positioned himself so he could see her as soon as she came out.

And she knew, as he watched her walking across the room toward him, that she was beautiful. He'd made her beautiful, there was no awkwardness in her anymore. The skinniness, the tiredness in her face were gone. Her face glowed, her hair was full and shining, her mouth sweet and expressive.

Ben got up, walked toward her.

He smiled at her and it was as if suddenly a vacuum had formed between them, a long tunnel of silence, as if all the sound had been sucked from the room.

170

They had lunch in the coffee shop. No one from the magazine ever went there; it was set back from the street and it was hard to see in the windows.

She endured the lunch while he talked to her about his piece. Then he went into a long criticism of his managing editor. There were a great many people at the magazine he thought were incompetent. She sensed he was right about these things, but his standards were so exacting that sometimes he irritated her. The fact was, he was the best writer there. There was no one else who could touch him, and he worked harder than anyone else. So perhaps he was right to think others were incompetent.

"How's Lisa?" Laura asked.

"Oh, she's fine."

"And Jesse?"

"He's just great."

"Sleeping any better?" Laura asked—meanly. She knew the child was sleeping badly, a sign of his distress, of Lisa's inadequacy.

"We're working on it," Ben said evasively.

He called for the check.

"Well," he said. "It's been good seeing you."

"Yes." Her face, her voice, she knew, were frozen.

"Oh my God, Laura," he said, reaching across the table. She felt again his small, strong, wiry hand, the skin tough and dry.

She settled back in her chair. Outside, it had begun to snow again. Slowly, as the white piled up, the city would become beautiful, all its flaws, its filth covered; its jagged lines, its ugliness given a soft uniformity, so that even Eighth Avenue would be beautiful.

"Let's go somewhere," he said.

It was the first of many visits to the hotels of the side streets of Manhattan.

Usually, she and Ben would have lunch first.

During these lunches, Laura would make helpful suggestions about Lisa. "Maybe you should get a baby-sitter during the day so she could work?" Sometimes she actually wanted to help her, she thought she really did. She could feel herself being drawn into the idea. She wasn't all bad. Yes, she was having an affair with him. But in her superior wisdom, her superior competency, she would join in the effort to improve Lisa's life.

"She doesn't want to leave him with a baby-sitter," Ben said. "She doesn't think it's right."

"But just a couple of hours . . . ," Laura said. "After all, no one should spend twenty-four hours a day with a child, full-time."

"She thinks he's too young. He's just learning to separate and she doesn't want to make it harder on him . . ."

Yet whenever he told her of some failing of Lisa's such as, "We've got to do something about that apartment. It's such a mess," or, "She just doesn't seem to be able to get any work done and then she gets depressed," Laura derived a secret satisfaction from it. But she knew if she criticized Lisa directly he would only clam up and rush to defend her.

Then, somewhere during the lunch, Ben would say, "We can't go on any longer," or sometimes, *she* would say it, because he was going to stay with Jesse and Lisa, because the stakes were weighed against her.

"This is it. The last time," he would say, or she would. And then they would go to a hotel.

She felt sometimes as if she were spinning at the end of a long rope, spinning out into space, out of control. Was this all just a game? A game in which the object was simply to take him from the other woman? And thereby herself become more beautiful, a better person?

She continued to visit him at his home. He would invite her over, or she'd have lunch with him and Lisa together. Why did he want them to be together? she wondered. Was it some ruse merely to keep Lisa thinking there was nothing between them? Or was it some need he had to believe he could love them both? Or some archaic, polygamous impulse on his part, to see both the women he loved together in the same room? Some pride of ownership perhaps.

And why did Lisa do it? Did she want to punish herself? Keep Laura under her eye? Satisfy herself that nothing was happening?

And what was *she*, Laura, doing? Parading herself in front of Lisa, emphasizing her own looks, her slenderness, her competency in the face of the other's inadequacy. A little bit of cruelty hidden under the guise of a friendly visit.

Laura would store up impressions, drop them, bit by bit, in front of Ben, damaging perceptions delivered to him under the guise of friendly advice. "Maybe you should get a cleaning woman. It would take some pressure off Lisa." Of course this just reminded him Lisa couldn't take care of her own home. Or, if he said Jesse was sick, she would say, "I think it sounds like Jesse's got an ear infection," as if she could somehow be a better mother to Jesse than Lisa.

She would say, "Look, I want to end it. We're hypocrites. Look what we're doing. We're not really this kind of people . . ." One night she said it when they were driving home from New Jersey—she had gone to watch him do interviews for an article on assembly-line workers.

"You're right," he said and he was silent. She looked

173

closely at his face and saw tears in his eyes and felt a wave of pity for him. He loved her, she knew. He was doing his best, caught in a struggle. She touched his shoulder, then his penis, and he pulled over to the side of the road.

In the darkness, with the lights from the cars sweeping over them, illuminating them, she sucked him off. It was dangerous, she'd never done this before, but the danger excited her and she kept on going, not caring.

There were scenes in taxicabs. Riding home together when he'd say, "We can't go on." Then he'd reach over and grab her and kiss her and they would practically be fucking then and there. She knew the cabdriver could see them in his rearview mirror, and normally she'd be embarrassed. But now she didn't care about modesty. "Let's go somewhere," Ben would say, and he'd tell the driver to change direction and they'd go to a hotel.

He'd make the cab stop a block away from the hotel and they'd go there separately—it was always during the day, at lunchtime usually, or at five, the end of the workday. He would scout the street first, she following behind him. The little pantomime made her angry. He was a coward, a hypocrite.

As if anybody, except Lisa, would care.

And then, after they'd made love, she would lie in the tiny room, resting her head on his shoulder. And she'd think of Barbara and Hal long ago, the two of them meeting furtively in their little hotels, hotels in the out-of-the-way areas of greater London, little hotels on the banks of the Thames, stolen moments, Barbara in her navy blue suit and her little hat with the veil, fragrant Barbara, and desperate because they couldn't help themselves.

＊

Ben and Lisa were going to rent a house in the country, a weekend place. "It'll be good for her to get away from her parents and for Jesse to be outdoors," Ben said.

He really was going to stay with Lisa. This made it definite.

In the coffee shop, she sat back in the chair. He reached over and took her hand, smiled.

On weekends, she imagined them in the country together. Perhaps they were making love—they *had* to make love sometimes. Once she thought she saw traces of Lisa on him, but she made love to him anyway. Maybe it was some perversion, she thought, two women joined through a man, but she didn't care.

He never mentioned his sex life with Lisa. Laura could only infer, hope, that it was lousy by the way he was with her.

One Monday, he told her, "I had a headache all last weekend. I think it's because I want to be in that house with *you*." He'd never before said it clearly—that he cared more for her than for Lisa. Always, it had been that he loved Lisa and Laura was just an aberration. "When I'm there," he said, "all I can think about is what it would be like if you were with me."

A film was being produced about the Vietnam veterans' meeting in Detroit. The filmmakers were cutting the movie in a house in the country outside New York. Since they both had covered the story, they were invited to see some footage. The screening was a pretext, and without admitting it to one another, they knew going to see the film would give them an opportunity to be alone.

175

They drove out together. The house was about an hour from the city. As soon as the screening was over, they left quickly, saying it was late.

As they were driving home on the highway, it began to rain. It was April, and still cold; the water swept in waves across the road. Laura wished they could drive like this forever, the rain lulling them, the car warm inside, the water enveloping them.

They talked about the film, about an article a woman they knew had written.

"Wasn't it a great piece?" she said.

"Well . . . ," he said, in that noncommittal way of his.

"But did you like it?"

He didn't answer.

She was angry again.

He always did that, refusing to comment when he didn't like something, as if by *not* saying anything, his criticism was somehow stronger. He would never admit that he was competitive to the death and arrogant in his knowledge that he was the best.

"Well, declare yourself," she said now.

But he wouldn't. It was a kind of game, his stubbornness exceeding hers.

"Why won't you say what you think?" she said. They both knew they were going to make love, and now they were fighting. She moved over to the far side of the car, as far away from him as she could. She hated this quality of his, his concealed aggression.

"That's the road we take to the house," he said, pointing ahead. "Do you want to go there?" he asked softly.

She didn't answer, but she knew they'd go there anyway.

He turned off onto the side road. They were in a forest of

spruce and fir now. They had both fallen silent, as if the exquisite seclusion, the privacy the mantle of water afforded them, the realization that sex was inevitable, had somehow overwhelmed their anger. It was a weekday, Lisa would be in the city, and Laura knew they were going to make love in the house, not in some ugly hotel. She knew they were going to take some time.

The rain poured down the side of the car, etching rivulets on the windows. Hush, rush. Down the gullies at the side of the road. Whish went the windshield wipers. No one knew they were here. For the first time in a long time, they were really alone.

"There's the lake," said Ben.

Ahead of them was a small lake, the water gray and dimpled in the rain.

"And that's the house." He pointed to a gray-shingled ranch house at the edge of the water. They turned into a dirt road between the evergreens.

"I hope we don't get stuck," he said. How terrible that would be, Laura thought maliciously—why they might be discovered!

They stopped the car in front of the house and sat still for a moment, not moving, while the rain increased around them.

"Stay in the car while I get the door open," he said.

She watched him run through the rain and grope for the key over the door. He found it, opened the front door, and beckoned to her through the wet.

Inside, the house was built like a log cabin, with timber beams and a stone fireplace.

But there was no furniture, except for a Formica kitchen table and two chairs, one of them with a broken cane seat. It was like their place in New York.

"You don't have any furniture," Laura said. "How can you stay here?"

"It's my fault. I should help her more," he said. "I'm away too much."

She pictured the three of them, Lisa and Jesse and Ben, alone by the lake, miles from anywhere in this bare house on an early spring weekend, Ben with his headache, Lisa trying to make him happy in that gentle, ineffectual way of hers. Suddenly she felt a wave of sympathy for all of them.

"I'll make a fire," Ben said, rubbing his hands together in the cold. He searched the house for kindling.

"There's no kindling," he said, coming back. "I meant to get some when we left last weekend, but everything was chaos."

He adjusted the thermostat on the wall.

She heard him open the back door. In a minute he returned with firewood.

"I think some of this is dry." He laid the wood down in the fireplace and began rolling newspaper up into logs. Then he lit it and the fire took.

"Is there anything to eat?" she asked.

"I don't know." They went into the kitchen. There were dirty dishes lying in the sink. He opened the refrigerator. Inside was a bread package with a crust in it, a container of yogurt. He lifted the lid off the yogurt and there was mold growing on top.

"Nothing," he apologized.

He opened the cabinet above the sink. "Here's some brandy." He smiled. He took a swig, handed it to her. "Tastes good."

"Where do you sleep?" she asked.

"In there." He pointed to the bedroom off the kitchen.

Laura saw a mattress on the floor with a sheet over it and an old comforter.

"And where does Jesse sleep?"

"He's been sleeping with us. We have to get a bed for him."

Laura had heard somewhere it wasn't good for children to sleep with their parents. But she was glad Jesse was sleeping with them—it meant they weren't making love.

"Should he be sleeping with you?" she asked, meanly, knowing the answer, but wanting to make him say it. "That's not supposed to be good, is it?"

"No. Probably not," he said grimly. "I don't want him to, but he has bad dreams and he gets up a lot. He comes to our room and gets into bed with us. If it's four in the morning you're just too tired to take them back. I try to force myself to get up and put him back, but then he just comes in again."

Now he sighed and looked at her, his face unsmiling.

"I love you," he said. His voice was weary, resigned.

They made love on the mattress on the floor, on a spare blanket. She didn't want her body to touch the sheets he and Lisa had lain upon together. Outside, the rain came down, thick and deep, covering the windows.

And lying there afterward, as Ben slept beside her, she thought, maybe there *is* such a thing as being meant for someone. Maybe there's some marking in the genes, some recondite programming, as inexorable as what is called fate, a joke played on human beings by nature, which determines whom we love. It didn't matter that he was married to someone else. It didn't matter what he or she might say or do to try to stop it. They were helpless, all their language, all their sudden insights, were useless, dust and ashes.

179

The following week, she was supposed to meet Ben for lunch. She waited in the restaurant, but after twenty minutes, he still hadn't arrived. She didn't understand it, he was always on time. She called his home, but there was no answer.

After half an hour, she ordered her meal and called again. When her lunch came, she couldn't eat. He had never done this before. It was totally unlike him not to show up for an appointment, not to call her if he would be late.

She could feel the fury building up inside her. Her throat grew dry, it seemed as if her eyes were bulging out of her head.

She took a cab back to her loft, checked her machine. There was nothing on it from him. She kept on calling him, but there was no answer at his apartment.

Finally, in the late afternoon, he picked up the phone.

"What happened!" she cried. Her voice was hoarse now with rage.

"Lisa's a little sick."

"Sick? You could have called me at least. I was waiting for an hour in the restaurant."

"I couldn't get to the phone." His voice was strange, guarded. "Are you all right, honey?" he called over his shoulder. Laura could hear the faint murmur of Lisa's response in the background.

"You couldn't get to the phone?" Laura almost screamed into the phone.

"Yes," he said, in an odd way, distant, as if he weren't really talking to her.

An alarm raced through her body.

"What the hell is going on?" she said.

"Nothing, everything's fine." He was lying.

The following day, she called again. Still, his voice had a studied casualness that she knew was false.

"Look, you don't have to say anything," she said into the phone. "Just answer yes or no. Is she sick?"

"Oh, she had a touch of flu," he said as if he were speaking to some distant acquaintance, not to Laura.

"I don't understand. Why didn't you call me?"

"I ran her over to the doctor," he said, as if he were talking perhaps to his parents, and not answering her question directly.

"I'll call you," he said.

He didn't phone. She couldn't understand it—he always found a way of calling her wherever he was. When he took Jesse to the park, he would call her, or when he was on assignment he would phone her from the highway.

She called him again. "Look, I have to see you. I just have to!"

"I'm going to take Jesse to the park around two," he said, as if he were talking to the mother of one of Jesse's playmates.

She met him at the playground near his building. Down below, she could see the Hudson sweeping by. It was a sweet spring afternoon, there was the scent of new leaves, a golden air. It was the moment just before the pleasant warmth would metamorphize into the blazing, brutal heat of summer. While Jesse played on the slide, Ben sat down on the bench beside her.

"What *is* it?" she demanded.

"She's been a little sick," he said, guardedly.

"With *what!*"

He paused. Then he said, "She's had a nervous break-down."

"A breakdown . . ."

"The other day, I found her letting Jesse eat some of her sleeping pills. She said she was hearing voices. I called the doctor and took her over. He said she had to see a psychiatrist at once. Her parents are with her now and we're deciding what to do."

His voice was controlled, distant. She could feel him trying to hold himself together.

Suddenly, he stood up. He ran to where Jesse was climbing the ladder to the slide and grabbed his arm. "Careful now," he said.

She followed him to the slide.

"I'm sorry," she said.

"I know," he replied.

"What are you going to do?"

"We don't know. We can't leave her alone. She's full of medication now and it's under control—but she needs extended treatment of some kind."

They watched Jesse as he ran now toward the sandbox. He was still a little unsteady on his feet; he moved with each leg held straight, his diaper big in his overalls, his pale blond curls bouncing. He smiled eagerly at the other children in the sandbox.

"I'm very sorry," Laura said again.

She could see, around his beard, that Ben's face was very pale, almost bloodless. There was a gray cast to it. She saw new lines, on his forehead, at the edge of his eyes.

"What about Jesse?"

"I'm not sure yet. We're debating that too."

"It's because of us, isn't it?" Laura said.

"No. When I spoke to the psychiatrist I realized that this

182

isn't the first time this has happened, only I was too stupid to understand. Just before we got married, I remember she said she thought she was hearing voices, magical voices—telling her to do things and I dismissed it. I took it as being just her—poetic sensibility." He looked miserable.

"It's come out now," he said, "maybe because of us. Maybe it's her way of showing anger. But it was always there."

"She's never said anything about us?"

"Never," he said, turning to her with a grim smile. "Except to say nice things about you." He frowned. "I feel I shouldn't be talking about it with you, because somewhere you're glad."

"How can you say that?" And yet he was right. She was stunned by Lisa's illness, yet somewhere too there was satisfaction in seeing her disintegrate, in seeing the enemy vanquished.

He looked miserable again, shook his head. "Forgive me," he said.

"Is there anything I can do?" she said. "I really mean that." Always trying to be of help, she thought, looking good next to Lisa's mess.

He smiled a hopeless smile. "I know," he said. "I'm sorry." She felt he wanted to touch her hand, but he didn't, in this public place.

He said Lisa's illness wasn't their fault. But she couldn't think of it any other way. The two of them, together, had driven her crazy. He wouldn't let her see Lisa. She had a vision of her, standing with that peculiar, rigid posture, the long, white-blond hair draped to one side over her shoulder, the smile that was almost like crying, like Ophelia.

If Ben didn't want to continue their relationship, she would understand.

She stayed away from the phone. She didn't call him. She had no right to make demands on him now, she didn't deserve to see him. At first, it had been just a love affair with all its forbidden delights—and all its little nastinesses toward Lisa—Laura's sly remarks about Lisa's incompetency as a mother, about her disorganization and her poor house-keeping.

But it was different now. It was grown-up, serious.

After two days, Ben called. "We're sending her to a place in Massachusetts. It'll be for ninety days, it's supposed to be very good. I'm going to let Jesse stay with my parents. I don't want to leave him with some baby-sitter all day while I'm working. Whatever my parents' faults, I know they love him and will take care of him."

Sometimes that summer when he visited Laura in her loft, they didn't make love. He simply lay in her arms, and she held him and stroked his forehead and his hair.

"Whenever I say good-bye to Jesse he just screams and screams," he said. He lay back on the bed, threw his arm across his eyes. "What have I done to him?

"But I can't stop seeing you," he said. "I can't."

She wondered if it could happen to him too, if he too might have a nervous breakdown.

Every other weekend, he visited Lisa in Massachusetts and returned grim faced.

"She seems to be getting better," he said. "I think she'll be home on Labor Day."

Laura knew that when Lisa returned, they couldn't

continue. Lisa couldn't recover if they continued their affair.

He brought Lisa home on Labor Day. He'd made careful preparations, having the house cleaned, stocking up on food. He had even bought some furniture, a new couch and dining table to cheer the place up—he'd asked Laura to go with him to buy the couch and she had helped choose it.

When Laura knew he was bringing Lisa home, she felt calm. She was prepared for whatever had to happen.

She thought of them making a new life together. It was beyond sex now, beyond desire. Something more serious, Lisa's life, Jesse's life. She had to behave, she had to let him go, not make demands.

She didn't hear from him. And she was almost happy. She made plans with friends, went out every night.

At the end of that week, he phoned her.

"It's no good," he said. "I can't take it anymore. It's not even that I love you now. I just can't be with her."

"I'm going to file for a separation," he said. "And I'm going to get custody of Jesse. He'll stay with my parents during the week until he's old enough to go to school. Then he'll come and live with me."

"A separation?" Somehow, the news took her by surprise. For a moment she said nothing.

"How's Lisa?" she asked.

"It's very strange. She's almost unresistant, as if somewhere she wants it too. Maybe that's how fucked up she is—she's not even expressing any anger. She's going along with it—at least for now. Until she gets well. She's going to live with her parents."

·)

The next day, he came to see her. When she opened her door, he stood there on the threshold, hesitating a moment.

There was something shy about him, tentative suddenly. She stared at him. It was as if all his mystery had been shed like a skin and now he stood before her in the light of day.

Laura blinked, trying to get him in focus. It was as if she were seeing him for the first time, in true daylight.

Here was his true face. He was smiling slightly, in expectation, in love. It was an ordinary face, and yet she loved him, for his sweetness, because he was a moral man, even after what he had done to his wife; she loved him because of sex, because her sexual life had begun with him.

She stepped toward him, and she embraced him, and when they were naked it was strange, because now they were allowed to be naked. She worried that the sex wouldn't somehow be as good. But it was the same, it was the way it always was, they didn't even have to try.

They told a few close friends they were seeing one another, although Ben said they had to be discreet because he didn't want problems with the divorce. One night, they had a dinner party at her loft, and their guests, a writer from his magazine, and his girlfriend, acted as if they had known all along that she and Ben were lovers. It had been a strange yet comfortable feeling, this quasi-legitimacy.

After their dinner guests had left, Ben took out his wallet.

"Here," he said. "Here's five dollars for the food. That should just about do it," he said.

"I paid more for the groceries than that!" she said.

"Well, I'm sorry . . ."

"Is that what you think you should pay?"

"I didn't know. It's *your* house." He handed her a wad of bills. "Here. Take what you want."

"That's not the point," she said.

"What *is* the point?"

"The point is you're stingy. That's what you really thought you should give."

He came up to her, put his arms around her. "Why are you doing this?" he asked. He *was* stingy on little things. And yet he had taken her out the day before and bought her a down coat. In big things, he would give her the world.

"What's going on?" he asked, holding her.

"I don't know . . . I don't know . . ." she said. And in truth, she really didn't.

On weekends, he collected Jesse from his parents. Usually, she went with him and Jesse to the zoo or to the park. She was drawn to Jesse, she wanted to hold him. She had fantasies of the day when she and Ben would be together and Jesse would go to school. She thought of taking him to buy school clothes, smart little stovepipe overalls. She thought he would soon be old enough to go to *The Nutcracker.*

But he only wanted Ben. He screened her out. When she tried to hold him, he walked away from her.

They were making love in the big, old, wrought-iron bed he'd shared with Lisa. Ben was touching her, bringing her to the very brink.

She heard a cry, a soft, faint cry coming from the depths

187

of the apartment. Was it Jesse? She wasn't sure. Ben hadn't heard it. She made a sound, encouraging Ben, arching her hips up toward his hand. It always worked, the sex, she thought.

Another cry. She was sure of it now. The beginnings of a wail.

Above her, Ben paused, listened. "It's him," he said.

"Maybe you should let him be," she said. "If you leave him maybe he'll put himself back to sleep."

Ben's thin body tensed, straining to hear. "He'll come in here if I don't go to him," he said. He climbed out of bed, moved naked across the room.

Where he had suddenly left her body, it was cold. It was as if a piece of her flesh had been torn away. And now there was an open wound, waiting for him.

She covered herself with the sheet, waiting. The murmur of his voice with the child came to her from the other side of the apartment. She could hear him singing, "Go to sleep . . ." The sweet tenor. "Go to sleep, little boy . . ."

She could feel herself closing up, drying up.

And now the rage taking over. It was as if the child knew, as if he just waited and did it deliberately when they were in bed together. They couldn't have one moment together.

"Go to sleep . . ."

And yet that was why she loved him, because he was a good father. Because he had kept his child, because he wouldn't give him up.

Now, lying there, she hated herself for what she had become, a monster, she thought, selfish. And she hated him for helping her to become that way; for giving her exactly what she wanted, for leaving Lisa.

Ben was coming back; he slipped across the room and into bed.

188

"I'm sorry," he said. "I think he's asleep now."

He put his hands on her body—they were cold. She pulled away a little. He began kissing her breasts. But she lay under him limp, unmoving.

"It's no good now," she said. "It's ruined."

"No, it isn't." He laughed, flipping her nipples with his tongue.

"It is," she said, holding herself stiff.

She heard the angry intake of his breath. He moved away from her, turned over.

"He should learn to put himself back to sleep," she said.

"C'mon!" he said. "What do you expect? He's a little boy."

"You're spoiling him," she said. "You can't make up for what's happened to him by spoiling him."

"Look, he's lost his mother and his father both at once. How can I not go to him?"

Suddenly tears burst from her eyes, the unexpected tears of a child, tears of shame.

"I'm sorry," she said. "I can't help myself."

He reached over to her, pulled her to him, held her. After a while, they made love again, and it was short and, as always, no matter what, no matter how much anger there was between them, it was sweet.

She wanted to love Jesse and yet she couldn't.

She looked at him and sometimes she saw Simon, she saw the pale, slanted eyes, a boy hard to reach, a boy who could be saved. She saw herself as a child, desperate and angry. Jesse needed her healing love and yet she couldn't give it to him. She should have known how to do it—because of Simon, because of her own past.

But she also saw Lisa's face shadowed in the depths of his face, she saw the shape of Lisa's jaw embedded in his, the shape of Lisa's nose, Lisa's circles under his eyes. She herself was just a child, Laura thought. What kind of person was she that she didn't have more sympathy, more kindness in her? That she couldn't love a child whose mother she'd helped drive crazy.

"You know, when the separation agreement comes through," Ben said, "we can live together. In a year we could get married and then"—he smiled and held her—"we could have a child."

A child? Was he forgetting how they fought? He still had hope. He was still willing to give it a try.

But she couldn't have a child. She wasn't fit to be a mother. Look at the way she was with Jesse. She was too selfish, like Hal and Barbara—cold, capable of deserting a child the way they had Simon, the way they had deserted *her* when they left her with her grandmother. She had learned on Barbara's knee that a mother could leave a child. Maybe there was something congenitally wrong in her, a gene missing, the gene for being a parent. It was a flaw passed down in the family line.

Would a child kill her, as it did Ruth? Would she die young, like Ruth, like Hal's mother? Maybe that too, the death of young women after bearing children, ran somehow mysteriously in the family.

"I don't know," she said to Ben. "I'm not sure I'm ready."

"We don't have to talk about it now," Ben said.

EIGHT

At Christmas, she decided to take Ben to meet Hal and Barbara. (Lisa and her parents had Jesse for the holiday.) Hal and Barbara had moved from the country—"It's too lonely," Barbara said—and were living in Washington, D.C., now, in an apartment in Georgetown.

She didn't want to admit to Hal and Barbara that she and Ben were lovers, so they spent the night before in a hotel.

They arrived at the apartment on Christmas morning. It was Hal who answered the door. "I'm afraid this is going to be a peculiar Christmas," he announced at once, with an apologetic smile. "We were out last night and your mother has a little hangover. So, I'm roasting the turkey myself. She gave me instructions."

Laura felt the anger tighten her face, but she said nothing. She didn't want to embarrass Ben, standing beside her. At least she could have prepared a meal, or stayed sober.

But she checked her anger. Still afraid of Barbara, she realized.

She walked into Barbara's room to say hello. The curtains had been drawn tight against the morning light because of

Barbara's hangover. She was the way Laura would always remember her, sunk back in the recesses of the four-poster, head propped on the pillows, eyes closed, the beige-pink coverlet over her, the familiar bedspread. The radiator hissed softly.

Laura walked over to the bed. Barbara heard her step and opened her eyes.

"Hello," Barbara said, her voice weak. She spoke as if she were sick. Barbara was angry at her. Why now, she wondered? Because she didn't want her to come for Christmas, because Christmas was too much trouble? Maybe Christmas made her think of Simon.

"I'm sorry you don't feel well," Laura said.

Standing in front of Barbara, she felt the old fear. She was always afraid when she heard that tone in Barbara's voice, of sorrow that hid anger just below the surface. She never knew what she would come out with.

Laura sat down in the chair at the edge of the bed. Barbara closed her eyes again.

"How *are* you?" Laura ventured.

"I've been better," Barbara said, with a little laugh.

"Can I get you something?"

"No." She sighed. "I'll be all right . . . Daddy's doing the turkey . . . Maybe you could give him a hand. It's one of those stove-top dressings. You just add water. The instructions are on the package. And there are those little frozen onions in the freezer."

"I'll take care of it," Laura said.

Barbara was silent, eyes closed.

Maybe she could interest Barbara in Ben, Laura thought, and she would get up to meet him. "Ben is the writer I told you about . . . ," she said.

There was no answer, so apparently she didn't want to meet Ben.

Then Barbara asked, "What does he think about your being in the same work?"

"He likes it," Laura said, surprised by the question.

"I always think the man wants to seem the more intelligent," she said. The "I always think" was a disguise, Laura thought, to soften into an opinion what she actually thought was fact. "Always let the man think he's smarter than you," she used to say.

"We have a lot to talk about," said Laura.

"Wouldn't he rather have the field to himself?"

"No," Laura said.

"Of course, he wouldn't tell you the truth," said Barbara. That was always her retort when she was hard up for logic.

"Of course he would say the truth," Laura said.

Laura felt the anger rise in her. She hated Barbara's idea of femininity. Barbara believed that the only thing she had in the world was her beauty, her identity as a femme fatale. When strangers, especially men, came to the house, Barbara still sucked her cheeks in to make herself more beautiful. She could have been so much more, Laura thought. And yet she presented to the world the image of a woman totally in the service of her man, a partner in a great love affair, her whole being created by her love for Hal, for whom she had given up her baby. It was as if Barbara were somehow fixed in time, still a twenty-five-year-old beauty, a romantic heroine out of a movie, someone from her movie annuals, who'd given up all for love.

She still spoke with an English accent—though she had been in this country eighteen years now and she had never gone back to England. Perhaps she felt that the accent was all she had.

Laura felt the anger push up through her forehead. She hated these "educated," saccharine tones of Barbara's. What Barbara really wanted to convey was that Laura had better not say anything about this hangover because *her* anger would make Laura's pale. She was suffering and Laura'd better fix on that. Not on the fact she had been drunk last night and would now spend Christmas in bed.

She could still be beautiful, Laura thought. A few years back, her hair had begun to turn gray. There was a crest of white growing down the middle of it. It might have been very handsome, but she had immediately begun to dye her hair blond, a fact that Laura found embarrassing. She was a bright woman, Laura thought, why would she want to fight her age?

Now the drinking was beginning to make her face puffy.

"Do you want to meet Ben?" Laura asked.

"God no! Not like *this*!" Barbara cried, although even with a hangover, Barbara looked good. Better than she herself did, Laura thought. Barbara would always be more beautiful, with her high cheekbones, her radiant complexion. Laura, with her tall, awkward body, her wild hair, would always be overshadowed by her.

Barbara closed her eyes again. They sat in silence. Laura wondered what was going on in her mind.

"You said he was getting a divorce?" Barbara asked.

"Yes," Laura said, surprised. Perhaps it was Barbara's unusual attention to detail. Like Hal, she was always preoccupied, absorbed by her inner life.

"And there's a child?" Barbara said.

"Yes." Something made Laura come alert.

194

"How old is the child?"

"He's about two and a half."

"Hmm," she said, eyes still closed, as if reflecting.

"That's a difficult age," Barbara said. "What's the child like?"

"He's sweet. I think he's had a bit of a hard time with the divorce." She didn't tell Barbara that Lisa had gone crazy.

Barbara's eyes were closed now, she was very still, breathing evenly. Laura wondered if she had fallen asleep. Maybe this was it, the end of the interview. Laura stirred, ready to leave. Then Barbara spoke.

"Were you having an affair with him before, while he was still with his wife?" Barbara asked. Her tone was innocent, expressionless, as casual as her series of questions had been.

Laura stalled. "Before?" she repeated.

"Before the divorce."

Barbara's eyes were still shut, her voice was very soft. There was a long silence.

"Yes," Laura answered, too surprised to lie.

"Well, now you know," Barbara said. She let out a grim little snort.

"All these years you've hated me and blamed me," Barbara said. "And now you know what it's like to want someone so much you'll ruin another woman for it—and leave your own child for him."

She sank back a little in her pillows. She sniffed. The sniff was a punctuation mark, an accent.

Laura waited to see what more would come, she held her breath, afraid.

"It's not the same," Laura said softly.

"How not the same?" said Barbara, eyes still closed.

"I don't have a child of my own. I'm not married," Laura said, watching Barbara carefully as she lay still on the bed.

She waited for Barbara to retaliate.

Instead Barbara lay in silence, eyes shut, as if she were in pain from the headache.

Laura still waited.

But nothing came from her. The prosecution had rested its case.

Laura sat quietly on the chair by the bed.

Then she stood up, "I guess I'll help Dad," she said softly.

But there was no answer. She began to walk away across the padded room.

At the door, she hesitated, waiting for Barbara to say something. But there was nothing.

Laura went into the living room. Ben was talking to Hal. Hal had pressed upon Ben a drink—which Ben had accepted, though he never drank in the morning.

It wasn't noon yet, but the sky was dark. The temperature had turned cold and it looked like there would be snow.

Today was Christmas, and there should have been music and decorations, Laura thought. Although the ceremonies of Christmas meant nothing to her—rationally—somewhere the child in her wanted them.

She sat down in the stuffed chair, the same blue-patterned armchair that had followed them from house to house. She knew Hal could feel her depression and Ben's discomfort. They needed the unifying presence of a hostess and a meal.

Hal looked from one to the other. "Hey!" he cried. "Why not go to the movie after we eat! *The Sting* is playing around the corner. We'll eat and we'll go."

"Fine," said Laura. She went into the kitchen to prepare

dinner. Barbara stayed in bed, behind the closed door of her room. Laura didn't disturb her further.

"I'm taking Ben down to Everett to meet Mama," Laura told Hal after they sat down to lunch.

"God!" Hal laughed. "That *town*! You better watch it, Ben. You'll have to go to church on Sunday. God," said Hal, "I hated that town. Just thinking about it makes me depressed. And the worst thing about it is you can't even get a drink!

"I remember getting there and just dying for a beer. But there's absolutely nothing for miles around. And then they all fall asleep at nine o'clock. And the food!"

He didn't want to be reminded, she thought, reminded that he had once been married to Ruth, a small-town girl. He didn't want to be reminded of what he had done to her. The town he came from was just the same, a small town, a humble house, Laura thought.

Just think of us as fallen aristocrats, he used to say.

He had married the actress, the woman with the English accent.

"I had fun there as a child," Laura said, reminding him he had left her there with her grandmother.

He caught himself. "Well, of course. Of course. It was great for a child."

Laura sat there cool, quiet.

She would always go back there—just for revenge, she thought.

"Well," he said, brightly. "Let's have another. Ben? Laura, how about you?"

Four years had passed since Laura had gone back to Everett. It was a five-hour drive from Washington. They climbed through

197

mountains covered in snow and dark evergreens, down into the valley where the town lay, then across the railroad tracks.

Before them was the town, the little frame houses lined up along the railroad tracks, the red-brick bank, the Newberry's. The depot, boarded up now.

Her grandmother had been watching for them at the window of the white house by the railroad tracks, and when the car pulled up she ran out onto the porch.

"Honey!" she cried, running down to Laura, arms outstretched to greet her, her favorite, baby of her baby.

As Laura kissed her, she could feel that her hands were soft now, no longer chapped and rough with caring for generations of children. Laura's grandfather had died four years before and left her with a good railroad pension. Her hair was soft, as always carefully set with a blue rinse in it. She had always been meticulous about her gossamer hair.

Ben took to her immediately, perhaps because he recognized that she loved Laura. Ben had grown up on Park Avenue. He had never spent time in a little town like this, in the remote mountains.

After dinner, Ben and her grandmother sang hymns. Her grandmother sat at the piano while Ben stood behind her, reading from the music. Her grandmother sang in her high quavery soprano, a little out of tune. Laura watched them and felt a surge of love for Ben, because he was being kind to her grandmother, because of his sweet voice.

That night, Laura slept with her grandmother, just as she had long ago when she lay awake for her. Ben was across the hall in the room that had been hers.

Before she put the light out, her grandmother read, as she

always did, from her daily Bible reader, while beside her, Laura flipped through *Time* magazine. Then her grandmother put her book away and turned out the light.

They lay still in the dark, not sleeping yet.

"You said Ben was married, honey?" her grandmother asked.

"He's getting a divorce," Laura corrected. She knew her grandmother wouldn't approve of divorce, but would love her too much to criticize her or anybody she liked.

"Are you in love with him?" her grandmother asked. Laura was surprised to hear the question coming from her, it was somehow so modern, so personal.

"I think so," said Laura. But she couldn't bring herself to answer directly, to say she loved him. For it seemed that even when they weren't fighting there was always a residue of anger between them. Although the cause of her fury had been removed—that for so long he had kept her waiting, insisting he loved Lisa—it was as if her anger now was a continuing echo of what had gone before, as if they had lapsed, in spite of themselves, into a pattern of relatedness that couldn't be broken.

But her grandmother couldn't understand these ambiguities. Her life had centered around her husband, his memory, her devotion unquestioning.

Across from them, on the dresser, were her grandfather's brushes, ivory backed, his change dish, lying on the white cloth untouched, as if he were still alive. Ever faithful, her grandmother's life was really over now that he was gone. She was simply waiting to join him.

Laura loved and honored her. Her grandmother had loved her with a deeper, truer passion that anyone else. Hal was about to give her up because Barbara couldn't stand the sight of another child in the house, a child who looked like Ruth. But something had made him take her back. Guilt? Love of his own child? Not wanting, finally, his own flesh and blood to be raised here in a hick town amid railroad workers and farmers. Fallen aristocrats . . .

If she had stayed in Everett, she wouldn't have become a writer, she would have married a local boy, had children by now. She would have been part of the interlocking web of connection, she would have been beholden to a community of others. She would have existed in an ordered world where obligation came first, even if the personal cost was agony. Divorces were rare in Everett. She would have been cherished by her grandmother—and she wouldn't be guilty.

But now the silence of the house oppressed her, the doilies, the dark, heavy furniture, the clutter of ornaments, salt and pepper shakers, and family pictures, the picture of Ruth at her high-school graduation. She understood now how Hal must have hated it, been suffocated by it, longed to escape it, to escape from Ruth, to marry Barbara, who was glamorous and foreign and different.

She had inherited some of Hal's contempt for her grandmother, for her small-town ways, her abstemiousness. She was a cosmopolitan now—a writer! She traveled to foreign countries, lived a life that her grandmother couldn't possibly understand. There was between her and her grandmother an insurmountable gulf. If her grandmother knew she had taken a man from his wife and child, that the child's mother had had a nervous breakdown . . .

They lay there on the high bed together, Laura twenty-nine now, like a child next to her grandmother. If I had grown up with her, Laura thought, if I had stayed here perhaps there would have been no uncertainty. But she wasn't like her. She was like Hal and Barbara, a wanderer, a person without a home. She was one of *them*. Maybe the only past she craved, she thought, was a past she had romanticized, re-created into a story, woven with her imagination into a distant and complete tale. But when she actually touched it, when it stood before her, she didn't want it.

Her grandmother's voice came to her in the darkness. "Maybe you'll come at Easter?"

"I'll try." But Laura knew she wouldn't come for Easter. Although her relatives were buried here, she had no connection to this place, except to her grandmother. The town had nothing to do with her.

"Can we open a window, Mama?" Laura asked.

"Just a little, honey."

Laura remembered she thought the night air was bad for you, so she opened it only a little.

Beside her now, her grandmother had fallen asleep, snoring lightly. Laura reached over and kissed her soft cheek, smelled the clean smell of Noxzema on it.

"Good night, Mama," she whispered.

"Good night, honey," said her grandmother, struggling for a moment up from sleep, too old to lie awake for her now.

The next day was Sunday. "You have to go to church, Ben," Laura whispered. "You have to *see* it." Her grandmother would be hurt if they didn't go and Laura knew she wanted to show her off to her friends.

There were only a handful of congregants left in the little church. Laura, Ben, and her grandmother sat near the organ pipes, which they had given in memory of Ruth. Who was Ruth? She would have been like her grandmother, sweet and dutiful.

In her childhood reveries, Laura used to imagine sometimes

that Ruth was watching her from heaven. At sunset, she would look up in the sky and think Ruth was up there in her crimson bathrobe, looking down at her.

When the service was over, they stood outside while her grandmother greeted the other congregants.

"Why, you remember my granddaughter Laura," she said to one after another, "Ruth's girl.

"Why lookee here!" she cried. "It's Mary Schiller."

Laura turned and recognized the wife of the funeral parlor director, Ruth's friend. She was middle-aged now, wearing glasses, dressed in a suit and high heels. Her clothes were slightly more expensive, the cut, the cloth a little better than those of the other congregants.

"Laura," said Mary Schiller. "Good to see you!"

"How is Irma?" Laura asked, remembering the intelligent-faced girl with the protruding eyes with whom she had played.

"You know, she's graduated from medical school now. She's in her residency," Mrs. Schiller said. So Irma *had* minded the dead bodies after all, Laura thought. She'd become a doctor.

"Why don't you and your friend come over this afternoon and say hello?" Mary Schiller said.

Schiller's funeral parlor was prospering. There was a new green awning extending over the sidewalk, and an outdoor carpet now, leading from the street to the front door. And the house was newly painted, a bright blue.

Mary Schiller took them into the living room, which was also used as an office and a reception room. On other days, a coffin would be placed in the center of the room. It was a formal, clean space, impersonal, with vinyl sofas and chairs. Shades darkened the windows, and hid the interior from the street. Somewhere, only a few feet away, Laura knew, was the place where the bodies were embalmed. She could see the kitchen just beyond the living room. She felt an impulse to giggle. Perhaps it was the proximity of death.

Mrs. Schiller poured them coffee.

"I see you've become a writer now, Laura. I saw something you wrote in *World* magazine, an article on that prison in New York?"

"Yes," said Laura, "Riker's Island."

"It was very good. Your mama must be so proud of your writing."

She looked at Laura. "You know you look just like your mother!" she said. "I want to show you a picture."

She got up, went to a bookcase, and took out a photo album and turned the pages. There was a photograph of two girls, Ruth and herself. They were about sixteen years old, standing together in prom dresses, posed in front of the railroad track, smiling gaily. So they had been good friends after all.

"That was our senior prom," said Mary Schiller.

"She's pretty," said Laura. Indeed she was, smiling shyly in the white lacy dress, which was fitted tight at the bodice, with a net skirt.

Mary Schiller looked at the picture fondly. "I went with Henry and your mother went with Johnny Johnson."

"Who was that?"

"Oh, he was quite a beau of your mother's. We were all kind of surprised she didn't marry him. He's down in Tylertown now, an attorney."

There could have been another fate, Laura thought. She could have married someone else and it wouldn't have happened.

Laura sensed here a treasure, a person who knew everything

203

about Ruth, knew secrets about her that Grandmother wouldn't know, knew all about her boyfriends, her small deceptions.

"What was she like?" Laura asked.

"Well, she was very interested in music," Mary Schiller said. "Did you know that?"

"No," Laura lied eagerly. Once before, Mary Schiller had offered her the same apparently innocuous fact. To say she knew it already might stanch the flow of information.

"She was very talented," Mary Schiller continued.

Behind them, the house was quiet, but for the ticking of a grandfather clock, a resurrected antique. Mary Schiller, being of the most prosperous family in town, had the knowledge, the leisure, and the money to restore the old objects that others might not value. Laura looked at her. Laura had never seen her dressed informally, she always wore a tailored dress and heels, as if she were about to receive a body. Laura wondered how she managed to put on an appropriate face of grief each time they had a funeral. Maybe her grief was genuine—this was a small town and many of the people she buried must be her friends.

"She used to play the piano real well," said Mary Schiller.

"Was she a good student?"

"Oh, she was a very good student. She got good grades."

"Was she pretty?"

"Oh yes. She was beautiful."

"There's so much about her I don't know," Laura said. "It's still not clear to me how she died."

"Poor thing," Mary Schiller said now, shaking her head. She hesitated. Laura paid attention.

"Your daddy must have told you about it," said Mrs. Schiller.

"I know she died in childbirth. He told me that," Laura said.

"Yes. Henry and I were running the funeral parlor then. We'd been married three years."

Mary Schiller was quiet. She poured more coffee, then pursed her lips. Laura wondered if she were finished. But she sensed that she wanted to go on.

"It was very strange," said Mary Schiller.

Her face clouded over. She leaned forward and handed Ben the milk.

"I couldn't understand it," she said, with feeling now, puzzlement, in her voice. Usually her tone was formal, vaguely impersonal, like her house, like her dress, like a doctor. "You know, I do the hair here and the cosmetics," she said.

"Your grandmother and grandfather wanted her to be buried here, of course, with her family. When she died, they sent her body over on Pan Am, and Henry and I went to New York to get it." She stopped, looked down.

"Oh my, that was hard. She was my best friend. I can't remember a time when I didn't know your mother." She paused.

"I think the English do things different than we do over here," said Mary Schiller.

Laura could feel the woman building to something. She sat very still. "Yes, I imagine they do," said Laura.

The woman was silent. She sipped her coffee. How quiet this room was, sealed off from the outside.

Decades of her professional duties had made her careful with language, Laura thought, had forged discretion in her bones. She had seen the rare suicide in the town, the rare death from alcoholism. She had seen faces blown open from gunshot

205

wounds, the hunter's mistake, bodies eaten by cancer, and she'd learned, as part of her professional duties, to say nothing.

Discretion was her stock-in-trade. But Ruth had been her friend, even before she married Henry Schiller, before she went into this business. This thing had been worrying her for years. Now she had a chance to tell someone about it. It had superseded the assumed behavior of her profession. Anyway, Laura would be leaving. She wasn't part of the town.

"I don't know," said Mary Schiller. "I'll just never understand the English," she said, as if she had thought often of the English. "You know, when she arrived, we were very—shocked. They had just put her body in a box, a plain wooden box. And when we opened it, she was completely naked. They put just a nightgown over her, as a cover. There was still blood in her hair from the delivery table. I couldn't understand it. We don't do things like that in this country. It may just be the way they do things in England," she said, as if making an effort to understand.

All through this, Ben had been politely quiet. Now, next to Laura, below Mary Schiller's line of vision, he took Laura's hand in his.

And Laura thought of the body, still soft from childbirth, still warm, placed in a box by a hospital attendant. She thought of the temporary coffin of unseasoned wood in the hold of a plane, passing through the freezing night, and Ruth, a young girl, a girl with blood in her hair, and the icy wind whistling between the planks of wood, the body jostled and broken, the bones rattling across the North Atlantic.

Laura sat in the room in the silence, the grandfather clock ticking. She and Mary Schiller didn't look at one another. They sat pondering. She could feel Ben next to her, watching her.

Then she stood up.

"Thank you for telling me," she said.

"I hope I didn't upset you," said Mary Schiller. "It's been bothering me so long."

"I'm glad you told me," Laura said. She took Mary Schiller's hand, and Mary Schiller followed them to the door.

"Will you be leaving soon?" she asked.

"Tomorrow," Laura said.

Now, as they walked to the car, Mary Schiller watched them through shining glasses with expressionless eyes.

Outside, Ben asked, "Do you want to go back to your grandmother's?"

"No, let's drive."

They rode in silence to the edge of the town. He turned up onto a hillside where the road had been plowed. It was late afternoon, there were streaks of orange in the sky, and beneath them now, they could see the village covered in snow, the scattered houses poking out of the white, the railroad tracks gleaming in the winter light. There was no sign of movement in the town, no sign of life.

Ben turned to her and took her in his arms.

She began to cry, and he held her as her body shook and her voice was wracked with anger. "That fuck!" she cried. "That sonofabitch! That *fuck*! . . ." she cried, over and over again.

They returned north. He called her every day from work. "Are you okay?" he asked. He was being gentle with her.

"Maybe we should go away on a real vacation," she said one evening. "Be really alone. We've never done that. Let's go to the Caribbean? We could go just for five days and you wouldn't miss the weekend with Jesse."

"I don't want to spend the money right now," he said.

"Why not? There are lots of cheap places we could go."

"I know, but I have expenses with Jesse. And I've got a piece due."

She broke away from him.

"You're such a tightwad," she said. She could feel the anger growing inside her again. "Why don't you ask your parents for the money? They can certainly afford it."

"You know I wouldn't do that."

"You know, your attitude towards money is really insulting to people who are really poor," she said. She couldn't help herself now, she was riding on something.

"It's the way I choose to live my life," he said.

"The money's there. Why not take it?" she said.

"They're already taking care of Jesse. I'm not going to ask them."

"Why can't we spend a weekend alone then, without Jesse?" she challenged him.

"I can't do that," he said.

"Just once," she said.

"Maybe you don't understand," he said. "He's my son. He's part of me. I *want* to see him," he said.

She watched herself with fascination, she couldn't help herself.

"Look," she said, "let's end it. It's obvious. It's no good."

She saw him hesitate a moment. Then he said, "Maybe you're right." To her surprise, he stood up, began walking across the loft to her door.

At the door, he stopped, looked at her. "Good-bye, Laura," he said.

But she wasn't ready yet. She couldn't do it. It wasn't dead yet between them.

At midnight, she called him. "I love you," she said. "Forgive me. I'm sorry. I don't understand myself."

And in the middle of the night, he took a cab to her loft and then they made love all night long and only stopped to sleep at dawn.

The next time they fought, the breakup lasted longer, for two days. Then he called and said, "I can't stand it without you," and she ran over to his place, pushing through the late-afternoon crowds to get to him, running back to him as if her very life depended on it.

They were driving uptown to deliver Jesse to Ben's parents' after the weekend. Jesse was asleep on the front seat of the car between them. Ben had read a piece she'd written in manuscript and criticized it. She knew he was right about what he'd said—she knew he was good, the best, at what he did. But she was angry because now she would have to rewrite the article and panicked because she wasn't sure she knew how.

"Listen, it's easy," he said. "You just do the lead this way," and he went on to recite a whole new lead for her. She felt him overbearing, superior—and right.

"But—"

"I'm right, I'm telling you! It's easy—"

She turned to him. "You just want to dominate. You want to be the big writer. Every time I open my mouth you interrupt me!" she accused.

He gripped the wheel, stony faced. "You're full of shit!" he said, between his teeth.

She felt dry with rage, carried away by a fury that was nameless, uncontrollable.

"I am *not* full of shit. *You're* the one who's full of shit!" she cried.

"For Chrissake!"

"You think you're better than anyone else. You think your work is holy and nothing else matters!"

She looked down at Jesse. She stroked his pale blond hair with her hand. His mouth was open a little, his hair was stuck to his forehead with the sweat of sleep, he was in the most serious, concentrated reaches of sleep.

"He only sleeps in cars," she said suddenly, interrupting her diatribe. Ben didn't answer, he was too angry to speak.

What a beautiful child he was, she thought, with his porcelain skin, his almost white hair, the violet shadows around his eyes. He was beautiful and strange. Like Simon, a cold child. Would he become a criminal? She wondered if the sound of Ben and her yelling at each other was being woven into the fabric of his dreams. She wondered if she would become a nightmare figure in his dreams.

Next to Jesse, Ben was rigid with anger, his lips tight, his eyes set on the road.

He dropped Jesse off. On the way back downtown, they didn't speak.

As they pulled up in front of her loft, she said, "It's not working. Maybe we're just too guilty." He said nothing, only looked at her with a long, dry expression.

She got out of the car. And then he drove off. He didn't call her as soon as he got home, as he so often did after these scenes, and then come back to the loft. Maybe he was weary too. Maybe he didn't want her anymore. She didn't care. She was relieved.

The next day, and on the ensuing days, he still didn't call, and she made no effort to contact him.

She didn't miss him, the tenseness in him. She was all dried up, and so was he.

During the following weeks, she stayed quietly in the loft, exhausted. She could feel her body becoming quiet again, it was as if a great calm were suddenly suffusing her.

An editor she knew at a travel magazine offered her an assignment to write an article on a resort on the western coast of Puerto Rico. The fee was very low; basically, she would get expenses. But Laura said she would go.

She traveled alone for two weeks, living in almost primitive conditions.

She had never traveled alone in this way, to a resort, and she kept to herself, not speaking to anyone but the proprietors she interviewed. At night she ate by herself, reading her book at a table in the restaurant.

She was amazed at the long periods of time in which she didn't think of Ben. Driving through the mountains to a *parador,* negotiating the dangerous and narrow roads of the forest by herself in the rented car, finding her way though she didn't speak Spanish, driving for miles without seeing anyone, she began to forget about him.

And yet, sometimes, suddenly she found herself narrating her experiences to him. He was her invisible audience, he would understand everything.

Later, after she returned to New York from the assignment, if she had a success, if an editor had been particularly pleased with something she'd written, she would tell Ben about it in her imagination.

Weeks went by, and she didn't think of him. She was astonished that she could have loved someone that much and forgotten him so easily. Every once in a while, after having not thought of him for a very long time, she dreamed of him. She dreamed of making love to him, and when she woke up, she would wonder why.

Once or twice, during the next few months, she saw Ben at parties, or on the street. On those occasions, he was formally, coldly polite. He asked how her work was, and she told him. He held back from her, and it was she who was eager and warm and friendly. She did find that, whenever she was in Chelsea, she would take the route past his building. It was a mean curiosity that motivated her. She wanted to run into him, and she wanted him to see that she was all right.

That summer, she met a man who owned a share in a restaurant on the Upper West Side. She'd been taken to the restaurant by a friend, an editor, for a drink. The man took her home in a cab and they sat and talked. The man had one surmounting dream, to sell his share in the restaurant and move to Colorado, where he could ski. She saw him again a couple of times. And perhaps out of simple curiosity one night she made love to him. The sex was good, much to her surprise. She had never before made love with a man simply out of curiosity, to satisfy a basic physical need. She slept with him two more times. Sometimes when she was making love to him, she thought of Ben, she wanted him to see it, she wanted to punish him with it.

Why punish him? Why did she want to punish him? Because he had left his wife, he had made his wife sick, she thought.

But after a few weeks, when the man who owned the restaurant called again, she said perhaps it was better if they didn't see each other. This wasn't a good time, she told him. She was still coming off another relationship. She wasn't ready. And she didn't see the man again.

She took every assignment offered to her, buried herself in her work. She'd never been happier, she thought.

Then, in early December, the anxiety attacks began. There was the sense of an illness coming on. She was coming down with something. And yet the sickness never materialized.

It was as if sometimes the air around her had a terrible radiance, as if there were an electric field trembling across her skin.

After three weeks of these attacks, she went to the doctor. The man examined her completely, took a chest X ray, and did blood tests. He could find nothing wrong and he quoted *Lear* to her.

In the first week of January she began to get the phone calls. At first she almost didn't notice. There were hang-ups on the machine, not uncommon. Then, once or twice as she sat at her work, the phone rang and she picked it up and there was only the sound of presence, static, sometimes the faint beep of a car horn outside a window. Then click—a hang-up.

There were a couple of phone calls in the middle of the night.

She went over in her mind the assignments she'd done. There had been the piece on the Adolescent Unit at Riker's Island over a year ago. But of course, she'd never given any of the prisoners her number. Also the article on the drug rehabilitation unit. None of the patients had her phone number. She had always been careful about giving it out to oddballs, always calling *them* when she was on a story. It could be some crackpot who'd gotten her number by mistake and then, hearing a woman at the other end, whoever it was had decided to keep on harassing her.

After a couple of days, she decided it was Hal calling her. The drinking had increased, had had a cumulative effect. The

213

discovery that Simon was a criminal, that he had disappeared, had sealed Hal and Barbara's fate, had proved the final blow to them and now, slowly, they were sinking more and more into the alcoholism.

But then, sitting at her desk that day working, Laura had begun to have the feeling that someone was watching her. That there was someone across the way in the windows of Rosenstein's Cord and Tassel. The windows looked almost solid against the reflected light, they were like mirrors, impenetrable. What accounted for it? What made you feel that someone was watching you? What made you suddenly glance up from your work and look toward a given spot? Were there invisible rays that emanated from a pair of eyes? That signaled to you that you were being watched?

That night, long after she had fallen asleep, there had been a phone call and, as she had picked up the receiver, there had been a pause at the other end, a brief connection, someone there, she knew. And then a hang-up.

But with morning, she'd almost forgotten about it.

The next evening, as she lay in the loft bed, she felt completely safe behind the great steel doors. Nobody could get to her.

Outside her picture window, the sky seemed lit with all the accumulated radiance of the buildings scattered across the boroughs. The glow from the sky penetrated the window of the loft and, lying up on the platform bed, gazing out of the window, Laura could discern the vague outline of the furniture in the room, of the refrigerator, her table, the wicker chairs by the window, her worktable. These pieces of furniture, these vague shapes in the semidarkness, were like living beings in a way, she thought as she fell asleep, old friends.

But then, in the early morning hours, the phone rang

again. Laura opened her eyes. The electric clock said 5:15. Nobody should be calling her at this hour. The best thing was to let it ring.

She clutched the pillow over her head, tried to smother the sound. She didn't want to wake up. Once she really came awake, she'd never get back to sleep. If she sat up in bed so she could reach the switch to turn off the phone, that would be it—she'd be wide awake and alert.

But even with the pillow pulled over her head, Laura could still hear it ringing.

She had to do the crash job on the piece about the black foundation executive tomorrow. She would be exhausted—she could never write when she hadn't slept.

From now on, she would remember to turn the phone off at night.

But it was still ringing.

Laura pulled the blankets over the pillow, creating a double barrier against the sound.

She'd fallen into the hands of a rapist, she thought. Someone was picking on her. At worst, it was dangerous. At best, whoever it was was trying to make her life miserable.

Maybe she should call a neighbor. There was the one-armed sculptor, the feminist poet. But she couldn't wake them now.

The phone was still ringing. Whoever it was was persistent, was insisting that she answer. Why was he doing this? Why was he trying to torment her?

She began writing her article in her head. "In the ten years since Winifred Green graduated from Wellesley," Laura wrote, "she has served as—"

But now Laura couldn't stand the ringing sound anymore and she reached across the bed and picked up the phone.

215

NINE

) Laura pulled on her jeans and sweatshirt and hurried
down the stairs to the front door. She slid the iron bar
across the outside door and opened it. There, in front of her,
she saw the dark shape of a man.

She stepped aside and he entered the narrow space at the
bottom of the stairs. She couldn't see his face, but only his
outline in front of her. And she could smell him, the dawn air
on his body, damp wool. As he passed close to her she felt the
cold from his skin.

"Simon!" she cried. She put out both her arms as if to
embrace him. But he stood stiff and still in front of her. For
a moment, her hands rested on his arms, which he kept at his
sides, unmoving. He nodded.

"I can't believe it!" She dropped her arms, let out a little
laugh. He said nothing.

"This way." She led him up the stairs in the semidarkness.

At the top of the stairs, they entered the loft. Now as they
moved into the lit space she could see him more clearly.

He was about her height, slender, wearing a raincoat with
epaulets, slightly faded, carrying a duffel bag.

216

He had thick, curly hair, worn long; and pale blue eyes, slanted eyes. Barbara's eyes. He had high, full cheekbones, his chin narrowing to a point. The area around his eyes was slightly puffy. His mouth was sensual; the upper lip was curved and slightly larger than the lower lip.

Cutting through the line of his eyebrow, Laura saw a faint scar. And for a second, she saw a picture in her mind, a body flopping silently down from the tree, bouncing on the ground, then lying there limp.

"My God!" she cried. He looked at her and smiled, it was a contemptuous smile, mocking.

She said, "Where have you come from?"

"England." He put his duffel bag down on the floor.

"Is it really you?" she asked.

He nodded, smiled.

"Please," she said, "sit down."

But he didn't. He continued standing in the middle of the loft, wearing his raincoat, his figure lit only by the one light she had turned on when he had called.

"Was that you calling me before?" she asked. "You were watching me, weren't you?" She could feel her voice breathless with excitement.

He smiled, nodded, as if it were a joke of some kind.

"You scared me," she said. "Why didn't you just call and say you were here?"

He shrugged.

"You frightened me," she said, but he didn't react. She remembered that he had gone to prison.

She stood a moment, awkwardly facing him. She searched for the proper thing to say or do. He was giving nothing. She turned, began switching the lights on in the loft.

He walked over to the window, looked out. It was as if he

217

were checking to see that it was safe. Outside the window, there was a faint, cold light rising, dawn coming.

She could see him better now. He had a tawny skin, his cheeks were flushed a deep red. English skin, she thought.

Still wearing his raincoat, he wandered around the perimeter of the loft, examining the prints and posters hanging on the wall, her books in their cases.

She watched him from across the room, blinked. It was a dream, she couldn't believe it. Simon. Here?

"God," she said. "How long's it been? Twenty years . . . yes, over twenty years.

"Have you spoken to Hal and Barbara?" she asked.

"No."

"Are you going to call them?"

He shrugged. "I dunno."

"When did you arrive?"

"A few days ago."

"Have you been watching me the whole time?"

He nodded.

"How did you get in across there?"

"At lunchtime. With the workers. I found an empty office and stayed there."

She could see that she was going to get nothing from him. She stood awkwardly in the center of the room for a couple of minutes, waiting for him to say something more.

Suddenly she was conscious of her pale, lumpy, morning face, her tangled hair.

"Let me just go and wash up," she said.

In the bathroom, she washed her face and brushed her hair. Usually, she shampooed her hair every morning in the shower, but now she didn't want to be naked under the water with him in the other room.

She came out and saw that he had sat down at last, one leg crossed over the other, jiggling his leg nervously.

"Well, what would you like to do?" she said. It was the only thing she could ask in the face of his silence. "I could show you around New York a little. Maybe you'd like to see the Empire State Building or something?"

"I don't want to go out," he said, quickly.

"You don't?"

"No."

"Well, then, take your coat off. Make yourself at home." He didn't move, just sat there, with a half smile on his face.

"Well," she said, "I have an appointment with an editor today. I could cancel it if you want."

"Could you?" he asked.

He wasn't going to let her go out, she realized. Did he want to hurt her? It couldn't be.

"I can't call till ten. None of them comes in before ten," she said.

There was a horrible taste in her mouth, she had to get something in her stomach. She walked over to the stove, put on water. She was conscious that he was watching her.

"Can I get you some coffee—or tea?"

"No thanks."

She made herself coffee. "I have doughnuts," she said. "Do you want a doughnut?"

"That'll be okay," he said. She brought him a plate with a doughnut on it.

He took off the raincoat. Underneath, she saw, he was wearing a big gray sweater and clean, black denim jeans.

"So, what do you do?" he asked.

"I'm a writer."

"What kind?"

"I'm a journalist. A free-lance writer."

"Make a good living?"

"Not a lot. But I like doing it. What do *you* do?" she asked.

"Oh, all sorts of things," he said, glancing around the loft.

"Like what?"

"I was in the antiques business for a while. But it didn't work out."

"Antiques?" She couldn't help a little laugh.

"Yeahr."

She imagined his antiques. Stolen goods, she thought, artifacts. "And what do you do now?" she pressed.

"I've got a few projects going," he said, mysteriously.

She wondered what his projects were.

Now, outside the window, the city was rising. She could hear traffic, the bang and clatter of trucks and cars.

Her eyes were burning, she felt suddenly exhausted.

She looked at him, shook her head as if to bring him into focus. Was it really him? "It's amazing, your being here," she said.

"Is it?" he asked.

"Did you know they wrote you a letter?" she said. "Did you get it, when you were twenty-one?"

He nodded, looking away again, around the room.

"But you never wrote back?"

He shook his head faintly, his eyes not on her.

"Why didn't you?"

"Nothing to say."

She thought of Barbara, writing the letter, waiting for him to reply. Hal and Barbara sitting in one of their houses—which one?—the silence between them, Hal pacing anxiously, worrying about Barbara, the ice cubes rattling in their drinks, waiting—and nothing came.

"I understand you were in prison?" she said.

He nodded.

"What happened? What did you do?"

He gave a little snort. "Now there's a story."

She knew he wasn't going to say anything.

He lit a cigarette, got up and began walking around the room again. She saw that his body was slender, almost slight. He glanced out the window.

"Seems like a pretty rough area," he remarked, with a kind of clinical interest. "Aren't you afraid of being robbed?"

Was he going to rob her? Or was he just speaking from professional knowledge? she wondered.

"Actually, it's pretty safe," she said. "There's no one around at night except other loft dwellers. And no one can get in downstairs because of the iron bar on the door."

She was going to get nothing out of him. She felt stiff and self-conscious, shy.

"Well," she said, "I have a piece due today. Maybe I should try and work on it. There are some books and magazines there. Help yourself. Maybe you'd like to see some of my work."

"That would be interesting."

She went to her file cabinet and took out a folder full of clips, handed it to him.

She put on the radio to fill the silence, and the sound echoed through the big space.

She sat down at her worktable with her back to Simon and began to try to write.

Usually, she worked in an orderly, ritualistic manner. First breakfast, then a shower, coffee, the papers. Then she sat down to write. But now her routine had been disrupted.

She sat, pretending to make notes on the article about the

black foundation executive. But after twenty minutes she gave up. She turned around and faced him where he sat on the wicker chair near the window, with his head of thick curls bent over her clips, reading.

"Maybe I'll just sort through my files," she said, and he didn't answer. She began opening up manila folders and throwing clips and letters and copies of old expense accounts into the garbage.

The morning passed and they hardly spoke. At ten she called the editor with whom she was supposed to meet and put the appointment off. He continued reading in the chair by the window. Having finished with her clips, he was now going through her stacks of magazines. She kept on working, stiff and self-conscious, sorting through her files.

When lunchtime came, she got up and stretched her arms. The strain of his silence was exhausting.

She made sandwiches and handed him his. The act of making him something, doing something for him, entitled her to open up the intimacy between them, she decided.

"You know," she said, "as you can imagine, I've often thought of you . . ."

"Really?" he asked, raising his eyebrows, seeming to suppress a laugh. Was he angry at her for never getting in touch with him? But the prohibition against contacting him had been so deep, even after she'd grown up.

"I didn't know where to reach you. Hal and Barbara—I didn't know . . ." Her voice trailed off. "You see, Hal and Barbara were so guilty, and I was afraid . . ."

He said nothing, left her to dangle there.

"I didn't see them in the phone book," he said, almost as if he weren't interested.

"Oh, they've moved to South Carolina. They've retired.

They move around quite a lot." She felt it incumbent upon her now to fill him in on the family history. She hurried on. "I hardly ever see them." A disloyalty, but she wanted to let him know she was not on their side.

"Hmm . . ." was all he said, going back to his magazine. There was a long silence.

"So," she asked, "you ended up growing up with your dad?"

"Yep," he said.

"They moved to America when I was around eleven or so," she volunteered. "Hal got transferred. I think there was some kind of problem about Barbara's divorce and their getting married. I don't think his career ever quite recovered from it."

He didn't say anything.

"Do you want to stay here awhile then?" she asked—needlessly, for it was obvious he wasn't going anywhere.

"Yeahr," he answered, smiling again. "I'll stay awhile."

She spent the afternoon with her make-do work at her desk.

At four o'clock, she got up, walked to the kitchen area of the loft, and opened the refrigerator. "I'd better go out and get some dinner. Is there anything you'd particularly like?"

He looked at her with his pale, slanted eyes.

"Don't go out," he said.

"Why not? It'll take a minute."

He smiled. "I'm paranoid."

"Why?"

He shrugged. "Just the way I am." Maybe he was simply paranoid by nature, a man for whom, by definition, there were always hazards.

"You mean you don't trust me—you just want me to—stay here?"

223

He shrugged again.

"Come on!" She laughed.

"For now it would be better."

Was he threatening her? She couldn't tell.

Perhaps she was simply, unconsciously, beginning to cooperate with his paranoia.

"Well." She sighed. "I'll make do with what I have. Do you like spaghetti?"

"Fine."

She prepared the spaghetti sauce, sautéing the mushrooms, tomatoes, oregano, and garlic together and letting it simmer. She poured them each a glass of wine and switched on the television.

Outside, she realized, the street had grown suddenly still. She could feel the wine gradually taking effect, the heaviness in her limbs.

When eleven o'clock came, she said, "Well, I guess we should go to bed."

"Where should I sleep?" he asked.

She was suddenly embarrassed. The loft had only one room, there was only one bed.

"You'll have to camp out on the floor there," she said. "I don't have an extra room. I'm sorry."

"Well," he said, the surly smile returning, "I've slept in a few strange places in my time."

I'll bet you have, she thought. She wondered what those strange places were. She wondered if he had a girlfriend.

"I have a sleeping bag and an air mattress. Will that do?" she asked.

"Yes."

She hesitated. What now? What should she do now? What was the etiquette between brothers and sisters? she wondered. Did they sleep in the same room when there was no other alternative? Did they get undressed separately? Did they see each other without clothes on? She'd never had any experience with brothers and sisters.

She remembered suddenly being naked with him, peeing with him, the pee dribbling down her legs, the hot shame on her face.

She went into the bathroom to take a shower. She wondered if he would undress while she was gone.

As she stood under the hot shower, the water pouring down on her naked body, she had a sudden fantasy of him walking in on her. But of course he didn't.

She washed her hair, blew it dry, and then dressed in her nightgown and bathrobe.

When she came out of the bathroom, he was still fully clothed, sitting on the chair waiting for her. The air mattress was blown up, the sleeping bag unfurled.

"Here's a pillow," she said, handing him down her second pillow from the platform bed.

"Thanks."

She felt again shy at the intimacy of it. He would rest his face against the same cloth where she had lain.

"Well," she said, pausing at the edge of the ladder that led to the platform bed. "Good night."

She climbed up onto the bed.

Down below her, he shut off the light. He went into the bathroom and she heard the water running, then the toilet flushing. He came out again, barefoot, wearing only his jeans, carrying his shirt in his hand. She could see the outline of his chest and back. His body was slender but not skinny, the frame narrow, the spine very straight, the shoulders round and smooth. He seemed nearly hairless, it was a young body. He

225

crossed the loft and slid down into the sleeping bag.

Silence now. Every time she moved in the bed, she was conscious of the sound. She listened for his breathing, but she could hear nothing coming from him. He seemed to lie absolutely still. He couldn't be asleep.

Her every bone and tendon ached with tiredness, and yet she couldn't sleep. Her mind raced. What did he want?

The air between them lay prickly and sharp. Each time she turned over, the sheets crackled and it sounded to her like an avalanche.

At last—it must have been very late, one o'clock or so—she slept.

In the morning, when Laura woke, he was up and dressed. The sleeping bag was folded with military precision—perhaps he'd learned this neatness in small quarters in prison. He had shaved and he was wearing a clean, unpressed white shirt outside of his jeans. He had done all this while she was asleep and she remembered the way he had been able to move so quietly when they were children, quietly like a cat.

She pulled on her bathrobe before climbing down from the platform bed. She didn't want to walk around in her nightgown in front of him.

"What will you do today?" she asked.

"Stick around," he said.

She went to the refrigerator. "Look, we really have a problem here. There's no food. I have to go out."

He hesitated. She said, "You can trust me."

There was the smart-ass, contemptuous smile again, but he didn't say no.

She dressed, bundled herself up in her parka, and went outside into the cold. The sudden daylight made her blink.

The winter light was flat and dull. It was cold, there were few people out, and yet those few she saw seemed far away from her, separated by an invisible wall of silence. As she walked along the narrow street toward the supermarket three blocks away, she felt as if she were walking in a dream, her feet not really treading on the concrete sidewalk, but pedaling slow motion on air.

She suddenly wanted to call someone, anyone, a neighbor. She thought for a moment of Ben, *he* should see Simon, But obviously, she couldn't call Ben. She wanted someone to see Simon, to be a witness, to make it real, someone to remember him, to say he had existed. But he didn't want to see anyone, that was obvious. If she brought anyone to the loft, he would run. She knew that. And she didn't want him to go.

When she got to the supermarket, cruising among the aisles, she saw the other, normal people beside her and she thought about him there in the loft, a man who had been a criminal, who didn't want to go out.

On her way home, she stopped at the tobacco store on the corner of her street to get the *Times*. The storekeeper, a Puerto Rican, greeted her nearly every morning of her life.

"Cold," she said.

"I got the heater on," he said. "I no see you yesterday."

"My brother's visiting," she said.

My brother. It was real. She felt a funny pride—absurd. She was thirty and proud to have a brother in front of this stranger. But *he* was ordinary, he had brothers and sisters, no doubt. And now she was like him, like other people.

When she returned to the loft she found Simon sprawled on the floor, listening to Patti LaBelle with the volume up high. For a moment she was startled, seeing him there. Somehow, she had expected to find him gone, but now she was glad, she realized, that he was still there, a thin, curly-haired man in jeans. She saw the high cheekbones, the curved mouth. He was tapping his knee in rhythm to the music, studying the liner notes.

"Hello," she said. But he hardly looked up, sitting there, sullen and insolent on the floor.

She settled in with her files again—at least her worktable and her files would be immaculate.

Then, after lunch, she suggested they play a game of cards. It turned out he could play gin. He turned the TV on while they played, one hand and then another.

"Do you remember the time when you were with us?" she asked, after an hour of this.

"Nope," he said, studying his cards. Was he lying? Or had he just repressed it?

"I remember it all very clearly," she said. "It was very important to me."

"Yeahr?" His eyes were on the TV set.

"Do you remember that little red car? The car they gave us?"

He squinted at the TV as if trying to remember, but said nothing.

It was useless.

That was it for today.

"I bought some steak for dinner."

"Good," he said.

"Then I got some ice cream for dessert. American ice cream. A choice—butterscotch or maple walnut."

"Good."

She cooked and served him the dinner, he sitting at the table while she moved around him serving the food. She was close to him, could see the back of his neck, his hair, the rich, thick, untidy curls. It was like having a child, she thought, or a husband.

When she went to bed that night, she knew she would sleep well. She had gone for two nights now without a full night's sleep.

And yet again, as she lay there, with him silently beneath her on the floor, unmoving, she couldn't sleep. Did *he* sleep? she wondered. What was in his thoughts? She wondered how long she could go on like this. She would never get the article written if she was exhausted like this.

Up on the platform bed, she tossed and turned. If she were alone, she might get up and put the television on, but she didn't want to let him know she couldn't sleep. She didn't want to speak to him, for they seemed to be observing some code of privacy, of silence, when the lights went out.

In the morning, she sat down to work again while he watched the early-morning television shows. The tiredness was so great that she could hardly sit up. She sat slumped at her worktable. She hadn't heard from the editor about the article. Maybe he hadn't noticed it was late yet.

"Throughout the ten years since she graduated from Wellesley," she wrote. Then, crossing it out, "All through the ten years—" she tried again.

It was impossible. Writing was a private act. She could never do it in front of someone else.

She swiveled around in her chair and looked at Simon. He sat on the floor, watching TV, his big, clean blue-and-white-striped shirt pulled out of his pants.

She began, retrieving a memory, any memory. She remembered sitting with him in the backyard in Hampstead, reading to him, he leaning against her, watching the page intently while she read. For one moment in his day he had been still.

"I remember you couldn't read," she said.

"They found out I had dyslexia," he said, watching the television.

"Really?" she prompted.

"I got away with it for a long time by pretending. I could remember the words in the book by getting someone to read them to me. I only had to hear it once or twice. Memorized the letter charts. Fooled them."

This sudden, brief confidence of his, his first acknowledgment of their shared past, emboldened her.

"How long were you in prison?" she tried again.

"Five years."

"Five years!" So, it was obviously for something significant. They didn't put middle-class people in prison unless they did something significant.

He smiled. "It would've been longer only I came from a good family," he said sarcastically. "And they hired a good lawyer."

"What were they like, your family?" she asked.

"Demented. Haven't seen them for years." The curtain drawn again. He got up, walked over to the television, and changed the channel.

"You know, I didn't have anything to do with it," she persisted.

"With what?" His eyes were still on the program. Someone was interviewing housewives who were kleptomaniacs. Their faces were in shadow so you could only see their silhouettes. He was concentrating on it.

"With her leaving you," she said.

230

He didn't comment.

"She gave you up because that was the only way your father would give her a divorce."

She pushed on.

"I hardly ever see them." Defending herself against an accusation he hadn't made. "Sometimes he calls me up on the phone and just listens to the sound of my voice. I don't know why. He's drinking a lot, maybe he's getting senile. I think he feels guilty." As she spoke, she realized no one else would have quite understood the parameters exactly.

She continued. "You know, I never understood what happened that day when you stopped coming to us. Suddenly, just like that, Hal said you didn't want to come anymore because your father told you the little red car was really for me. But I can't believe you'd think I wouldn't have shared everything I had with you. Didn't you think about me? What it would mean to me never to see you again?"

"I dunno," he said.

His taciturnity was a petty device and now it suddenly angered her. Why had he come all this way if he wasn't going to talk to her? Here he was arriving at her doorstep, just like that, expecting to be let in, after making anonymous phone calls and frightening her all night. Just like her family! To arrive suddenly and expect you to pick up the pieces. Hal coming to America after having disappeared for months, just disappeared and then taking her from her grandmother, then expecting her to be his normal daughter again. Hal suddenly arriving in New York, telling her Simon had become a criminal—and expecting her to forget that fact and go on as before, being a dutiful daughter. Now here he was, when everything seemed to be going well, coming to disturb her peace.

She turned back to her work, angry, feeling the heat rise in her.

That night they watched television again. She sat on the couch in the darkness, while he lay on the floor in front of her. His back was to her and she could see his hair haloed by the blue light, his legs stretched out in front of her.

The next morning, on the fourth day, as they were drinking coffee and reading the papers, she the *Times* and he the *Post,* she said, "Look, I really want to know some things."

"What?" he said.

"Like what happened when you stopped coming to see us?"

He stared off into the distance, as if trying to remember.

"You've got to talk to me!" she said.

He paused, seemed to be thinking.

"Owen promised me a Lionel train set if I didn't go with her," he said. "A complete set, the whole works—barnyards, animals. I figured I might as well get a train set out of it."

So he did remember.

"Then?" she asked.

"Then?" He smiled at her. "Nothing," he said. An I-don't-care smile, distancing her.

She waited for him to go on. But he had stopped dead. She was afraid to prod him.

She sat down again to write her article, took a deep breath, and began typing.

By lunchtime, she had written a first draft. It wasn't her best work, she thought. But she'd revise it in the afternoon, put it in the mail, and call the editor to say it was done.

That night, Simon took out a tobacco tin and papers and lit up a joint. He offered her some and she took it. Darkness had fallen around the loft, and silence, and once again they were alone, each of them sitting in a wicker chair, opposite one another.

She felt the pleasant sensation of the dope perfuse her body.

"What about your father?" she asked.

"Faggot," he said.

So he knew.

"Always fawning over me," he said. "He had a bookshop in Brownlee. One day on my way home after soccer practice I stopped at the shop. It was closed, but I could see there was still a light on. I went round the back. The door wasn't locked. I saw him there with his—assistant. They were—in a compromising position, you might say . . ." He smiled, ironically, taking a drag on the toke, his pale eyes squinting in the smoke. "After that, he could never really look me in the face. My Aunt Edna lived with us, raised me. Supposed to be a more normal environment. You know, mother, father. I got to be the kid. Lucky me. Strange pair," he said. "She died four years ago. Anyway, I don't care."

"I don't believe you," said Laura.

He smiled, almost smugly.

"I don't," he said. "I don't have normal feelings like other people."

Laura laughed. "C'mon!"

He rolled another joint, sucked, offered it to her. She took it, then handed it back.

"You must care about some people," she said.

"Maybe in my life, there've been one—two people," he said. "Norman. He was my friend, the one who turned me in." He looked at her quickly, seriously. "I didn't do it." It was the first time he had referred to prison without her asking and he seemed to assume she knew the story.

"Do what?" she asked.

But he didn't answer.

"Tell me about Norman," she said.

"I knew him in Brownlee," he said. "We used to hang out together. He was older than me. His dad was rich, in the meat business, tied up with the mob somehow.

"Norman was fun. He had a motorbike. Spoiled boy, was Norman. Looked like Paul Newman, or—who's that French star, the one with the broken nose?"

"Jean-Paul Belmondo?"

"Yeahr. Him. Like Paul Newman, only rougher."

"Did you like Brownlee?"

"Dismal place! Always cold and damp, even in summer. There were no jobs. They were going to put up a convention center. What a joke! They even had a press conference, but the money never came through. Norman left, everyone did. I couldn't take it anymore with Edna and Owen. When I was sixteen, I ran away to London. I'd heard this rumor that Norman was living in a suite in the Portman-International—of all places. I looked him up. He was running an escort service out of a bar, you know, sleeping with rich women for money. I didn't have anywhere to stay. I was sixteen, only I looked older. He made me a partner!" He laughed.

"An escort service?"

"It was very high class. We wore only the best clothes, suits made to order and all that. We even had business cards.

Sometimes . . ." He paused a minute, took another drag. "Sometimes we'd do double duty with a woman and her girlfriend. The money was great. They'd come to town, we'd have dinner, drinks. We did them a service. We were gentlemen. Sometimes I could make a couple hundred quid a night with tips and all."

She watched him in the semidarkness, his slender figure opposite her. She didn't want to turn on the light, she was afraid of interrupting him.

He was smiling now at his memories, not looking at her. "Good times," he said. "Then Norman started to branch out. He had another thing going, running a stable of girls for someone in a house near Grosvenor Square. I was his assistant. It was also very high class. He never touched the girls himself, and I didn't either. It was work, you know. We were always straight with the girls. I was sort of like their pet, a mascot like. Some of them wanted to sleep with me, but I never did because it was work. You don't shit where you eat, as the saying goes . . ."

"Quite a saying," said Laura.

"You should've seen it, the best antiques. The house was owned by a viscount and they rented it from him. I used to sit at the door to keep order, though you rarely had any trouble with that caliber of person. If a girl got upset, she'd come to me and know she'd be safe. I'd never try anything.

"I lost all contact with Owen and Edna. They wouldn't have known where to find me. Anyways . . . one day we got into a spot of trouble. One of our girls was trying something. Some of the people we had coming in were very high class, businessmen, there were a few MPs, that sort. Rich—had to be with those prices. One of our girls started getting ideas and was trying to blackmail a customer. It was stupid, it would never have worked. But we had to put a stop to it or it would ruin business.

"Norman wanted me to go with him and straighten her out. We went over to her place and Norman began to talk to her, real easy-like. But she suddenly started screaming at us, attacking us physically, hitting on us. Norman belted her one. You had to do that kind of thing now and then. I didn't like to, but sometimes that was all they understood. They're like children that way. She started calling us all sorts of names, dirty names. Called us dirty faggots. That's when I kind of lost control. I admit it—I hit her too. She tried to fight me and grabbed my hair, pulled a whole handful of it out. Then Norman got in between us and threw her off me. Well, she fell in a funny kind of way. I don't know how it happened, but she must have broken her neck . . .

"When the police came, I told them my part—I wouldn't say anything about Norman—as I said, he was my friend. My best friend. Every time they brought his name up, I just kept my mouth shut. But I guess old Norman didn't do the same. They found the hair in her hand—my hair—and he turned on me and I got the whole rap for it. I was innocent—and I promise you that. I struck her once, that was all. Norman got time off for turning on me . . .

"Anyways," he continued, "I got sent up. I got five years because of my age and because Owen and Edna got me a good lawyer."

"It must have been very hard," Laura said quietly. "They prey on young men . . ."

He said nothing, didn't look at her.

She didn't press. He and Norman had been lovers, she guessed. Like father, like son. Maybe, for a brief time, this

Norman had been a proper father to him, maybe he had, for a while loved him, taken care of him.

And then, like everyone else, he'd betrayed him.

Simon went on. "Afterwards, when I got out of prison, I went to see Norman. I wasn't going to hurt him or anything like that. I just wanted to understand . . . I'd hit her once, but he had hit her several times. He threw her against the wall, for Chrissakes! I knew he was the one who struck the—deathblow. I wanted to understand why he betrayed me. But when he saw me at his door, he was terrified. He practically shat in his pants. 'Oh God, Simon, I—I'm sorreeee!' " He did a perfect imitation of the frightened man. "He said he did it because I was so young and he knew I'd only get a short sentence."

"Were you going to hurt me and Hal and Barbara?" Laura asked.

"I didn't know," he said. "Didn't know what I was going to do." Maybe he really didn't, she thought. He wasn't someone used to rational action, to planning.

It was 2:00 A.M. She got up and went to the cabinet, took out the brandy, poured two glasses and brought one to him.

"You know," she said, with a smile, as if to make a joke, "I used to think they murdered my mother." It was that time for confession, the dark hour, she thought.

Now he didn't hesitate, miss a beat.

"Maybe," he said.

"What?" she asked, surprised he'd taken her seriously. She'd always thought it was a fantasy. Now he was saying maybe.

"Could be," he said. That frightened her. He didn't laugh it off. After all, he knew about such things. He had been in prison.

"How would you prove it, though?" she asked him rationally, in a kind of dream now.

"Well," he said, calmly, "to begin with, you want the official cause of death. You need some kind of evidence."

"Evidence? What kind of evidence?"

"I don't know. . . . Maybe the doctor knows something?"

"The doctor? He's probably dead now."

She remembered the little brown bottle of pills, Hal running into the kitchen, the car idling out front. Simon was crazy. It couldn't have been. She knew that it had never happened, it was a fantasy, a projection of her anger at Hal and Barbara. At this hour, in the dark, in her exhaustion, anything was possible. She shook her head awake.

"So why did you come here anyway?" she asked. "Why now?"

"I had a job to do," he said. "My way was paid, you might say."

"What kind of job?"

He nodded toward his duffel bag. "See the bag there. Open it."

She stood up, walked over to the bag.

"There's a package inside. Lift it out."

She unzipped the bag, reached in, pulled out a package wrapped in brown paper and taped.

"Open it."

She switched on a small light. Hesitantly, she tore at the wrapping. Inside, she could see thick, neat stacks of hundred-pound notes.

"What's this?" she asked.

"Money."

"I can see that."

"There's a hundred thousand pounds there."

238

"Where did you get it?"

"I'm delivering it for someone. . . . It's illegal to take more than twenty-five pounds currency out of the United Kingdom. I brought it out of the country for someone who doesn't want to pay taxes," he said.

"What a stupid thing to do!" she cried.

He shrugged, smiled, a smile of bravado and indifference.

"Why would you do that?"

"I get a cut. It's a job. I needed money. It's an old associate. . . . They gave me a passport . . . a forged passport."

"You came here on a forged passport?"

He smiled. "I was convicted of a crime."

Stupid, was her first thought, only the stupid do things like this. Crime is for the stupid. Would she somehow be implicated in this? Was she an accessory? This kind of thing had nothing to do with her.

What was she doing here? She looked at him. Was she *like* him? Was she the same thing in some way? Was there something in her that was the same? There, but for the grace of God . . .

"Jesus," she said. "What an idiot thing to do . . ."

"Don't worry. . . . When I leave here I'll drop it off, pick up my cut and the return ticket, and that's it . . ."

"Aren't they—whoever they are—the people who are expecting this money—aren't they waiting for it?"

"Yeahr."

"Well, shouldn't you just take it to them now? Aren't they liable to misunderstand if you keep it?"

"They trust me. They'll wait."

She sat down on the couch, silent.

There was a moment in which she thought—this is an

adventure. An adventure the way hanging out with the Vietnam vets was, pretending in some way she was one of them, or being with the students in Paris, or the prisoners on Riker's Island.

She couldn't call the police. She knew that. He was her brother.

He smiled at her, his pale eyes crinkling. "You're not going to rat on me, are you?"

She looked at him. "No," she said.

It was three o'clock now.

"Maybe we should get some sleep," she said.

He stood up from the chair, walked over to get the sleeping bag.

She went into the bathroom and undressed.

When she came out, she felt suddenly shy again with him, a tension between them. It wasn't that she judged him, but some other tension, some lack of ease between them.

He had taken off his shirt and was wearing just his jeans. He was barefoot.

She remembered sleeping in the bed with him when they were kids . . . the way his toenails used to scratch her legs, the feel of his body next to hers.

He always waited until she was undressed and the light was out before he took off his clothes, slipping out of his jeans inside the sleeping bag.

For a moment, she took his modesty as a rebuke. Didn't he find her attractive?

"Good night," she said.

" 'Night." He glanced at her a moment. His eyes rested on her. She looked at him.

His eyes were questioning, tentative.

240

She shifted her face. He turned away.

She got up into the bed. In the half light, looking down from the loft, she saw, for the moment before he climbed into the sleeping bag, his chest, the smooth, hairless skin, like marble. Young skin. He had young skin. He turned his back to where she lay. She could see the indentation of his spine, like a knife cut to the waist. Lying in bed, watching him, she thought that he was beautiful.

He eased himself into the sleeping bag.

Now she could hear his breath, the delicate inhalation and exhalation.

There was much to know, and in the privacy of the dark, they could talk.

He was only a few feet below.

She could get up, go to where he lay, touch his cheek with her hand. They were both a little high, no one would know. The inevitable conclusion to their relationship. Their strange, undefined relationship. Brother and sister, not quite brother and sister.

She lay under the blankets, the loft like a cavern around her, the windows shut tight against the cold, outside only the muffled sound of a car, an engine roaring past.

Who was he? Brother and not a brother. Can you fuck your brother if he isn't really your brother? He was a person whom, under ordinary circumstances, she might not even *like*. Uneducated, inarticulate. But they were alone, they might never see each other again.

But if she got out of bed and climbed down the ladder, if she moved across the room and took him in her arms, tried to make up to him for all they'd done to him . . . she'd only be betraying him. Her own need would come first. How many

241

others had preyed on him? Men too, she knew. In prison of course. Everybody's barter.

She couldn't be like the others.

She would be there for him always, a sister. That was the reason you couldn't fuck your brother. Sex was fickle, but the love of a brother or a sister was a constant thing.

They couldn't talk now. They mustn't connect. It was necessary that a barrier be raised between them, remain until daybreak, until it was safe to talk again.

During the next few days, they began to settle into a routine. It turned out that he was handy. He fixed the toilet, which had been running, and replaced the faulty tap in the kitchen sink.

"Prison," he said, his face scrunched up, from under the sink where he was working. "You learn a lot in prison."

When she left the loft, she always turned on her answering machine because he refused to pick up the phone. If she were out and wanted to tell him something, she called and spoke into the machine, knowing he'd hear her.

In the morning, after they had gotten up, Laura went out to buy food and to do essential errands.

He still refused to leave the loft. He had a total capacity for absorbing himself in trivia. He was very sedentary. He had discovered American television, and the set was on for hours at a time. Sometimes he would simply stare at the picture with the volume turned down. In the morning, he watched cartoons and "Sesame Street," then soap operas. He watched it all with a kind of detached interest, never reacting to it.

Nothing could get him out of the loft. One morning, he awoke complaining of a toothache.

"I have a great dentist," she said. "He doesn't believe in

pain. He even puts cotton wool around the needle so you don't have to see it."

"No," he said. "It'll be okay. Got any Darvon?"

He took some Darvon and swore the pain was gone.

A dream seemed to permeate the loft, a curious light to slowly fill the space. As she gave him a second helping of dinner, stood over him filling his plate as if she were taking care of a child, she could feel herself being drawn inexorably into an illusion. She pretended, just as she had as a child, that he *was* her real brother, who'd come to visit her.

She started to talk like him, with an English accent—not an Oxford accent, but in his hybrid tones, half cockney, half educated. "Yeahr," she said.

He appeared to be happy. He never seemed restless. He seemed content to be with her always, and never to go out.

She'd always thought of this, she realized, of being in a room with him, he'd be the perfect companion, the brother who'd stick up for her at all times.

She'd never lived with anyone before. She had had lovers but never moved in with them. Maybe she was incapable of living with someone else. Perhaps the solitude she was used to had become a craving, a necessity.

But she didn't mind the loss of solitude with him. They could go for hours at a time without talking. Both of them could tolerate long periods of quiet, they didn't have to fill the space with sound. They always seemed to want to eat at the same time, to go to sleep at the same hour. She prepared meals now without even asking if he was hungry.

It would have been a perfect marriage, she thought. They never fought or disagreed. In many ways they weren't like a normal brother or sister, she realized, or even a husband and wife. Their relationship was different, a special entity, perhaps experienced by very few others.

It was deep winter now and the sun never seemed to rise fully, but always to lurk just below the horizon.

A blizzard swept across the city, putting it entirely out of commission for two days. Outside, the wind blew hard off the river, deep drifts built up on the streets. And then came the silence. The truckers didn't come to deliver in the morning.

They were like two prisoners in a remote outpost of the Arctic twilight, Laura thought, trapped together in a shelter.

The remnant of her fear had evaporated. She had stepped with him across a kind of boundary, she realized, into a realm without law. This was the real world now, the world of her family. Not your typical middle-class family, belonging to a community of others to whom you were responsible in an interlocking network of obligation, whose laws and customs you observed. Their family lived outside the normal limits of society, in a kind of netherworld, hidden from those around them, appearing normal to all, but secretly strange. A family who had one another followed by private detectives, a family with a secret child.

She began to realize that she was content.

She had stopped thinking about work. She hadn't been contacting editors. One day she realized with a small shock that she had only six hundred dollars left in her bank account. So when an editor called and asked if she wanted to do a piece on adoption, she said she would. She made a few phone calls, went to the library, but she couldn't get interested in the article.

It was as if she were in a state of hibernation, all growth and normal life processes stopped. What mattered now was being with him. Their world was only one another now, and the light, changing from dull gray in the morning to fulminating gold in the late afternoon. This man, he was her brother. He would never hurt her, he had to be on her side—even if he *had* murdered someone.

"I need a haircut," he said. "Can you do it?" It was at the end of his fourth week with her.

"Sure," she said. "I can cut hair."

She fetched a towel from the bathroom and the scissors from her sewing basket.

"I think these scissors are pretty sharp. Sit here," she said, guiding him to a dining chair, feeling his shoulders beneath her fingertips.

She tucked the towel around his neck. She could smell him—his hair and skin, the light, young, clean smell. Sometimes he showered twice a day. He was only a couple of years younger than she, Laura thought, only he seemed much younger.

"How do you like it?" she asked.

"Coming down over the ears like that."

She propped the mirror from her bureau on the table so he could watch what she was doing. He lit a joint.

"I can't do it if you smoke."

He stubbed it out obediently.

She began to cut the hair. As she worked, she watched the two of them framed in the mirror. She saw her own fine, long, curly hair, standing out from her face, her skin very pale. Her eyes were round, a vivid china blue. His hair was dark blond, thickly curled, his skin tawny, his eyes slanted, a much lighter blue than hers. They didn't look like brother and sister at all.

Underneath her hands, Laura felt his hair. She remembered when he was a kid, especially when he was tired at night, when he'd let her comb it. He was her living doll. It must have soothed him. It did instead of stroking or caressing. He wouldn't let anyone else comb it.

"Your hair was so much finer as a child," she said. See, see, we did exist together. She remembered the texture of his hair. "It used to be like silk. Now it's so thick."

He said nothing, watched her carefully in the mirror as she began to thin the hair. It needed thinning.

She curled a lock around her fingers. "It's all sorts of colors. White-gold, even a little black."

Outside it was snowing again, a late-winter storm, perhaps the last, a sheet of white falling across the window. They couldn't even see across the street.

"Not too short," he said.

"I won't. I'm good at this."

She cut slowly, prolonging it. "Remember how you used to let me comb your hair?"

He didn't answer.

"You were like a dog," she said. "You just used to lie there and let me groom you. . . . And that red car, it *was* for both of us. It wasn't just for me," she said.

He laughed, not dismissing her.

Then she remembered what he had said. "Who was the second person you cared for?" she asked.

"Well," he said quietly. "When we were kids, there was you. We were sort of in the same spot, weren't we?" He smiled.

She felt a small fire kindle in her—he *had* cared. She reached over and touched his hand. But he didn't respond. He let his hand lie in hers.

"I could help you," she said. "I could try and get you a job. You can stay here as long as you want while you get yourself together."

"I can't stay," he said.

"Why? Why can't you?"

Such was the peculiar dreamlike state she was in now that she actually didn't think it would be ridiculous, unnatural, for him to live with her forever. To have, at her age, a man living with her who was both her brother and not her brother. In this strange, unreal suspension in which they were living, where all rules, obligations, sense of time, had simply evaporated, she'd accept him under any conditions.

He looked at her seriously. "You know, one day you're going to come home and I'll be gone . . ."

"Don't," she said.

"It's the best way," he said. "I promise," he said, like one who was used to disappearing.

"Don't make it be now, though," she said.

He said nothing.

"Why *did* you come, anyway?" she asked.

He paused.

"When we were kids . . . ," he began, as if telling a story, "one day I came to their house—it was after Barbara had gone and Edna had told me she'd left me for someone else, for a man, and she didn't care about me anymore. Barbara came and got me. She had a black car, I remember. We got to her place and I walked in and I saw you there. Skinny little thing you were, pale, pigtails sticking out." He looked at her, smiled. "I looked at you and I knew we were in the same boat . . ."

"We were," said Laura.

"I used to think about you when we were growing up. From time to time." He smiled, teasing her, a brother. "All of them—they were busy doing their own thing, selfish. They didn't care about us. You were the only one I cared about."

He shrugged.

"Thought I'd drop in and say hello," he said.

"Not very revealing, are you?" she said.

"Sure I am." He smiled.

"But I want to know. Tell me. Where are you going?"

"Don't you worry." He reached out and squeezed her hand. It was the first time he'd touched her voluntarily. Then he pulled his hand away.

"Is it going to be now?" she asked.

"Not now."

She finished cutting his hair and lifted the towel carefully from his shoulders, shaking the loose hair into the wastebasket. She had an impulse to keep a lock of it for herself, a piece of his tissue, proof to herself he'd been there. But she was afraid he'd laugh at her.

He got up, walked over to the long mirror on her wardrobe. He peered at himself, running his fingers through his hair.

"Not bad," he said. "Not bad."

The next morning, Hal phoned.

"How are you?" he asked.

Simon is here! she wanted to yell. But she didn't. She couldn't do it unless Simon let her, and he hadn't given her permission.

"What are you up to?" he said.

"Nothing much," she said. "How are you and Mom?"

"Everything's fine. The heat's a little much down here for me, though. We miss the change of seasons, you know, the real autumn and the snow . . ."

They were going to move again, she knew. She could tell it. Before each move there was a complaint. The house was too big, or too small, or they wanted to be in the city now, or the country.

"When are you coming down?" he asked.

"Maybe in early spring," she said. Though they would probably have left by then. She hadn't gone to see them in South Carolina. She didn't want to get attached to some house of theirs—and then never see it again.

"Well," she said. "I have to run now. I've got a friend here."

She hung up and turned to Simon.

"Are you going to see them?" she asked Simon.

"Doubt it."

"Why?"

"Why should I?" He smiled ironically. "They probably don't even want to see me."

"Of course they do," she said. But inwardly she thought, Maybe they don't.

"Simon, I think we should tell them you're here."

He said nothing.

"I think we have to tell them," she said. "I'm going to call them."

TEN

Laura stood looking down from the window at the street below. She could see, in the flat light, the pedestrians passing underneath, a traffic jam of cars and trucks. Through the window, she could hear the dull roar of the city, the honking of horns.

When she had called them back, she had said to Hal, "Are you sitting down?"

"Is everything all right?" he asked.

"Well, it's pretty big news."

"Just tell me."

"Simon's here."

"Simon!"

"Simon. Barbara's son. I think you better tell her."

"When did he come?"

And she'd told him. He had hung up, and then called back twenty minutes later and said they would get the next plane out of Charleston.

"Are you nervous?" she asked Simon now.

"No," he said. Indeed, he seemed very calm, lying back in

250

the chair, contemplating his cigarette smoke. But she felt herself excited, her heart racing. It was as if she were going to have a treat, a birthday party or something. But she knew what the excitement was. It was revenge, showing him to them, showing them what they had done.

She watched out the window.

Down below, Laura saw a yellow cab pull up in front of the loft. She dashed down the stairs and outside.

She saw Hal get out of the cab; behind him the cab was empty.

"Where is she?" Laura asked.

He stood on the sidewalk. "Hi," he said. He shook his head. "I'm sorry," he said. "She was all excited and then, just before we were going to leave, she pulled her back out. It's completely out. She can't even walk, she's flat on her back."

She watched his thick fingers count out the bills for the driver, the cab idling next to him.

"You mean—she's not coming!"

"I'm afraid so. She's just devastated. She's hoping Simon can come down to us."

Staring at him, she suddenly thought she saw a pinprick of white light. She felt the rage boil up in her, a white rage. For a moment she couldn't even speak. She stood there and felt powerless, like a child again. As he bent toward the driver to get his change, she saw where the flesh above his collar line was reddened from the sun and she had a vision of strangling him, throttling him, wringing his neck with her hands.

Her throat was dry. "I can't believe it," she said, finally, into the air.

"Believe me, she feels just awful about it," he said, straightening up, looking grim.

She could feel hot tears rising up behind her eyes, tears of fury. She turned and went before him up the stairs. He followed her. He was carrying a briefcase, wearing a raincoat. He seemed to be more stooped than before, to have shrunken slightly with age.

They climbed the stairs to the loft.

Inside, Simon had risen to greet them.

"She's not coming," Laura said at once. She paused, trying to get the words out. "She hurt her back."

"Simon!" Hal cried, stepping forward, hand outstretched toward Simon. "Good to see you! Gee, I'm sorry about this," he said, pumping his hand. "Barbara is just beside herself! So disappointed! I think it happened when she was packing, she picked up the suitcase and then——. Now, what I want to do is to make immediate arrangements for you to come down," he said, turning, looking for a chair.

"Mind if I sit down?" he asked Laura.

"Sure," Laura said coolly, smiling now, she knew, contemptuously, at the absurdity of this.

He took off his raincoat and handed it to her, then sat down on the couch opposite Simon, who had seated himself on the wicker chair by the window, and had, so far, said nothing. Simon was clean and fresh and shaven for the occasion of his mother's arrival, his curly hair damp from the shower. Laura saw a little nick on his cheek from shaving.

"How *are* you?" Hal beamed at Simon.

"Fine," said Simon from the back of his throat somewhere.

"How was your trip?"

"Fine," he said again.

"What did you fly? British Airways?"

Simon nodded. Hal looked from her to Simon, smiling, as if this were a happy occasion.

"Well, we hope you'll be able to come down and visit us," he said, pleasantly.

Simon didn't answer.

"I don't think Simon will be able to make it down," Laura said, speaking for him, his protector.

"Why not?" Hal cried, almost cheerfully, as if she were joking.

"He doesn't like to travel," she said.

"He doesn't like to travel!" He turned to her. "But he's here, from England. Right, Simon?"

"Yes," Simon said, then shrugged, smiling faintly, as if he were amused.

"Laura, I'd love a drink," Hal said.

"What do you want?" she said coldly. "Coffee, tea. A real drink."

"Oh, I'll take a vodka and tonic," he said. He glanced at the clock. It was before five. He touched his stomach, frowned. "The plane ride was kinda bumpy."

Now he turned to Simon cheerfully, vigorously. He went to open his briefcase, took out a small notepad and a pen as if to make notes.

"What your mother—Bar—" he hesitated, as if confused himself as to what to call her. "We want to work out a specific plan of financial assistance. We'd like to help you out. But first, tell me what you've been up to."

Simon didn't answer, but Hal didn't seem to notice.

Laura brought him the drink, set it down on the spool coffee table.

He took a sip. "Ahh! Good," he said.

He looked at Simon again.

"I trust your father—Owen—is well," he said.

"I dunno."

253

"Do you get to see him often?"

"No," said Simon, smiling to himself as if over some private joke.

"And your Aunt Edna?"

"She's dead."

"Oh, I'm sorry to hear that.

"You know, we wrote to you. Your mother wrote to you. Did you ever get the letter?"

"Yes," said Simon.

He looked at Simon with a little smile. There was almost something cute about the smile, Laura thought, as if he were reprimanding a naughty boy. "We hoped you'd reply."

Simon said nothing.

"You know this was an awful tragedy," he went on. "An awful tragedy for your mother," he said. "She's never gotten over it." He shook his head. "We fought and fought. We had the best lawyers in England involved. But the courts, they were just against us. I was an American citizen and there was a lot of anti-American feeling then. There was no way." He looked at him intensely.

Simon didn't respond, but Hal seemed not to notice his silence. Only she understood it.

"We wanted very much to have you," Hal said. "But, when we went to get you that time, you were only eight, but you just didn't want to come. You screamed and screamed. We understood, of course, your father, perhaps, had been talking to you. . . . But we felt it would be bad for you to put you in all that conflict."

Simon sat stony, in the blue light from the window, like some kind of statue, she thought. He reached his arms behind the back of his chair, and tilted his chin up. His hair was a mass of curls, his eyes very cool.

Hal sat forward on his chair, wearing his houndstooth sport jacket, no tie.

There was a long and terrible silence. Laura could feel herself shrinking back into her chair with embarrassment.

"So what have you been doing since?" Hal asked.

"A few things," said Simon.

"A few things. . . . Oh," said Hal. He took a breath. "Well," he said brightly, looking from Laura to Simon. "Have you had any college?" he asked.

"No," said Simon.

"Well, that's one thing we'd like to help you with, college."

"I'm all right, thanks," Simon said.

"Well, of course, college is essential. I mean, we did that for Laura."

Simon said nothing, remained stubbornly silent.

"Gee," Hal said, "it's just too bad your mother couldn't be here. It really is. I know she's feeling just awful about it. Now, how long do you plan to stay?"

"I don't know," Simon said.

"Well, maybe we could make a plan for you to come down?"

"I told you, I don't think so," said Laura. They should have come to him. How dare they?

She was speaking again for him, she realized. But he refused to talk. And he was, in some way, defenseless.

Now there was a large silence in the loft. The windows were dirty, she noticed, the blue light coming in. Down below, the muffled sound of traffic, shouts from the delivery men, but here, just the huge space and silence.

The awkwardness hung between them, her fury, Simon's insolent indifference. Hal looked from one to the other.

"Well," said Hal. "Think about it. I can understand—everything's kind of a big surprise. Think it over and let me know."

He looked at his watch. "Well, I just wanted to put in an appearance to tell you we were with you and in person how sorry Barbara is about this thing. . . . I guess I should think about going. I'd like to get the five-thirty back. I'm worried about Barbara. She's completely helpless down there. What I want you to do, Simon, is think it over and I'll give you a call," he said. "Think the whole thing over. The money's there."

Hal rose, smiling still. "Where's my raincoat?" he asked Laura. He had been there less than an hour.

She went to the hook and got it for him.

He put the raincoat on, closed up the briefcase.

"I'm sorry to run," he said. "I know you'll understand. Laura, you think I can get a cab?"

"Yes," she said, nearly speechless. "On Canal maybe."

He walked up to Simon, shook his hand.

"Please," he said, "we'd really like to see you. It would mean everything to your mother. I'll give you a couple of days to think about it." He turned to Laura. "Maybe it would be better if you called *us*, Laura."

He walked to the door. Laura opened it for him, followed him down the hall, speechless with anger.

Down in the entryway, she faced him. "I don't believe you did this," she said.

He turned, as if genuinely surprised. "What do you mean?"

"You know what I mean."

"I don't!" he said, with all sincerity.

256

"How could she? Is she a total wreck?"

"Who are you talking about?"

"I'm talking about Barbara and you know it. What's the matter with her? Is she totally incompetent?"

"Please don't talk about your mother that way." They stood in the close entryway, nearly touching. She could see his hair, almost gray now, thinning over his high forehead, his jaw jutting out a little with age.

"She's not my mother!"

"How can you say that? After all she's done for you!"

"Done for me! Look what you've done! He's been in prison. He has nothing. Look what you've done. Don't you care about him? Don't you care about him at all?"

"Laura." He stood, smiling. "Of course I care. Your mother hurt her back. She couldn't *walk*."

"Stop calling her my mother. She isn't my mother."

"I can't have you talk this way about her."

He turned, as if to go.

"Listen to me," she yelled. "Let me talk. I can talk any way I like about her."

"Not in my presence," he said, his hand on the outer door.

"You just don't care about anything, do you? You just care about yourselves. He's her son, for God's sake! What's the matter with her? Is she sick or something? Is she just a great big—blubbering—infant!"

She realized she was disappointed. She wanted Barbara to be here, to *show* her, and she'd been deprived of that opportunity.

"Laura, I must ask you again not to speak about your mother like that," he said.

257

"Why can't you face what you've done? Why can't you look at it? Look what you did to him! Look what you did to *me*! Look what you did to my mother!"

She saw his lips tighten, he was angry now.

"How can you live with yourself?"

He paused, stared at her for a moment, his eyes narrowing, his mouth tightening. He seemed at a loss for words. Then, "You little bitch!" he said.

He stepped forward, clenching his fist. She saw the powerful fist and for a moment, she was afraid, afraid the way she'd been when she was a child, afraid of his fatherly rage, afraid that he was going to strike her.

"You think you can win, don't you!" she cried. "You think you can have it your way, get out of it! . . ."

Suddenly, he composed himself, straightened up. "Laura, I really must go. I have to catch a plane."

She snorted. "You amaze me, you really do. You just amaze me. You're stronger than me, you really are. I can't win, can I?"

And he looked at her, a cold, angry look, but there was a little smile on his face, a smile to show he was above it all, a smile of fatherly indulgence—a smile of triumph.

And then he turned and walked out the door and away from her, down the street.

She came up the stairs. Simon was standing, alert, near the door as if he had heard them.

He moved toward her, put his hand on her arm.

"That shit," she said. "That shit. I'm so sorry, Simon. I'm so very sorry."

She moved toward him, put her head on his shoulder. He stood quite unyielding, erect and stiff, but he raised his arm and touched her back.

After a moment, he stepped away.

He looked at her, they stood still, watching one another. He was bent over, she saw, almost slumped. She could tell he was exhausted, and so was she. They stood saying nothing, watching each other, and then she turned away.

She went into the bathroom, drew a tub full of water. She poured Vitabath in it and lay there, soaking herself.

That night, she lay awake, aware of him below in his sleeping bag, listening as always for his breathing.

At 4:00 A.M., in her half sleep, she woke up. He was lying on the wooden platform next to her mattress, beside her. He was wearing jeans, his chest was bare. His body was separated from hers by inches. He was staring at her.

She could just make out that his eyes were open. She wondered how long he had been there watching her while she was sleeping. It was like when they were children, and he'd get out of bed in the middle of the night and walk across to her side of the room, like a cat, with no one hearing or seeing him, and then he'd stand watching her.

For a moment, she said nothing, just watched him in return.

The outline of his face was visible, the high cheekbones, the pointed chin, the ring of curls.

She reached out her hand, began to stroke his hair, running her fingers through the tight curls. His body shivered, it was cold.

"You're cold," she said. "Do you want to get inside?"

She opened the covers and he slid into the bed, next to her body in the flannel nightgown. His feet were icy on her legs. She reached around his body with her arms, and pulled him against her.

The shampoo smell of his hair came to her, the soapy smell on his skin. His skin was smooth and young and she remembered again that he was younger than she.

She reached up, kissed his forehead.

When he went inside her he let out a little cry. A cry of sorrow and frustration, not a physical frustration, but a frustration at not being able to talk. It was a sorrow that went out beyond them into the night, into a region she couldn't know, a dark and limitless place. Because, finally, there was no comfort for him anywhere and she was simply a vessel through which he had to pass to some other place where she could never go.

And while he was on top of her, she found herself for a moment disassociating from the experience. She was above them, on the ceiling, looking down, not here with him, but removed, watching them. He was, she thought, still the most beautiful living creature she'd ever known.

In a moment it was over. He pulled out of her and turned away, instantly, as if he were ashamed, as if somehow he were heartbroken.

"Come," she whispered. She hooked her right arm around his shoulders, he turned toward her again. With her left arm, she brought his head to her neck and rested it there, her hand on his face. They lay without talking. She kissed his forehead. He didn't respond but lay there still and watchful.

Soon, she could feel his body growing loose against her, he was falling asleep. There was a sudden spasm in his limbs, the kind of spasm she used to have when she was a child just at the moment she was falling asleep. He came awake for a second, stirred. She could see his eyes opening, he lifted his head, looked around as if he didn't know where he was.

"It's okay," she whispered, "go to sleep." He settled in

again against her body, his arms reaching around her now.

And although he was heavy against her, she was afraid to move, she didn't want him to pull away to the other side of the bed. And she lay for a long time, uncomfortable with his weight, holding him, running her hands over his hair, stroking him.

Afterward, when she thought about it, she realized, of course, that it wasn't about sex. It was about comfort; it was finishing things off the way they ought to be finished.

And finally, it was a cry of mutual frustration, a recognition of the limits of their experience together, that, in the end, she couldn't help him.

When, at dawn, she came awake, he was still there. He lay on his side, his back toward her. She sat up and looked down at him and saw his mouth open slightly with sleep, his back rising and falling. She studied his face, the high cheekbones, the slight puffiness around the eyes, his body, square shouldered, slender, not much taller than her own. She noted and memorized one by one all of his features, the exotic, curly hair, the high, Tartar cheeks. Where his leg extended out beyond the covers now, she saw his tawny skin that was almost tanned, the sinewy man's leg. She'd never had a chance to study him this closely before. She put her nose in his hair so she could smell it.

He stirred and sat up, then climbed down from the bed. In a few moments, she followed him. She didn't try to talk to him or to touch him.

He said nothing, but went into the bathroom, ran the shower for a while, then came out wearing his jeans.

"Do you want something to eat?" she asked.

"No," he said. She saw that he was frowning slightly, avoiding looking at her. She ate her cereal in her bathrobe while he walked over and switched on the TV, standing there, watching it, rubbing his wet hair with a towel.

She finished her breakfast, and as she passed him to go into the bathroom and get dressed, she stopped and said, "You don't have to think about it again. Don't worry about it."

He looked up at her and suddenly he smiled. The smile was soft, tenuous, uncertain, and she saw that he was afraid. But then he moved toward her, he reached out his hand and touched her cheek, resting his hand against her face. She bent her head toward his palm and for a moment, they stood there, looking at each other, she with her cheek against his hand. She saw his eyes narrow, squinting at her slightly. But the eyes weren't really focused on her now, it was as if he were looking beyond her for something.

She reached up and touched the hand, squeezed it, and then she released him.

She didn't try to touch him again, didn't go up to him and put her arms around him, or try to seek some kind of affirmation, the way she might have from another lover in the morning.

In the bathroom, she showered and dressed. When she walked out, he was as usual absorbed in the TV.

They would be brother and sister now, she figured.

"Okay," she said. "I'm going out to buy some food. Want anything?"

"No thanks," he said.

She went to the closet and took out her parka. She found her purse and keys and went to the door. As she opened it, she glanced behind her and saw him lying sprawled out on the floor, in his fresh morning clothes, shaved and clean, watching the TV as always.

It took her an hour to do her shopping. When she returned home with her packages and the paper, she glanced up from the street at the loft window. The light was on.

She unlocked the outside door and climbed the stairs.

As she opened the door to the loft, the space seemed suddenly stuffy.

"Simon," she said.

The loft stretched out on either side of her. It was neater than it had been in months. He had cleaned it. He had vacuumed, dusted, straightened the books and magazines, puffed out the pillows. He must have worked very fast.

She walked around the loft. There wasn't an unwashed glass in the sink, or a coffee cup.

He'd even cleaned the bathroom.

Not one little sign. But like some expert criminal, he'd removed all record of his existence—she wondered if he'd even erased his fingerprints. His entire presence had been eradicated, softly removed from her life. His bag was gone, of course, all his clothes, the paperback biography of the Stones and a book of Patti Smith poems she'd bought him, hoping to interest him in something other than TV, to connect his culture and hers—he had taken them too.

She took off her coat. The only sound in the loft was the hum of the refrigerator. A room, even with only one other, silent body in it, has a different sound than a room that is empty, she thought.

For the rest of the day, she waited. She didn't try to work. She switched the television on, the way he would have. There'd be a phone call. He'd come back. It was an errand. He'd change his mind.

She made phone calls for work. In the afternoon, she went out again, to the bank and the stationery store.

Returning home, standing down in the street, she looked up again at the window. It was beginning to grow dark and yet there was no welcoming light. He hadn't come back. And, as she entered the silent loft, he wasn't there, of course.

She didn't bother to turn on the lights. She sat on the chair by the picture window, looking down at the street. The day had been warm and the snow had begun to melt. Now the slush shone on the sidewalk in the street lights. She waited, the silence of the loft behind her.

ELEVEN

The late winter slowly turned to spring, the ice melted, there were warm days when she could go without a coat.

She knew he wouldn't come back. And yet, sometimes when she wasn't on guard, she found herself waiting for him.

No doubt he had gone to deliver the money, collected his cut. And then what? Returned to England, lost himself somewhere in London, into his old life, whatever it was. Or gone on a vacation, in some warm climate.

She began to go back to her routine of work.

For a while, when she came home to the loft, she would pause for a second in the street below and by habit glance up at the window, half expecting to see it lit.

And when she entered the loft, automatically turned on the answering machine, and listened to the voices, she realized that she was listening for him. But his voice wasn't there.

Curiously, she wasn't sad. He had warned her. She knew there was no other way. He couldn't have stayed.

Sometimes, though, as she walked along the street, she would think of him, and suddenly, involuntarily, tears would spring to her eyes. But they were tears of rage, rage at what had been done to him.

She decided to call Hal and Barbara. She hadn't spoken to Hal since the day he had left her loft. He hadn't phoned again to see if Simon was coming down to South Carolina. Simon was right, of course, they hadn't wanted to see him after all.

When she dialed their number, it was Hal who answered.

"He's gone," she said, her voice cold.

"Gone? Where?" he asked.

"I don't know."

There was a pause. "Well, I'm sure he'll come back."

"He won't," she said.

"It's probably just a temporary thing," he said.

Her voice was icy, furious. "Did you tell Barbara about him?"

"Of course I did."

"And what did she say?"

"Well, she was very concerned naturally that we make provisions for him."

"But he doesn't want your provisions. . . . Didn't she have some curiosity about seeing him?"

"Naturally. . . . We asked him to come and visit us."

"But don't you think—after what you did—you should have come to *him*?"

"Laura, I told you the situation. You know about Barbara's back. She couldn't walk."

"But didn't it get better? You could have called then."

"Laura, we've done what we can. We made every attempt."

She could feel the wall, stone cold, extending high above her.

She sighed. "You know, I can't believe this. I really can't."

"I'm sorry, Laura. But that's the way it is." She sensed that underneath it all he was telling the truth now—that Barbara was too afraid to see Simon and never would have.

"Good-bye," she said, curtly.

"Good-bye, Laura," he said with a sigh, wearily, as if this were just something she would have to get through.

Three months passed. One day, the editor of the travel magazine she sometimes worked for called and asked if she were free to go to England on assignment. The magazine wanted a piece on the southeast coast, the chalk downs, the old seaside towns, something funky. The British Tourist Authority wanted to promote the area. As usual for this magazine, the fee was low—five hundred dollars—but it was a free vacation.

She had never gone back to England. None of them had, except Hal, once, on business. Barbara had never expressed any desire to return, to see old friends. For most people, Laura thought, England was a country of fine cathedrals and sloping downs and thatched cottages. But to her England was the country where Ruth had died, where Simon had been taken from her, where other children had tormented her for being American.

England was the past, inchoate, impenetrable, a wall of matter, solid, frightening, the reality of Ruth's death rising up at her.

Yet, as she made plans for the trip, she grew excited—it was a spring vacation after all.

She flew into Heathrow in the early morning and passed through customs easily because of the hour. After a day's rest in London, she drove down to Lymington, where she met the photographer.

They took the ferry to the Isle of Wight, then back again to the mainland, driving along the coast through Bognor Regis, Littlehampton, Worthing, Brighton, Eastbourne, Hastings, and up to Ramsgate.

She had stepped, without incident, onto English soil. And in fact, the trip was a pleasure. The photographer was an older man, in his fifties, who had seven daughters. What are their names? she had wanted to know. "I can only remember them if I do it alphabetically," he said. "Let's see—there's Clarissa, Edwina, Marigold, Phoebe . . ." And he had regaled her with stories of the girls and his days with them.

None of England was recognizable to her. She loved the cool, green downs, the quaint Victorian hotels of the coast, even the shabbiness of it. The weather had been intermittently poor—there was just enough sunshine for the photographs.

On the last leg of the journey, as they were driving on A259, she noticed a turnoff for the town of Brownlee. She caught a glimpse of buildings on a distant hill, a martello tower. But they didn't stop because they were on a tight schedule and Brownlee wasn't really an important town. As they drove by, she turned around in her seat to look back, as if to see something of Simon, the house where he had lived perhaps. Of course, there had been nothing.

The trip ended in Ramsgate. They finished shooting in the morning, and she said good-bye to the photographer, who returned home to his remaining daughters in Croydon. She had a day left now, on her own.

In her hotel room, after lunch, she picked up the phone by the bed and dialed information.

The operator refused to give her Owen Reed's address, she would only tell her his phone number. She would have to call Reed directly to find out where he lived.

As she dialed the number, she could feel her heart pumping, her palms sweating. Thirty years old, and still she was afraid of him.

"The Book Shoppe," said the voice of a man. He had a crisp, Oxford accent.

"Is this Mr. Reed?" she asked. Her voice was breathy with nervousness.

"Yes, it is."

"I'm sending a check for a bill. I just wanted to make sure of the address."

"Number ten. Duke of York Street."

"Uh—how late are you open, by the way?" she asked.

"Until five o'clock."

"Thank you," she said, and hung up.

His voice was curt, a voice she associated with older homosexuals, bored and haughty. And yet she thought she detected in it too, even from this distance, a kind of hurt.

She drove back along A259, then took the road heading south, toward Brownlee. It had been an overcast day and now rain began to spatter the windshield. She turned onto the coastal road. On her left was the ocean, a dirty gray color, the waves sending up a fuming spray. The water looked oily and unfriendly, the frothy waves filled with dirt.

On her right were houses. They stood incongruously without shelter on flat, sandy land that must once have been wasteland. They were Tudor style, trimmed with black beam.

She slowed the car and peered out at the houses, searching for Simon's. But it had been night when she had gone with

Barbara to get him, and she didn't recognize any of the houses as his.

Now, on her left, there was a pier on wooden pilings and the remains of an amusement park with a domed roof, boarded up now. Along the boardwalk were kiosks and sweet shops, closed now. A band shell with a latticed roof sat in disuse, grass growing up through the floorboards. In the distance, through the mist and rain, she could make out the ruins of an old martello tower.

The road was climbing now, and she was coming into Brownlee proper. She saw rows of Regency houses painted pastel colors, and narrow stucco-fronted buildings with heavy timber beams, and cobblestone streets. Signs in fake antique lettering hung over the shops, part of a recent restoration perhaps. Down below was the harbor.

Laura stopped and asked directions to Duke of York Street.

She continued on, made a left onto a narrow street, wide enough only for one car. She saw a sign marked THE BOOK SHOPPE. She pulled the car to a stop, parking it partially up on the pavement.

The rain had stopped, and a thick mist had arisen, almost like rain itself. As soon as she got out of the car, her hair and skin were coated with wet.

The building was probably very old, she thought. Like the others, it was made of white stucco and black beam. She could see a light burning in the window. She wondered if he would offer her a cup of tea.

As she pushed open the shop door, a bell tinkled. The shop was very small, lined with books from floor to ceiling. It was close and hot, and smelled of old paper and a little bit like unwashed hair, like a bedroom in the morning. An electric heater was going in the corner, and it was, thank goodness, warm. A big wooden table served as a desk, and on top of a pile of papers a Manx cat was asleep. No one seemed to be home.

A doorway leading to the back was curtained off by a piece of dark green velvet. Laura stood in the middle of the room awkwardly.

Perhaps he'd gone out. In a small English seaside town like this, they probably weren't worried about theft. She glanced at the books. There was a set of Mommsen in faded dark red binding, and Stendhal's *De l'amour*; a stack of *Illustrated London News*, back issues, probably for collectors. A sign on the wall in a black chipped frame said, "A good book is the best of friends, the same today as forever."

It looked as if no one ever came in here. She wondered how he paid the rent. Perhaps he dealt mostly with collectors.

Then she heard a sound. A man pushed aside the curtain and entered the room.

A cigarette dangled from the corner of his mouth. He was wearing a stained cardigan, and gray trousers shining with age. She could see where his hair had once been gleaming black, but now it was flecked with white. His eyes were very dark. They had a sad, voluptuous expression, full of hurt.

"Yes?" he said, his voice curt.

She took a breath. "Are you Mr. Reed?"

"Yes," he said, weary, as if he knew this encounter wasn't going to produce any sales. But if he was rude like this to everybody, Laura thought, he probably didn't sell much anyway.

"Can I help you?" he said.

"Mr. Reed, I don't know if you'll remember me—"

She saw his eyes flicker as he focused on her.

"My name is—" She stopped, took another breath. "My

271

name is Laura Fiske. I'm Hal Fiske's daughter, and Barbara's stepdaughter."

For a moment, he looked as if he'd been struck. His hand flew to his chest. He lowered himself onto the desk chair next to the table, dropping cigarette ash all over the invoices. The cat stirred and complained.

"Please, could I sit down?" she asked.

He said nothing but she took this to be assent. She removed her raincoat and sat opposite him.

"You're Simon's father," she said.

He stared at her. "Yes. Do you have any news about Simon?" he asked, quickly, eagerly.

"No. I was hoping you would have some . . ."

"I don't . . . I don't." There was a desperate sound in his voice. He shook his head, then his face set suddenly in anger. "I've given up on him. His aunt and I, we tried our best."

"He came to see me in New York," Laura said.

"New York!"

"Yes. Where I live. He stayed with me for a few weeks."

"He was in New York?" he asked again, disbelieving.

"Yes, three months ago."

"I knew nothing of it," he said.

"Had you been out of touch?" she asked.

"I haven't seen him for over a year," he said now. He stopped as if he couldn't stand to finish the thought. "After he got out of prison and went back to London."

"Do you have any idea where he could have gone?" she asked.

"I don't. He's always been very uncommunicative. I have no idea." He shook his head. "After he went back to London, he didn't call. He didn't write. There was nothing from him."

They were silent for a moment in the stuffy air, in the warmth of the electric heater.

Reed looked at her.

"When he left you in New York, did he give any indication about where he was going?" he asked her. He wanted information from *her* as much as she wanted it from him.

"None," she said. "He stayed with me for a few weeks," she said. "But he made it clear that at some point he would have to leave. Then, one day, I came home from work and he was just—gone."

He shook his head, looked away at the table.

"That's like him," he said. "He never told anyone where he was going."

"Does he have any friends? He mentioned someone called Norman."

"Him!" Reed snorted. "He's a petty criminal. I tried to contact him too. He's disappeared. Probably changed his name and gone off to the south of France," he said, scornfully.

Laura watched him, Barbara's husband, the feared one. And now they sat, without preliminaries, in the hot room, the sea outside, joined by mutual concern.

"Why *did* Simon go to prison?" she asked.

"It was never clear. The charge was manslaughter. You know he was accused of killing a prostitute in London? This Norman was involved in it. Simon used to hang around with him on the boardwalk. He let Simon take the rap for it and then disappeared. All the evidence was stacked against Simon."

"Did he really do it, do you think?"

"He denied it. I don't know. I don't think we'll ever know." He paused, his worried eyes searching the desk. "In the past year I've done everything to find him. I've contacted the police, Scotland Yard, the Missing Persons Bureau. I've tried to find Norman Savage, advertised in the London *Times*. . . . To me . . . to me . . . he died years ago . . ."

He loves his son, she thought. He loves him, like any father.

He wiped his face with his hands. There was silence. The Manx cat got up, stretched, then leaped off the table.

He buried his face in his hands.

"Can I get you something?" she asked. "Are you all right?"

"Yes," he said. "I'll be all right." He looked up, seemed to recover, lit another cigarette.

"Here, I'll show you the letter I got from Scotland Yard," he said. He opened a drawer in the old, chipped table, took out an envelope, and removed a letter from it. "Dear Mr. Reed," the letter began, "In response to your inquiry of August 10, 1975, I am very sorry to say—"

Just then the bell tinkled and the door opened behind Laura. She turned and a young man entered. He was wearing a dark green windbreaker. He stamped his boots on the floor and pulled the hood down, revealing neatly cut blond hair and a rosy, healthy-looking complexion. He was tall, and wore gold-rimmed glasses. He glanced from her to Reed.

A fearful, regretful look flashed across Reed's face.

"Oh, Michael, I'm busy," Reed said irritably. He shot an anxious look at Laura. It must have been hard to have lived the life of a homosexual in this small town, she thought. He must have always been afraid they'd take his son away from him. Even though the laws and customs had changed, the fear was embedded in him. She wondered if this was the man Simon had caught him with.

"That's okay," said Laura. "Please, perhaps I should go now." But she didn't move, she remained sitting in the chair.

She realized suddenly, she wanted Reed to ask her something about herself. She wanted him to ask her *fatherly* questions. It would connect Simon to her more. She hoped he would at least offer her a cup of tea. But, she supposed, she was still associated in his mind with *them*, with Hal and Barbara.

The young man took off his windbreaker and smiled at her. He was in his early thirties, she calculated.

"Michael," said Reed sharply. "That new shipment came in. Please see to it."

Michael smiled at her again and went into the back room.

Reed looked at her fearfully, covertly.

"Barbara and Hal are in good health," she said, as if he would care, wouldn't wish them dead; as if, after all these years, civility could now intrude.

Reed said nothing.

"Well, you have work to do," she said. "Maybe I should be going."

He didn't try to stop her.

She stood up. She knew Reed wanted her to go. It was no use.

"Thanks for your time," she said. "Can I leave you my card—with my address in New York? If you ever hear from him, would you let me know?"

He said nothing, simply watched her. She rushed on. "I always thought of Simon as my brother . . ."

He didn't react. Her words seemed to have no effect.

He took the card from her hand, put on his reading glasses, which hung on a cord around his neck. He read the card. "Very well," he said, his eyes dark, his voice cold—cold through time.

"Thanks," she said again. She turned and walked to the door, opened it.

Down in the street, she glanced back. She saw Reed standing in the lighted window, peering out at her, and behind him, the young man, Michael, who had come out from behind the curtain, looking over Reed's shoulder, not quite touching him.

Suddenly, she was exhausted. She could feel the tiredness pulling at her arms and legs, pulling her down.

Up ahead was a tea shop. She approached it and entered. The proprietress was wiping down the counter.

She ordered beef soup. It was good and nourishing, with big chunks of meat in it and whole carrots. The warmth spread through her body.

The fog had dampened the windows, and the moisture trickled down the glass.

Sitting there, staring out at the gray sea, at the headlights of the cars flaring in the mist, she thought, Where are you? Not even the decency of a proper farewell, a punctuation point to the story, a phrase: "That was the end of him. This is what happened." She imagined him in some backwater hotel in Spain or France. Maybe he'd taken his money and gone on a warm vacation. Maybe there was someone with him, a lover, a man or woman, who probably didn't even know his real name.

And then what? He would drift. He would make some kind of a life for himself, perhaps a life of petty crime. Involved in schemes. His life wouldn't be long, she knew that.

Perhaps he would think of her, but only fleetingly. He would see life only as a series of short moments, of eating, sleeping, making love. Surviving. There would be no long moments, no reflection. Little brother, brother of my heart. Allowed to hold him only once, briefly. And now it was as if he had never existed.

She thought of him as a speck in the sea of humanity, an aspect of her past, a connection lost, that no one would ever understand. And she thought, for a moment, of her own aging, of time passing. One day his memory would fade and recede until perhaps it would become affectless, the sparest shadow on her consciousness, fade and recede like dye bleached in the sunlight, like the pattern on a piece of brightly colored cotton, fading, slowly, subtly so that you almost couldn't tell it had ever been.

Outside, the fog had cleared, temporarily blown away by the wind from the sea. Above her, the clouds raced across the sky, and a white sun beamed feebly through. The air was chilly.

In the car, she studied the map. If she drove directly north on A22 toward London, she would go right through Stownorton.

She set out, driving for an hour, until she came to the town. There were rows of shops, low-storied nondescript buildings with false fronts, a bank in a heavy gothic style, a gas station, and an auto dealer. She recognized none of it.

She stopped at a pay phone and looked in the directory for the doctor's address. There was an address for his surgery. So he was still practicing.

His office was in a long row of attached red-brick houses. They were new, she guessed, built in the past ten years. Cement paths led from the street to the front doors. There was number 45 and a brass plaque, THOMAS SEVERANCE, SURGERY—she didn't remember this office. Obviously he had moved. As the suburb had prospered, he had prospered with it, moving into new offices. She rang the bell.

A nurse, a tall, gangling woman with pale skin and a red nose, answered the door. "May I *help* you?" she asked.

"Yes. My name is Laura Fiske. I want to see Dr. Severance."

"Is it a medical matter?" the woman asked.

"No. It's personal. My father, Mr. Hal Fiske, was a friend of Dr. Severance's. We used to live in Stownorton, twenty years ago. I've come back on a visit and wanted to say hello."

"Please come in."

There were several other people in the waiting room, women, most of them slender, sporty looking, prosperous, wearing good jewelry. The walls were lined with hunting prints.

Laura sat down and waited, leafing through the old copies of *Harper's & Queen* and *The Economist*.

The other patients were ushered into the office ahead of her. She waited—she couldn't very well expect him to come rushing out immediately upon hearing her name. At one point, someone left the office and she heard a voice. It was jolly, booming—she recognized it from long ago. An old dislike came flooding back, a distant memory of icy instruments on warm skin, of her skin peeling and crusted.

Had he known about the affair? Had he deliberately fronted for them? Was he incompetent, the way her grandmother had said? "If she hadn't gone to England, she wouldn't have died. Doc Baldwin said so."

She wove a fantasy—doctor enjoys friendship of rich American, senses the winner, provides a cover for the love affair. Perhaps he was just a voyeur, enjoyed knowing what others didn't. And then he'd gone and fouled up. With sheer

English incompetence, he had messed up the delivery—at least that was what her grandmother had always believed.

They had lost touch with him too, the way they did with everyone. They didn't want to be reminded.

The nurse came into the waiting room, interrupting her thoughts. "Dr. Severance does indeed remember you and your family. Please come this way."

She followed the woman into the office. She saw him sitting behind his desk. He rose to greet her.

"Laura, how do you do?" He pumped her hand. His grip was too strong and hurt her fingers. "How *are* Hal and Barbara?"

She saw the little mustache, the eyes pale green like peridots, the round, reddish face, the hair sleeked back. He was wearing a sport jacket, not a white coat. She recognized him.

His voice came to her from far away. "You must give me their address," he said. "I really ought to drop them a note."

She looked at him across the glass-topped desk, the little plastic model of the cardiovascular and pulmonary systems by his notepad. On the walls, she saw pictures of him standing with long rows of men holding golf clubs. There were trophies on top of a cabinet next to medical books.

He had said he wanted their address, and now she reached into her purse for her address book. There were three for them under F, two crossed out. She hadn't memorized the third yet.

"And what's become of them? Are they well?" he was asking her.

"My father's retired and they've moved down to South Carolina."

"I'd love to get to the States sometime. Oh, those were great times, they really were," he said, shaking his head nostalgically. "After the war, all sorts of fun times. Now it's all hard work."

She looked at him, listening to him chatter, and it seemed that he was at the very end of a long tunnel, his voice echoing.

"And what do you do for a living?" he was asking her.

"I'm a writer."

"Oh. What sorts of things do you write?" He was genial, a club man, never making waves. Medicine was just a sideline to golf and his club, she thought.

"I'm doing a travel piece now. I do political things. You get to be an expert on just about everything." The words extruded from her, floated across to his desk.

She had to stop the chatter. "I've come for a reason," she said.

"Are you feeling unwell?" he asked.

"No. It's not that. . . . I've come because I wanted to ask about my mother. You know, she died when I was very young."

His face clouded. He looked professionally troubled. "Of course," he said. "A terrible tragedy." He sighed.

"I was here in England," she said. "And I wanted to go over it with you. I guess I wanted to understand it better, what happened."

"Of course," he said solemnly.

"You wouldn't by any chance have her records?"

She thought she saw him hesitate. Just a tiny hesitation. But perhaps he wasn't used to being asked for the specific, the concrete.

"Let me ask Miss Beeforth."

He pressed the intercom. "Miss Beeforth, could you get me the records of a Mrs. Harold Fiske? That would be 1953, inactive, in the storage room, I think."

The atmosphere now, in the room, had almost imperceptibly chilled. Outside his window, through the venetian blinds that were drawn for privacy, she could hear the sound of children playing on the sidewalk, racing past on bicycles.

"Well, who do you think your next president will be?" he asked.

While they waited, she tried to say something intelligent about the election. Her throat was very dry. All she could think about was soon the records would be here. Connected to her by paper.

Miss Beeforth entered, carrying a torn and yellowed manila folder.

"Ah, thank you, Miss Beeforth."

He opened the folder. "Yes. Here it is." He studied the chart a moment. "Ah yes," he said, as if reminded, and then read out loud, " 'blurred vision, hyperemesis'—that's uncontrolled vomiting—'weight gain, water retention'—all the traditional symptoms of toxemia. By the time we got her, she was severely toxemic. When, finally, she did go into labor, the situation was very serious. The baby, we discovered, had died in utero. She went into convulsions on the delivery table. She was bleeding badly—"

"Why didn't you do a cesarean?" she asked.

"Well, when you have toxemia, the clotting factors in the blood are all used up. One is reluctant to operate under those conditions. Just the operation can be fatal."

"But why didn't you take her to a bigger hospital when it got like that?"

"There wasn't time." He sat back, coolly. "Besides, we felt we were capable of taking care of her."

Her questions were growing heated now. "But why didn't you go in earlier, before it was—so dangerous?" She tried to keep the heat of her interest down. She didn't want him to stop, feel threatened, clam up. "Don't worry," she said quickly, "I'm not going to sue you."

For a moment, he looked surprised. Then his face hardened. He sighed suddenly, heavily.

"Miss Fiske, I don't know if you know this but until your mother went into labor, she refused all medical treatment of any kind. You can see it on her records if you want."

"She did? Why?"

"All I know is that she refused to let me or anyone else examine her. She was very adamant about it."

"But *why?*"

"I don't know. Several attempts were made. But she absolutely refused. She had no prenatal care of any sort. Your father tried to get her to see a doctor. He was very concerned. But she would have nothing of it."

She wouldn't let him examine her because he was fronting for them, Laura thought, fronting for Hal and Barbara.

"You must have known my father and Mrs. Reed were having an affair," she said.

He looked down at his papers, shuffled them. He pursed his lips. "Well, I wouldn't know about that sort of thing," he said.

Perhaps he actually hadn't. Or perhaps he enjoyed it, the sexual spark of it, the thought of it, enjoyed it without defining it to himself.

Now he looked at her. She saw the red face, the gray sleeked hair, the little green eyes. "Miss Fiske, has it ever occurred to you that your mother *wanted* to die?" he said.

The room seemed suddenly to grow very quiet all around her.

"Wanted to die?" she repeated.

"Yes," he said. He tightened his mouth, as if he had committed a great indiscretion in order to save his reputation and now wished to say no more. "I think she did. She was a nurse. She must have understood the meaning of her symptoms and what the outcome would be if they were untreated."

Laura thought of her legs, swollen and big and round, the big shape lying there high up in the bed in the darkened room, the little voice a whisper.

She wanted to die because of them, because of the affair. Because she was helpless. There was nowhere to go but death.

Laura thought about murder. There is murder involving direct action. And then there is another kind. When you torment someone so much that they want to die.

But had they set out deliberately to *kill* her? They wanted her to die but they didn't even articulate it to themselves. And in a way, they hadn't bargained for her death. They hadn't thought it would happen and it had taken them by surprise. It was more than they had bargained for.

Her death, then giving up Simon, had tainted their love forever.

Now, in front of her, Severance was looking at the chart again. "The cause of death is listed as 'internal hemorrhage secondary to eclampsia.'"

"Could I see the chart?" she asked.

He handed her the chart and there it was written. There was her name, written on the graying paper. Written in the early morning hours, the moment of her death. The date was August 23, 1953, the time 3:00 A.M. Laura imagined the smooth summer dawn, Hal awakened by the phone call, Severance exhausted, the orderlies quietly covering the body.

And the reason Hal hadn't gone back to see her was because he couldn't bear to look her in the face. Because he was afraid of what she might ask him, accuse him of, at the moment of her death.

She thought about revenge. What did she owe her, what revenge? she wondered. How could she love a father who had done this. She thought of Hal, orphaned boy, running too soon to Ruth's arms. And Barbara, trapped with Owen Reed, searching for salvation, a better life. But instead, they'd made their own punishment, self-created, a life of isolation and loneliness and regret.

She felt exhausted again.

She handed back the chart.

"It was what we call in medicine 'a catastrophic event,' " he said.

A catastrophe, she thought. A sudden, unquenchable, overwhelming event, overturning the order of things; the final moment in a drama or romance, a violent and widely extended change . . .

"I do have another patient," he said. "Are there any more questions?"

"What about the baby?" she asked. "What happened to the baby? The baby wasn't buried in America."

"At that time, when a baby was born dead, the hospital would have disposed of the body. No doubt, the body was cremated by the hospital."

"There was no funeral?"

"There would have been no funeral. Since the baby had been born dead, it had, in one sense, never lived."

Laura sat still for a moment. The phone on his desk buzzed softly. He answered it. "Yes," he said. "Miss Fiske is just leaving."

ɔ

It was warm outside, nearly dusk, a humid late-spring evening. She could feel the change of seasons, the summer to come. Above her, the sky was tinged pink.

Following the road, driving slowly, she passed new housing, shopping centers.

She came to an area of large suburban homes, built in imitation of various classical styles, set back from the road in neatly tended gardens.

The houses had a certain uniformity, but with individual variations as in an American development—here neo-Georgian manse, there heavy Tudor.

Somewhere along here was Cambridge Road, she knew, and the hospital where Ruth had died, the tennis club where Barbara and Hal and Dr. Severance used to play. An excuse for Hal and Barbara to see one another.

The trees grew thick above her head now, the gardens were lush and close with spring, the new leaves thick and gleaming.

Now, as Laura drove, the memory of the place seemed to seethe upward through her body. She could feel a kind of alarm spread through her, a tingling on her skin.

The road was dark, the sycamore trees forming a canopy of branches over it. Above the line of the trees, the sky was lit up pink and silver.

That was the house. Number 10, Cambridge Road. She stopped the car.

It stood before her. It was a large house, like its neighbors, built of whitewashed brick, with a green roof and Palladian windows. A privet hedge ran the full length of it, separating it from the road.

There was something impermanent about it in its cleanness, its smooth blandness, Laura thought. It was supposed to seem old, yet it looked quite new. It had probably sheltered several executives from London and their families since she had lived here.

Laura sat in the darkened car, looking up at the house. There it was, brick and mortar.

She remembered the summer night long ago, the light shining from the second-floor window, a square of inaccessible light, and in the garden below, while the summer swirled around her, she'd stood trying to reach her.

Laura shivered, suddenly cold.

The sky was darkening, a car passed her, its headlights blinding her for a moment. The house was a great wall now, and from the angle where she sat, it seemed huge, to reach up into the sky.

"She was a lovely person . . ." That was how it would end. And Simon . . . he was simply gone. There were no endings, Laura realized. She sat for a few more moments looking up at the house.

Now, suddenly, she felt hungry. There was a reservation for her at a hotel in London. She would drive to London, go to the hotel, order room service, a big meal, and then have a drink and a very long, hot bath. And tomorrow, she would get on the plane for New York.

TWELVE

One June day, about a month after Laura returned from England, she was walking on Twenty-third Street. She was heading for the flower district, she wanted to buy a tree for the loft, a nice, big ficus. She was heading west, and the sun was shining in her eyes, sparkling off the buildings in shards of light, almost blinding her as she went. It was like a Seurat, she thought, or a Braque, the colors bleached out by the sun.

She tilted her head down, away from the sun. Her eyes were fixed on the pavement. But she knew her way so well around the city by now that she could almost get by without seeing. Some automatic radar made her stop when she came to a street crossing, made her look up, and when she had crossed, she looked down and turned inward again, thinking about her work.

She was writing a profile of the director of a new Broadway show; it was destined to be a hit.

As she walked, she could smell, amid the exhaust fumes and smoke from the street vendors, the faint salt tang of the river, the sweet smell of new leaf flesh. There was the noise of a radio playing from a window, the crash and clatter of the city in spring echoing off the buildings.

Laura's head was turned down when she heard the sound of children, chattering and shrieks and laughter, a sound she associated with the end of the school day. She looked up, saw the children clustered together, wearing their backpacks, pushing each other, running in circles around one another. A group of them came toward her as she walked. She glanced at them.

She saw a boy of about four or five with pale blond hair, bangs to his eyebrows, milky white skin, and delicate violet shadows around his eyes. He was wearing a red-and-white-striped T-shirt and a denim jacket and jeans.

She stopped, watched as the boy ran over to another child and an older girl of about sixteen. Laura saw the boy reach into his pocket and pull out a wedge of bubble gum and break some off, giving a piece to his friend, a plump black child, who took it. The two boys laughed and exclaimed. The young girl, watching them, smiled. She must be the baby-sitter, Laura thought.

She recognized the blond-haired boy. It was Jesse, Ben's son. He glanced up at her. For the merest second, Laura saw him focus on her, and she returned his glance. She saw him squint at her a moment, as if remembering something.

But then, just as quickly, he turned away, and became absorbed again in his friend.

He hadn't recognized her. She was a stranger to him, she realized.

He had turned out to be a beautiful boy. She stood, studying him. He was trying to blow bubbles now at his friend, and the bubble gum flattened against his mouth and the other boy laughed. He looked just like Lisa, Laura thought, only without the strain in Lisa's face, the craziness. Ben must have him now, she thought, now that he was nursery-school age, and the girl must be taking care of him after school.

Laura stepped back a bit behind two adults, and she watched him. Ben lived two blocks away. It was funny how she still walked near his place whenever she could. She did it almost without thinking. And when she passed his apartment, she always crossed to the side of the street where his building was. She was still drawn to him.

And she dreamed of him sometimes. When an important event occurred in her life, she found herself wishing she could tell him about it. He traveled a great deal still, she imagined. And when she did run into him, they usually stood in the street and talked for ten minutes or so. He was always friendly and courteous—but cool, and he avoided talking about anything personal. She was usually overly warm and friendly— she wanted him to know she was okay. That was part of the cruelty of it, she thought, part of that undefinable punishment she felt she had to inflict upon him, the punishment whose reasons she didn't completely understand—or she only understood when she thought hard about them—to let him know she was happy.

A few months ago, she had heard that Ben had another girlfriend, and when the news reached her, she had been consumed with jealousy. And when she'd heard the relationship had ended, she had been relieved. Maybe there was still hope, she thought.

Hope. She smiled to herself now at the thought. Maybe it would be when they were old. Maybe they'd have to marry other people first. And then, when they were old, they would come together. They'd meet in the park, Laura thought. To him she would still be twenty-eight, and beautiful. To her he would still be the one man in whom it had all come together, the man for whom she'd felt the perfect ratio of love and sexual longing. There would be no more anger, no more guilt. They'd just be glad to see one another—though there'd still be sex, of course.

Now, standing back in the street so that Jesse couldn't see her, she continued watching him. He was stamping his foot like a pony and the other boy began imitating him, and now they were circling around, pretending to be ponies, chasing one another, backpacks flying. The baby-sitter called to them.

What a beautiful boy he was, Laura thought.

He hadn't even recognized her, he was oblivious to the fact that she was standing there watching him, that she was part of the story of his life, that she had loved his father and that his father had loved her in return. He had repressed the memory of her screaming at his father in the car, of her at the airport taking his father away from him onto the plane.

Strange how children forget, she thought. Maybe it's nature's way of protecting them, because children are consigned to remember the longest.

The baby-sitter was gathering them up now. She grabbed their hands and began walking away, in the direction of Ben's place. The two children walked docilely for a few yards and then, first Jesse and then the other boy, broke free and began to run down the block.

Laura stood watching them. For a moment, their figures were blocked by the crowd. She could see the baby-sitter running after them. They were swinging their backpacks at one another now. She saw the baby-sitter stop and call out something to them.

They began to walk more quietly now, a few feet apart. She could see them looking at one another, laughing at something.

Laura watched as their figures receded, nearly lost now amid the crowd on Twenty-third Street. She stood there, she watched them, and she was glad that he didn't remember.